the
CORNUBIAN

Britain's Next
BESTSELLER

First published in 2015 by:

Britain's Next Bestseller
An imprint of Live It Publishing
27 Old Gloucester Road
London, United Kingdom.
WC1N 3AX

www.britainsnextbestseller.co.uk

ISBN 978-1-910565-05-6 (pbk)

Cover Photography by Lorraine Butler
Author Photograph by Eunice Matthews
Edited by Rosemary Carr of Exactus

Dedication

For Sadie.

You have always been, and always will be, my dearest friend.

If, when we are old ladies, we should ever find that looking at the young men should grow dull, then we shall have this book, and Martin MacBride.

"Can't wait."

THANK YOU

MY determination and perseverance alone would not have been enough to ensure the success of this book. The result was a culmination of many good friends' selfless time and effort.

Thank you to the official Cornubian photographer, *Lorraine Butler, The Happy Clicking Chick,* who shot our cover photograph and all videography, and also to the incredible talents of photographer *Abi Lyes* for capturing the inspirational visuals of the book down at the fantastic Olde Church House Inn at Torbryan. Gratitude also to her niece, *Rachel Treagust,* for her beautiful Cornish photography that we were given permission to use, and to *Myke Winters* of *Planet Penwith* for his stirring shot of Marazion churchyard used in the opening sequence to the promotional video.

Thank you to *Raisa Miles* for composing the haunting accompaniment to the campaign video, and for her cheery optimism and faith in me.

To the delightful *Polly Ferguson*, the tenacious *Ali Bennett*, the sunny *Lisa Smith* and the lovely *Jen Bignall*, thank you all for your tireless promotion.

Thank you so much to the wonderful *Simon Read* who allowed us all the time and room we needed to film 'The Smuggler Dance' on his stunning replica of 'The Golden Hind' and to *Gillian Hoult, Steven Myers, Alistair Hailey, Megan Russell, Beki Spiller, Kyle Spiller, Sue Butler* and *Jennifer Haines* who joined us there.

Thank you to the world's best line-editor, **Rosemary Carr** of Exactus. When many other line-editors and proof-readers laughed at my puny budget, you took heart, stepped up to the mark and provided a faultless service.

To the incredibly talented **Eunice Matthews**; thank you for making me feel gorgeous. Your skill with makeup is second to none, and I feel so blessed to have met you and worked with you throughout this enterprise.

To the selfless **Jon Lees** and the ever generous **Carol Holbrow** for promoting the book through your businesses as well as online – thank you.

To my fellow writers, **Elliot Thorpe** and **David 'Hellbound' McCaffrey**: you worked so hard to help me achieve my goal, for no benefit of your own. You restored my faith in author support, and made this world that I have taken a step into a little less intimidating. Thank you for your words of encouragement when I needed them.

To intrepid tweeters **Mike Coles, Jay Richardson** and **Leanne the Lilac Lady**: you did not know me, but you pre-ordered and you promoted my book for me. You made the difference. Thank you so much.

To the fabulous **Kate Norris**, who expertly updated our website day and night, despite giving birth to a baby in the middle of the campaign – your hard work is very much appreciated and I feel so much stronger for your support.

To my beloved husband, **William**, and my ever bright and patient children, **Jess, Jennifer** and **Rafe**: I am so sorry I have had a laptop glued to me these past six months. Thank you for your support and love, and thank you for believing in me.

To the illustrious **Julian Fellowes** for his words of wisdom and his backing – I will always be grateful that you went against protocol and offered your support.

To each and every person willing to part with at least £11.49 of their hard-earned cash in order that we might succeed, I've said it before and I'll say it again: *each and every one of you counts.* Not because of your order, but because of your faith in me.

And lastly, to my long-suffering and unpaid P.A., *Nikki Collings*, who has given me so much of her time in order to get this project off the ground. Your skills are far more honed than mine in relation to all things technical. For producing the filming to proofreading the finished article, and for generally holding my hand and reminding me to breathe, Nikki, you are an angel. From the bottom of my heart, *thank you*.

The literary world is renowned for being closed off and hierarchical, but we made it through.

My deepest gratitude to you all.

THE CORNUBIAN'S SUPPORTERS

Tina and Dave, Jo Algar, Jen Bignall, Raisa Miles, Fay Simcox, Jennifer Haines, Dawn Donovan, Kay Drake, Will Haines, Jane Lugg, Rebecca Spiller, Elaine and Richard Spiller, Kate Norris, Gillian Hoult, Tracey Veacock, Michelle Corkovic, Lou Honeywell, Nathalie Honeywell, Richard Parnell, Rita Parnell, Jon Lees, Natalie Shaw, Steve Dore, Polly Ferguson, Jane Hodges, Tim Whittle, Kim Holmes, Beverley Kelly, Karyn Jeavons, Emma Light, Becky Lees, Louise Thomas, Gary Robinson, Carolyn Chamberlain, Jo Kirk, Rebecca Baker, Fiona Cornwell, Donna Lang, Xanthia Kunaszkiewicz, Andrew Stocks, Janey de Nagle Costello, Lisa Southwell, Emma Aydemir, Lockie Story, Leanne Morrison, Diane, Janet Armstrong, Abi Lyes, Lorraine Burt, Michelle Spiller, Keith Greatrex, Erica Parrott, Keiley Hollinson, Carol Holbrow, R Treagust, Sandra Jay, Sally Whittle, Ali Bennett, Lisa Barton, Linda Dillon, Tracy Ryan, The Great Ben Robinson, Stephen Fuller Kayak Guide, Lisa, Marlene, Emma Parrock, Dean Fullalove, Norman Evans, Anthony Lount, Ali Hailey, Lorraine Butler, Ann, Hilary, Neil Norris, Janet Webb, Cecilia Smith, Charlotte Bebbington, Carol-Ann, Victoria Hurford, Dayna Shearman, Paul Woolgar, Trina Carter, Michael Heather, David McCaffery, Gemma Hubbard, Compton Pool Farm, Ann Stocks, Jenny Stocks, Elliot Thorpe, Jane Glanfield, Sarah Dudley, Barbara Steventon, Anais Hay, Elaine Goff, Stewart Rodger, Janet Goff, Julie Timlin, Katy Meek, Francesca Johnson, Chris Libby, Robin Bornoff, Philip Smith, Linda Silvey, Stephen Nicholls, Clare Niven, Cassandra Brooke, Valerie Lunday, B&J Heaselden, Charlotte Lentern, Jane of the Giants, Maureen Monk, Katharina J. Rayner, Simon Read, Amanda Nelhams, Claire Cornish, Janet Jones, Jill Elswood, Gemma Bond, Frank Armstrong, Rodney Moorhouse Ltd, Shaun Northey, Kristina Spiller-Smith, Gavin Yeoman, Bekki Pate, Julia Gale, Mrs. J. Powling, Jay Richardson, Meg Fenn, Andrew Dillon, Liz Lithgow, Emma Wright, Mike Coles, Sophie Jenkins, Michelle Diana Lowe, Julia Sutton, Irene Thorpe, Ellie & Martha Haines, Rosy Yates, Clare Welsh, Lyham Douglas, Sue Lees, Rachel Keeley, Jane & Robert, Matt & Lisa, Emma, Frank Sale, Kyle Spiller, Ian Turbutt, Rosemary Carr, Mike Coles, Essential Chiropractic, Mark Gaughan, Tracey Veacock, William Mallett, Juliette Lessware, Gfive Design, Adam Spiller, Rebecca Sill, L.S. Kingsley, Michael Kiff, Paresh Jivanji, Melvin Saunders, Jason D Gregory, Lisa Dickerson, Stephanie York, Gareth Haywood, Anne Birks, Debbie Flack, Catherine Atwell, Sheila Rice, Caroline Stabb, Lucy Sellors-Duval, Kate Richards, Roxan Tucker, Gillian S. Elliott, Eunice Mathews of Eunice Makeup, Gwen Pulle, Jane L. A. Collins, Donna Harding, Trisha Flack, John & Viv Arscott, Karen Dore, Malcolm Armstrong.

Prologue

Cornwall, 1787

WARM candlelight penetrated the gloom of the heavily beamed bedroom. Flickering shadows were cast along its slanted ceilings as Josephine Bryant untied the string that encased the crumpled parcel. The stained, waxy paper and underlying tissue fell away to reveal a length of carefully folded lace. Jo drew it out and, turning towards the mirror above her dressing table, held it against herself. A smile spread across her face as she wrapped the delicate fabric around her shoulders and fingered the white and cream scalloped edge that draped over the soft skin of her chest.

A dark shadow appeared in the doorway. She became aware of another presence and turned abruptly.

"Another gift from MacBride?"

The voice was gruff, heavy with a sneer. It was Cardinham, her lover.

"It's for our wedding, John."

"It's to win your affection."

Jo turned back to the mirror, re-adjusting the lace.

"He's happily married, as we are both very much aware."

Her calmness incensed him further. Within a moment he was beside her, digging his fingers into the soft skin of her shoulders as he turned her to face him. His bloodstone ring grazed against her neck.

"For pity's sake, Jo, open your eyes! These are smuggled goods!"

She pulled away from him, her eyes flashing defiantly.

"Can you afford such a fine lace?"

John Cardinham fell silent. His mouth formed a thin line. He took a step away from her, then, as if changing his mind, lunged back and, wrenching the lace from her grasp, ripped it in two.

"He'll be swinging from the gallows before the next moon!" he shouted over his shoulder as he swept out of the door, slamming it shut behind him. He thundered down the stairwell, bellowing as he went. "Shanley! Step aside, men, and fetch me Shanley!"

Jo grabbed the oil lamp from her dressing table and hastened out of the room and down the narrow, wooden stairwell into the crowded tavern of Pensilva Cellars. Cardinham's furious appearance only a few seconds before her had drained the warmth from the convivial air.

"Where is Shanley?" he shouted.

"He's just left," replied a punter over the rim of his tankard.

"John," hissed Jo. "This man is our friend!"

Cardinham spun to face her, his craggy face contorted with rage.

"MacBride is no good. He's a bloodsucker, creeping to procure your affection and he thinks he can do so under my very nose!"

"Oh this is madness!" cried Jo.

More punters stopped drinking to stare as the sound of her voice intensified.

"He is a villain!" cried Cardinham, "A shameless villain! A deplorable highwayman! And as an honourable member of this community I intend to see that he pays for his crimes."

Jo narrowed her eyes at him.

"This is still about Lamorran, isn't it? That she chose Martin over you."

"She was mine! He's always wanted what I have."

"He does not want me! That is just a lie you have spun in your mind. He is devoted to Lamorran. I am of no interest to him."

"Devoted is he?" yelled Cardinham. The slim figure of Cole Shanley finally appeared in the low, wooden doorway of the inn, but Cardinham did not notice him. "What a guileless child you are! He is corrupt to the core, thinking he is above the rest of us, thinking he can trifle with what's *mine!*" Jo gasped. She was not owned by anyone. "Let me tell you this, woman, I will kill him with my bare hands! I will rip his throat out and savour every moment I watch him suffer if he dares to take one step into my inn again!"

Jo slapped him across the face. The hollow sound rang out across the inn and the remaining chatter fell to hush. There was a moment's pause as Cardinham's twisted expression melted behind one of shock.

"This is my inn," said Jo. "It will always belong to my family – to the Bryants." She surveyed him bitterly. "And I want you out of it."

Silence hung in the air. Jo held Cardinham's stare, her decision firm.

At last, Cardinham kicked over a table and stormed out past a surprised Shanley, sending a cask of cider crashing on its way and as he did so.

* * *

An authoritative voice broke through the hubbub of the courtroom, calling for order. The grubby, jewel-adorned hands restrained in iron cuffs twitched and the prisoner shuffled uncomfortably.

"What's the matter?" whispered the clerk standing beside him. "Afeared?" The prisoner known to all as "Sparky" because of his love of gunpowder turned to him, his dark eyes twinkling maniacally. His look was scornful. "Afeared of dying?" the clerk continued, a grim smile playing upon his lips.

Sparky turned back to face the courtroom.

"I've lived to face more frightening things than death."

"Such as?" enquired the clerk.

"Two days without a drink," came the grim reply.

The clerk rocked back on his heels to glimpse again the tell-tale shaking hands in their cuffs, then landed back on his soles, staring curiously at the pirate at his side.

The courtroom door was thrown open and an elegant figure stepped in. Her face was hidden under a black, floppy hat. She took a seat near the front, removing her hat and allowing ebony, tousled hair to cascade over her shoulders and down to her waist.

A whistle escaped the clerk's lips.

"Just look at that fair maiden who's taken up seat," he said.

Sparky glanced briefly in the direction of the clerk's gaze.

"'Tis my wife," he said, without hint of emotion.

The clerk's jaw fell as the judge climbed the podium and the room fell quiet. Running his eyes over the large, leather-bound book in front of him, the judge turned and addressed the pirate.

"Captain Jose Vaquero," he began, his voice ringing clearly over the heads before him. "You have been found guilty of all the charges brought against you; that you did feloniously and in a hostile manner, attack, engage and take twelve merchant vessels, assaulted their skippers and stole their cargoes; that on the high sea about four leagues from Nombre de Dios, you shot at and took a schooner commanded by Captain James Lawes; that you did raid, plunder and burn the town of Venta Cruces and put the inhabitants in corporal fear of their lives; and that a league from the coast of Rum Cay, you did board a trading schooner, taking both the cargo and crew, murdering the first mate and the boatswain, and selling the remaining number as slaves." A low murmur spread through the court. "I am afraid, Vaquero, you leave me no choice but to insist you go from hence to a house of incarceration, and from thence to the place of execution, where you shall be severally hanged by the neck until you are dead. And may God in his infinite wisdom be merciful on your soul."

4

The judge snapped his book shut and made preparations to leave.

Sparky's wife threw her husband a pitying look, but one dripping with sarcasm. The pirate returned it with an insincere smile as he was led away. The clerk, unable to help himself, glanced back over his shoulder at the striking female, now carefully replacing her hat. She caught his gaze and held it coyly through her lashes.

* * *

The clerk threw open the iron door of the cell.

"Your witch of a wife stole my purse!"

"Ha!" said Sparky. "Thought a man of court would have known better than to trust a woman."

The clerk scowled.

"There's a gentleman here to see you," he muttered, standing aside to allow a formal-looking officer to enter the room.

The officer removed his hat and placed it under his arm, briefly clearing his throat.

"Captain Vaquero," he announced, "I am here on behalf of His Majesty King George. He wishes to engage you as a privateer to serve to protect his kingdom. You shall be given an armed vessel, and you shall be licensed to attack and capture enemy shipping." He replaced his hat. "If you care to follow me I shall take you herewith to be awarded the Letter of the Marque."

Sparky registered no surprise as he followed the officer obediently from the cell, but the clerk let out a whistle of disbelief as they passed.

"Well! You were born under a lucky star, to be sure!" he said, and was treated to a departing wink from the pirate.

Chapter One

Cornwall, 1791

THE morning was fresh and breezy. A pale sun reflected onto the ocean and gulls wheeled and shrieked noisily over the harbour. The ship was landing, battered and ravaged by the wild sea. A man not yet passed his prime leapt from the deck onto the jetty. Soaked from head to toe, his long leather boots were stained dark with oil and his rough clothes were ripped and torn, but his countenance was glowing. He raised an arm to the surprised harbour master and bounded onto the launch.

Hemlock Street had not changed in his absence, and yet as MacBride stepped into its narrow mouth he could feel at once that the place for which he had been longing these past four years had a strange emptiness about it. The early morning sun had not yet risen high enough to sink its warming rays between the cottages, leaving the winding alley shadowy and cool. Nobody was about, with the exception of a long-haired, scruffy mongrel that sat loyally outside a green front door about halfway down the street. The dog's eyes stared, unblinking, and when MacBride frowned, the creature lowered its head and let out a small series of whines. MacBride walked up the street, taking time to look about him. There was an uneasy silence, and someone snapped shut their curtains as he passed by. He reached the dog, crouched down and ruffled its matted fur.

"Duncan," he whispered. "What's happened to you, boy? You've come all bones."

The dog, recognising its master, licked his hand. MacBride smiled then glanced up and noticed that the green door was hanging off its hinges. He rose to his feet and eased it open, his hand resting on the knife in his belt. Dusty floorboards stretched before him. The cottage was empty.

"Morrie?" he called, and his voice reverberated around the empty walls. He took another step in. "Morrie!" This time he bellowed, his voice filled with fear. He ran up the staircase, rotten planks splintering beneath his boots. "*Morrie? Lucy?*"

Each room was like the last. A shell. Empty, dusty and cold. Duncan followed at his master's heels as though afraid to let him out of his sight. MacBride returned to the kitchen, his heart full of fear, and leaned back against the dresser. A small growl escaped Duncan's mouth as the back door began to creep slowly open. MacBride slid his knife silently from his belt. He took a step backwards hiding himself behind the door, and stood perfectly still. Only his fingers moved, flexing and tightening on the handle of the blade. The door opened wider, and the cautious intruder placed a foot inside the room. MacBride ducked out from behind the door and pinned the man up against the cupboard, flicking his knife to his throat. Just in time he realised who it was and released his grip. Duncan let out a bark and wagged his tail.

"Oh, Marty, me boy!" cried the man. Doug Coby grasped the top of MacBride's arm in relief and embraced him. He then drew back and took in the man before him again as if to check it was really him. "I thought someone had broken in, so I did, someone having no business here. Oh my boy! You're back at last! I never once gave up hope for ye. The towners, they said ye were dead, they did, but I knew ye weren't! *'You wait, he'll be back!'* I tells 'em. '*No one gets the better of Marty!'*"

MacBride slapped his old friend on the back.

"Tell me ... Where are my wife and daughter?"

There was silence. Doug lowered his eyes. MacBride's heart pounded in his chest.

"I'm so sorry, Marty. They're dead."

* * *

MacBride sat in a worn, old armchair in Doug's cottage, a glazed expression on his face. All around him were the mementos of a fisherman's life and a large fire roared in the hearth. Martha, Doug's wife, opened the top drawer of her dresser and lifted out a dark green jersey, thick and coarse. She handed it gently to MacBride, who unfolded it.

"This is my jersey," he frowned. He stared at it, fazed. "Yet it can't be mine. I lost mine off the coast of Africa."

Doug and Martha exchanged glances. MacBride looked up at them.

"They took it to Lamorran," Doug said. "They told her ye were dead." Martha dabbed her eyes with a rag. "You were away for so long," continued Doug. "It had been over two years. They were living in poverty. They came here every night, we fed them all we could afford, but she was a proud woman. She …" He took a sharp intake of breath. "It was your jersey, you see. The local pattern for Newlyn – and ye the only man missing. She walked into the sea the night they told her."

"And Lucy?" croaked MacBride. "What of my daughter?"

In reply, Doug handed him the little, woollen hat he had found floating on the waves.

MacBride hardly glanced at it. He didn't need to. It was instantly recognisable as Lucy's.

"They never found her body, mind. But she being small must have got carried away by the waves."

MacBride looked away, staring blankly ahead, his lips slightly parted, mouth dry. He opened his mouth to speak, but no words came out. He shook his head at his own inadequacy and returned his attention to the object that had brought about the destruction of his family.

"That isn't my jersey. It can't be. I've been set up. Someone must have made a duplicate." His stare came back to rest on Doug, his voice now level and purposeful. "Who took it to her?"

Doug and Martha exchanged anxious looks.

"Cardinham," came the reply. MacBride nodded slowly as he digested this last piece of information, and then leaped up and charged out of the door, slamming it behind him. Doug hastened after him, but MacBride was already halfway up the street, Duncan scampering in his wake. "Marty!" cried Doug. "He doesn't live in town anymore!" But MacBride ignored him. Doug hurried inside and plucked his jerkin from the hook. "I'm going after him!" he called to Martha. "Who knows what he might do if there's no one to stop him."

* * *

The stable courtyard at Sanmoor Farm was flooded with early morning light. As MacBride strode across the quadrant, he heard a loud whinnying and the sound of hooves battering a stable door. His horse could sense his return.

"Morwellham …" he whispered, softly stroking the horse's nose. He unlatched the door and patted the horse on the neck before vaulting onto its back. "No time for fond hellos, old friend." He gave the horse a kick and they galloped over the cobbled yard and out of the gate, just as the farmer, a portly man in his middle years, came running out of the farmhouse door, a half-eaten chunk of bread in hand.

"Oy!" yelled Farmer Rogers. "Come back!"

His wife hurried out behind him, her skirts in her hands.

"Did you see the blaggard?" she panted.

The farmer paused, straining his eyes as he stared through the dust into the distance. When he finally turned to look at her there was surprise in his eyes.

"Looked like MacBride," he said. "I think the scoundrel's back."

* * *

Pensilva Cellars was a great hulk of a building that stood on the edge of the cliff between the little fishing communities of Newlyn and Mousehole. Half-built into the cliff behind it, its tall chimneys emerged from the natural rock above it, small wisps of swirling smoke escaping from their tops. The inn gleamed darkly in the weak morning sun, now almost swallowed by giant, black clouds that swept the horizon.

MacBride galloped up the steep, uneven road that twisted its way to the tavern through a scattering of withered, wind-bent trees. The great, iron-studded door was shut and barred. MacBride hammered with all his might.

"Open this door!" he shouted.

There was silence. MacBride pummelled the door still more loudly and shouted again. At last, footsteps could be heard approaching.

"We're closed!" came a woman's voice.

"Open this door, Josephine, or I swear to God I'll break it down!"

This was followed by a moment's pause.

"Who is this?"

It was a demand, but there was a shadow of uncertainty to it.

"It's Martin."

At once there was the sound of a bar being lifted and bolts being shot back. The door opened and MacBride found himself looking into the face of Jo Bryant. He felt unnerved by the sight of her again – her slender body, her long, dark hair uncharacteristically loose and cascading down to her waist. The only change in her was the stillness of her eyes that once harboured sparks of mischief which had danced like jewels in her face. She was bewitching, and for just a moment he paused to take in her beauty. Then he pushed past her into the tavern. He glanced at the familiar retreat around him before turning to Jo again. She looked both sorry and anxious. Shivering slightly, she wrapped her thin, grey dressing gown protectively around her waist and tucked her fists under her arms.

"Oh Martin," she whispered.

The sound of her voice brought MacBride back to his senses.

"Where is he?"

"He doesn't live here anymore ..." began Jo, but MacBride cut her off, turning and gripping her by her shoulders.

"WHERE IS HE?"

"I don't know."

"Don't you do that, Jo, don't you do that to me."

"I don't know! I promise you I don't know!"

"You're lying to me, you're lying to protect him!"

"I swear I am not! I've never lied to you!"

MacBride let his arms fall and strode across the tavern, through the doors and up the winding, rickety staircase, Jo hurrying in his footsteps.

"Martin, I don't know where he is!" she cried, following him as he searched one room after another. "He left. He's gone away. Martin, I know what he did to you and I'm sorry. I don't know what happened to him. He was so jealous, he cracked up. Lost his mind. Martin ... *Martin! Please listen to me!*" She caught him and shook him but MacBride pushed her away.

"You let him!"

"No!" cried Jo, roughly brushing away a tear with the heel of her hand. "No! I didn't know!"

MacBride felt his knees buckle as though the sudden surge of strength he had experienced that morning had deserted him. He was suddenly overwhelmed by tiredness, and wondered how long it had been since he had slept, so keen had he been to return home as quickly as possible. He slid down the wall to the floor and hung his head.

Jo fell to her knees and lifted his face so that his eyes met hers.

"He's taken everything from me," said MacBride, hoarsely. His eyes shone with tears. "And he can't even stick around to face me."

She put her hand over her mouth in despair. He was broken; nothing but an empty shell of the man she used to know. Her heart ached, knowing there was nothing she could do, no words of this world that she could utter that would comfort him. She lifted her hand to brush the tear from his cheek, but he pushed it gently away and, without a word, rose slowly and walked out of the room, leaving Jo on the floor with her own silent sobs.

* * *

From the moment MacBride stepped out of Pensilva, the rain pelted down upon him like poison, and he stood with his arms wide and his mouth open and turned up to the heavy skies, as though he could wash away his pain. When he'd had his fill, he led his horse down the twisting path away from the inn, his dog trotting behind him. Doug was hurrying towards him. The old man tore off his jerkin and wrapped it tightly around MacBride.

"Come on, son," he said, leading him away.

MacBride spent the remainder of the day sleeping deeply in Doug and Martha's attic bedroom. When he woke it was dark. He sat up, trying to recall where he was, to whom this vaguely familiar room with sloping roof and small, arched window belonged. But no sooner had he remembered where he was than the knowledge of his wife's and child's deaths descended back onto his shoulders like a lead weight. He laid his head back down on the pillow and closed his eyes in a bid to slip back into an ignorant sleep.

It was no good. He was no longer tired. He made his way down to the kitchen where Doug and Martha were sitting in chairs beside the fire. MacBride wordlessly filled a pot with water.

"You must stay here for the time being," said Martha, firmly.

"I'm going home," replied MacBride, shortly.

"Don't be daft, boy, ye can't live there," said Doug. MacBride did not answer. "Stubborn as his wife," muttered Doug to Martha. Then, turning his face back to MacBride, he added, "Even yer blasted dog refused to come for food most nights, insisted on looking after himself! What's the matter with you all?"

"I'm going down *The Anchor*," said MacBride, and he disappeared out of the door.

The rain had ceased and the night was clear and starry. MacBride's breath hung in the air.

"Hold on, Marty, I'm a-comin' with ye!" Doug called. MacBride stopped and obediently waited for his friend to reach his side. They fell into step. "This is no time to be on your own," said Doug.

MacBride stopped and turned to him.

"I will not rest until the death of my family has been avenged. I will see to it that Cardinham settles his debts. With God as my witness, let that be my vow."

He strode on. Doug caught him up again.

"Did ye think I didn't know that?"

"Do you really want to be a part of this, Doug?"

"You are a son to me. Lamorran was like a daughter, and little Lucy a granddaughter. Do not make the mistake of thinking ye are the only one who has lost their family. Whatever ye do, my boy, I will be there to help ye all I can."

* * *

The Anchor Inn stood on the quayside – a rowdy place, heavy with smoke and the hushed voices of smugglers discussing their illicit business. Situated at the bottom of Hemlock Street, MacBride had frequented it often. It was an unspoken rule of the locals to talk of all things innocent whenever a stranger entered. MacBride felt like one of those strangers now as he walked in from the cold. Little by little, the inn fell silent as the fishermen in their high-necked jerseys turned and stared at the man they all believed to have perished at sea some four years earlier. First they looked upon him as a stranger; then they looked upon him as a ghost. At last a tall, stocky man at the bar thumped down his ale and cried,

"So, Bridie! You've decided to come home at last!" He clapped him heartily on the back and a large cheer rose up. MacBride smiled unconvincingly and shook his old friend Cattermole's hand.

"Some home I've come back to," he said.

Cattermole nodded then brushed his greying hair back off his face.

"Aye. That evil bastard! We knew something wasn't right about it, but she had gone before any of us knew what had happened. He was a fool if he thought she'd go running back to him just 'cos you weren't around." He paused awkwardly, wondering if he'd said too much. "Well?" he added. "You gonna tell us where you've been?" He beckoned to the innkeeper who produced an ale for the smuggler. The innkeeper nodded at the tankard, signalling the ale was on the house.

"Algiers," said MacBride, sitting down at an old table in a dark corner. His sea-faring friends gathered around to hear the tale, leaving Doug still grudgingly buying his own drink at the bar. "I was captured in the Mediterranean by a privateer and sold as a slave. It wasn't pleasant."

"I don't doubt," chimed in Jack North, one of MacBride's old crew, "I've heard tales of Algiers and their patroons."

MacBride nodded and took a sip of ale.

"I watched them tie people to stakes, cut off their limbs, smother the stumps with honey and leave them to be eaten alive by the insects." There was a humorous grimace from Doug as he finally found a seat. "But what they did to me is nothing to the torture I've come home to."

"If there were enough insects in this cursed country I'd vote we do the same thing to Cardinham. If we could track him down," Cattermole said.

"He'll come back," said MacBride.

Doug looked up.

"What makes you so sure?"

"Because I've come back."

Cattermole slapped MacBride on the back and grinned.

"And just what are you planning to do with yourself in the meantime?"

"Just what I've always done. Churchyard still haunted, James?"

"Aye, and phantoms still walk the moor road, and Morte Bay still full of dead ships, Cap'n," replied Cattermole.

MacBride drained his tankard, thumped the table and rose to his feet.

"Nothing's changed then. Let's go."

"Where?" asked Cattermole.

"To repair my ship." He glanced at Doug who gestured to the fact that he had only presently sat down. "Get off home, old friend, you must be tired."

MacBride led the way out of *The Anchor*, Cattermole and North following in his wake.

"Now?" said Cattermole. "Don't you sleep?"

"Slept all day."

Cattermole turned to North and shrugged. They followed him to the quayside. It was cold and quiet. Everything was still. As the approached the glossy water they saw a decrepit cutter bobbing beside the jetty. Duncan leapt seamlessly onto it.

"Bugger," said North. "That's not *The Mevagissey?*"

MacBride jumped aboard.

"She's in a bad way," said Cattermole, "Do you think she'll make it round to Morte Bay?"

"Aye, she'll make it," replied MacBride, reeling in the ropes. "She's carried me all the way from Africa. If I have to row her there myself, she'll get there." He flung the ropes onto the deck. "I'm mending my ship. She's all I got now."

Something caught his eye hurrying along the jetty behind him. It was Doug Coby.

"Hey laddie!" he panted, hailing him. "Wait laddie, I'm a-comin' with ye!"

Morte Bay was drenched in darkness. Moonlight picked out the shadows of shipwrecks, some half submerged under the waves. MacBride guided *The Mevagissey* through a safe passage into a cove, where they dropped anchor and rowed ashore. North and Doug were armed with lanterns, while MacBride kicked at seashells that had been swept ashore amongst the shingle. His manner was matter-of-fact, but inside he felt as though black hands were twisting around his heart. Waves whispered loudly across the shore, taking MacBride back to when he had last walked here. The same waves and Lucy, dear little Lucy, running along the shingle, screaming and laughing as the icy water nipped at her toes, darting down to grasp pretty shells which she carried in the folded hem of her white skirt. MacBride heard his own voice break through his reverie as he ordered his men to check the rudder and keel of the skeletal hull of a wreck that had been thrown against the cliff.

"I'll see what condition the bowsprit is in," he added.

They salvaged what they could. Later, when carrying parts back to the rowing boat, MacBride stopped suddenly.

"Did you hear that?" he hissed to Doug who was looking worried at his side.

They stood still for a moment or two, but the tide was in and the breaking of the waves and the swishing of shingle being dragged back into the sea confused their ears. MacBride sniffed the air.

"Nothing here, my man," said Cattermole.

"Put your lanterns out," whispered MacBride. The men did as they were asked. MacBride strained his eyes. The dark shadows of the cliffs towered above them. Beside them, the rowing boat bobbed gently, moonlight picking out *The Mevagissey* silently waiting on the horizon. "Keep walking," said MacBride, quietly.

They reached the boat and began loading what they could. Then with a flash they were bathed in the light of a host of lanterns. Cattermole shielded his eyes with the back of his hand. After blinking once or twice he could see the figures of five men before him. Four of them were preventative men, and the local coastguard accompanied them.

"Hello, boys," said one of the customs officers. "What's going on here then?"

"Out for a stroll," said North as Cattermole announced that they were building an outhouse.

MacBride, who was bent over the stern, straightened up slowly. As the light fell on his face, the nearest officer stepped back in surprise.

"Well, well, well!" he said. "Mr MacBride! I heard you were dead."

"It would be easier for me if you stuck to that," said MacBride with an amiable grin.

"Yet here you are, large as life."

"Or perhaps you merely see my ghost before you?" suggested the smuggler, opening his arms wide in gesture.

The officer grinned and poked him with a stick.

"Solid ghost. I shall have to pass the word back down to Shanley."

"No skin off my nose," said MacBride carelessly, pushing the boat into the water.

The customs officer waved his lantern from side to side in an attempt to see what was going on.

"And what business do you have here tonight, Mr MacBride?"

"Fixing my boat," replied MacBride, sloshing through the shallows, "Surely that's no crime?"

"That ship belongs to us," broke in a second officer, nodding towards the wreck.

MacBride followed his finger and raised his eyebrows.

"Good luck," he said. "I have a feeling even mine will sail better than that rotting carcass."

"And what, may I ask, are you going to be using that little cutter for?" asked the first officer. "Going back to your old ways?" As he spoke he glanced at Coby, Cattermole and North wading out to the rowing boat. He knew their faces. "I am afraid I have no choice but to place you under arrest," said the officer, producing a restraining belt and advancing towards MacBride.

"For what?" asked MacBride, with feigned surprise.

"Now, now. You're going back to smuggling! You're a smuggler and don't try to deny it."

"A smuggler?" repeated MacBride with a puzzled look on his face. "Oh, you mean one of those brave free-traders? I've heard all about them." He smiled wryly. "Never met one though."

"Bloody rubbish! Even the local vicars are in with the smugglers!"

"Ah! Then they must be good people."

The customs officer leaned closer.

"They are *not* good people. They are dirt. *You* are dirt."

MacBride stared at him quizzically, leaning forward so he could whisper.

"My good officer, you know, and I know, that all I have ever been is an honest fisherman."

"And I'm the King of England!" cried the officer.

"Well I'm willing to go along with that," shrugged MacBride, "but I think my story is more plausible."

"Shut up, MacBride!"

The officer was losing his patience.

"Well come on, Officer! What are you going to arrest us for? The wrecking of a wreck?"

"I will bring you down, MacBride, I will bring you down for illegal import."

"You catch me at it, Officer, and I'll go quietly."

"That won't be a problem," growled the officer. "There will be revenue vessels stationed at sea within the month. They'll be able to intercept every boat in every creek and every little harbour along the coast of Devonshire and Cornwall."

"That's very impressive," smiled MacBride, "but all you are going to find in any boat of mine is pilchards. Now if you'll excuse us, gentlemen, as much as I am enjoying our conversation, I have a ship to fix." He turned and waded back to the rowing boat.

"You just stay cocky, MacBride!" shouted the customs officer as MacBride clambered into the boat. "You just stay cocky!"

When they had rowed out of earshot, MacBride glanced at Cattermole.

"So they're intercepting at sea now?" he grunted. "You failed to mention *that*."

Chapter Two

MacBRIDE worked on the boat day and night, and slept hardly at all. After two weeks, *The Mevagissey* was sea-worthy once again. MacBride made the announcement that he would be leaving for Cherbourg at first light.

Doug Coby was anxious.

"Marty, you must sleep. Ye can't go that distance without a good rest."

"Leave it, man," grunted MacBride, tossing a couple sacks of wool over his shoulder. "This is something I must do."

True to his word, early the following morning he left with his team of twelve men, Doug Coby's young nephew, Isaac, amongst them at the tender age of fourteen.

Doug and Martha waved them off from the jetty. Doug gave a deep sigh.

"Be merciful, sweet Jesus, and bring them back safe."

"We must put our trust in Martin," Martha reassured him, wrapping her arm around his shoulder.

"It's Martin I'm worried about," replied Doug, gruffly. "He's got a death wish now, that man."

Nevertheless, *The Mevagissey* returned in just under two weeks carrying a large contraband of brandy. When they were approaching land, MacBride lashed the kegs together in pairs and attached a heavy sinker to them before throwing them overboard into the black water.

"How do you remember where they are?" asked Isaac.

MacBride laughed.

"I've been doing this since I was eight and landing here since I was seventeen. I could find the spot blindfolded now." He pointed to the silhouette of a mine on the hill. "They are exactly south-south-east from that mine."

"When will we come back for them?"

"Tomorrow night," replied MacBride, "But only if the coast is clear. After the run-in at Morte I have a feeling there are going to be a lot of eyes looking out for us."

All looked quiet on anchoring in the harbour. MacBride threw out the rope and secured the ship. Isaac was the first on dry land and Cattermole handed him a box of pilchards, nodding towards a little office on the waterfront. Isaac obediently took the crate and was followed by another five of the crew, similarly laden.

"All looks good at present, Capt'n," mused Jack North.

MacBride did not reply.

* * *

Later that day, the crew sat in *The Anchor* sipping ales. Only MacBride was missing. He was making a detour to the town church.

It was within the walls of All Saints church that he had married Lamorran over fourteen years ago. She had looked like a piece of Heaven; the most beautiful creature he had ever laid eyes upon. She was dressed in white silk-velvet with autumn leaves wound into her hair, her cheeks pinched and glowing. It had been a cold, crisp day in December, the fields and houses white under a sparkling of frost, and they had left the church laughing under a shower of winter petals.

MacBride didn't pause for a moment to take in his surroundings now. He walked straight under the arch and into the church, the heavy door swinging back with a thud behind him.

Father Malone was kneeling at the altar, praying. He was known amongst the free traders as "Mops" because he always cleaned up after them and hid their tracks. The clergyman, hearing footsteps, stood and turned to face him.

"So, you've come to see me at last! They told me you were back." He beamed and held out his hands. "How are you, my son?"

"In one piece," MacBride assured him, grasping his hand.

Mops shook it vigorously and clapped him on the back.

"Yes, and praise the good Lord for that! They told me you were taken to Algiers! God has smiled upon you, my boy, for few come out of there in one piece. He has doubtlessly been watching over you."

"I'd rather he had been watching over my family," said MacBride as they began to walk back down the aisle. "I'm quite used to taking care of myself."

"Ah, yes, that was indeed a most unfortunate story." Mops shook his head soberly. "I cannot make sense of it." When MacBride did not answer he placed a hand on his shoulder. "You must never feel alone. There is always a place waiting for you here in God's house."

"God isn't part of my plans right now."

"A friend then."

MacBride turned to face him.

"Ay, a friend. That is why I came to see you."

"Oh?"

MacBride dropped his voice.

"Is there still room in the crypt?"

Mops frowned and glanced over his shoulder towards the door. When he turned back there was a smile playing about his lips.

"Going back to your old ways, son?"

"Never left them."

"Always room in the crypt, Marty. So long as there is a cask of brandy in it for my own medicinal purposes."

MacBride winked.

"There's eighty kegs lying just beyond the harbour as we speak."

Mops face broke into a broad smile. He unhooked some keys from the belt slung below his waist and handed them over.

"I must say, it's good to have you back!"

* * *

The church clock struck two as MacBride and his crew made their way towards the graveyard. With them came eight borrowed farm horses, their hooves muffled, three of which were pulling carts laden with brandy. It was a hushed procession that made its way through the inky night. Not a word was spoken, only the soft rumbling of cart wheels gave them away. Six men were given the job of lookouts and positioned themselves at observation points in the road and around the graves as the gang crossed the graveyard to reach the entrance to the crypt. MacBride took Mops' keys from his coat and swiftly unlocked the iron gate. It creaked. He struck a match and lit a lantern. Directing the men to commence unloading the carts, he stepped in and took a quick look around.

The crypt was sizeable and as yet remained a secret to the preventative men, despite suspecting Father Malone of involvement with the smugglers for some time. There were several steps leading down into the crypt itself, which was cold and empty save for one coffin at the far end.

MacBride made his way quietly towards it and pressed his ear to the wood before carefully opening the lid and shining the lantern inside. He grimaced.

"All right, Capt'n?" whispered a nervous young member of his crew, Eli Abe.

"Indeed." MacBride replaced the lid. "You can't be too sure of what may have changed when you've been away for some time."

"You don't trust the Father, Capt'n?" Eli was surprised.

"I do now I know no one is waiting for us," he said and pushed by Eli to signal the all-clear to the other men.

It was half past three when the last of the barrels had been loaded safely into the crypt. The horse and carts were driven away as soon as they had been emptied, and as the final cart trundled softly out of the churchyard just eight men and two horses remained. MacBride was fishing the keys from his coat to lock the gate on his way out when he heard a low and urgent whistle from somewhere near the east wall. In an instant the remaining smugglers disappeared, blending into the darkness, their horses with them. MacBride silently turned the key in the lock and withdrew quickly. He ran towards his horse, swiftly removing the muffles from its hooves, and then, giving the restless Morwellham a pat, he vaulted onto his back. He left the silent graves and trotted laggardly to the churchyard gates.

The tree-flanked lane beyond was even darker than the churchyard, and the oppressive silence prevailed with only the rhythmic clacking of the horse's hooves on the stones penetrating through. But MacBride was well aware that he was not alone. He kept his focus ahead of him, unsure of exactly where the officers were, although he could almost hear them breathing in the suspended stillness. He slowed his horse to flush them out. A lantern was lit and two officers stepped out of the darkness.

"Halt there!" commanded Officer Pentlan.

"Whoa!" called MacBride, obediently. At this command the horse reared up and galloped off into the night. "I can't control him!" MacBride called over his shoulder as they were swallowed by the shadows. "Not very well trained I'm afraid!"

"*Not* very well trained," muttered the second customs officer.

Officer Pentlan caught his eye and raised a brow.

"Indeed, Roberts?" he said. "I think you'll find it's quite the opposite."

* * *

Officers Pentlan and Roberts caught up with MacBride the

following afternoon. They found him sat alone in *The Anchor*, sinking a pint of ale. He smiled and waved to them as they entered, and despite the tavern being almost empty – a good many of the fishermen had gone to sea – the eyes of those who had dropped in for an early libation followed the officers as they made their way to the corner where their quarry was settled.

MacBride raised his foot under the table, pushed out a chair for each of them and gestured to them to take a seat. The officers sat down.

"Won't you have a drink?" he asked amiably.

"We're here on business," said Pentlan.

"Fair enough. Don't have a ha'penny on me, as it happens." He waved towards his tankard. "I only got this because they felt sorry for me."

"I presume it is no coincidence you're here on your own today," said Pentlan, removing his hat and placing it on the table. "You often take nocturnal journeys, MacBride?"

"It's odd that you should know my name despite my never having had the pleasure of setting eyes upon you before," mused MacBride. "Well, before last night, that is."

"If you were a decent man, I probably wouldn't," said Pentlan.

"A *decent* man would introduce himself," said MacBride with a smile.

"Officer Roberts, Officer Pentlan," said Pentlan, gesturing first to Roberts and then to himself.

MacBride shook their hands in turn.

"What can I do for you?"

"You can start by answering the question, MacBride."

"I'm trying to keep busy," replied the smuggler nonchalantly. "Sleep doesn't come too readily at the moment."

"I must admit I did not expect to find you so close to town. I had men posted on some of the more remote roads."

"Well, thank you for that enlightenment, but why would I be there? If you had wished an audience with me, you could have just dropped in at my cottage."

"I am no more a fool than you, MacBride," said Pentlan, leaning forward. "You know quite well to what I am referring."

MacBride mirrored the officer's motion by leaning forward himself and lowering his voice.

"Officer Pentlan, I have just lost my wife and only child. You will excuse me if I do not behave conventionally for some time."

"Not conventionally?" echoed Pentlan, rising to his feet and replacing his hat. "On the contrary, I saw nothing to which I did not expect."

He stalked towards the door, Roberts following in his wake.

"Officer?" MacBride called after him. Pentlan turned. "John Cardinham. You heard of him?"

Pentlan paused.

"I have not," he said curtly, and left the inn.

MacBride finished his ale and disappeared through a door beside the bar. The innkeeper, an unexpectedly diffident man called Lurret, left the bar and hurried after him as he made his way down the passage. He knew MacBride would have questions for him.

"Who are those men? Where's Shanley? Isn't this still Shanley's patch?" MacBride asked.

"He's still here, Marty," replied Lurret, falling into step beside him. "But I tell you, be careful. They're sending down more and more gaugers by the day, and they're getting more hard-nosed and more hard-bitten, each and every one of them."

"They're intercepting at sea," said MacBride.

"Aye, I heard that," said the innkeeper. "And I heard they may even be enlisting dragoons if the situation spirals any further out of their control. They're recruiting more and more. That young 'un that was in 'ere with Pentlan, I haven't seen him before. I tell you, they're coming down by the day."

"*Welcome home*," MacBride muttered.

"I wouldn't serve them, lad, if I didn't need the money," said Lurret, apologetically. Then he chuckled and gave him a poke in the ribs. "But why turn away good paying customers when you can sell them some authentic free-trade brandy! Word's about you have some a-begging?"

"I do indeed, sir," replied MacBride, "What's your requirement?"

Lurret handed MacBride the lantern. "Give me two dozen," he said, rubbing his hands together.

MacBride took a diversion and made his way down the steps.

The cellars that lay beneath *The Anchor* were not the great cavernous chambers that Pensilva concealed, but they did have one redeeming feature; they harboured a trapdoor which led into a tunnel, a tunnel which ran from the beach up to the church tower. It had been hollowed out many years ago by smugglers for smugglers, and provided a safe and hidden pathway from shore to store. At the bottom of the steps, MacBride shifted a barrel of spirits to reveal the hatch below. He took a long metal pike from the wall and used it to lever up the trapdoor. Then, once he had lowered himself down, he reached up and carefully slid the hatch back into place.

MacBride held up the lantern, revealing a tunnel running into the distance. The roof was low, demanding he stoop slightly. The walls were no more than compacted earth with granite muscling through here and there. It smelled musty from lack of fresh air and there had been a small fall of earth half-way along that MacBride had to pick his way over. It was a passage that seemed to grow longer the more times you walked it. It ran in a straight line with a few curves and twists where the granite protruded from the ground and walls. The church was nestled into the steep heath land behind the tavern, and this allowed the secret tunnel to run directly through the hillside and into the church tower. There were a series of wooden staircases that led from the end of the tunnel up to an old door, disguised on the vestry side with cut stone which blended with the tower walls and had, in any case, the added protection of an eight foot tapestry adorning it.

MacBride slipped out quietly from behind this tapestry now. He made his way across the vestry and was just about to slip through the curtain into the church itself when he heard a familiar voice just inches away on the other side of the screen.

"These are dangerous men, Father," the voice was saying, "I urge you to send word to me at once if you see anything suspicious afoot."

"Gracious!" came the voice of Mops. "Have you presented this request to every soul in town?"

"We have reason to believe that MacBride's gang have been working specifically in the area of this church. We met him on the road outside in the early hours of this morning."

"By the church?" nodded Mops. "A grave crime, indeed."

"Do not mock me, Father," said Pentlan, growing agitated.

"I mock you not," said Mops. "Although I fail to see what is so unlawful about being in the vicinity of a church, albeit in the dead of night."

"MacBride is a villain and a smuggler."

"Both?"

"I do not like your tone."

"I do not care much for yours."

"You are aware, Father, that consorting with smugglers is not just an offence but a sin?"

"And may I remind *you*, Officer, that this man, a man I hold in great esteem, a man well-known as a devoted friend to me, has just returned home to find his family gone? Has it escaped you that this is a church, somewhere where he might find a little solace and relief from the relentless suffering, from the demons that will be biting at his heels from daybreak to nightfall? Only God can provide him with that peace at this time. For goodness' sake, man, there is a stone commemorating his wife and daughter in the graveyard. He can sit here all day and all night if it so suits him!"

"He didn't seem distressed to me," put in Pentlan. "The deaths of his loved ones provides quite the timely justification for his presence here, don't they? How advantageous."

"Guard your tongue and judge not that of which you know nothing," said Mops. "MacBride is not a man who wears his heart upon his sleeve. Has it not occurred to you that he visits their memorial at night when he has the assurance that nobody else will be about to witness him grieve? You have only just encountered the man, do not make the mistake of listening to embellished rumours and condemning him of lacking all respectability! If he were such a man, I swear he would be no friend of Father Malone. Now if you'll excuse me, I am a busy man today."

"Thank you, Father," grunted Pentlan as Mops began collecting two or three books of psalms from the pews.

"And may God grace you with a little more insight," called Mops gruffly as the two officers left the church.

As soon as they were out of sight, MacBride emerged from the curtain causing Mops to start violently, almost dropping his books.

"Lord preserve us!" he muttered. "Don't creep up on an old man."

"My apologies, Father," said MacBride with a grin, "I was coming to warn you of two nosy customs men but I see I am somewhat overdue."

"They are rather fresh at the job."

"Fresh?" asked MacBride.

The reverend smiled.

"They want me to keep a dedicated watch for you when the miners take leave and come to town at the end of next week."

He gave a little wink.

"The miners?" enquired MacBride, lifted by the prospect of an affair with the ocean again. He nodded thoughtfully. "Must be time to put back out."

* * *

It was dusk. Pensilva Cellars towered grandly on the cliff.

Josephine stood by the open window, a soft breeze caressing her hair. She watched as the small fleet of fishing boats sailed out of Mounts Bay, their lamps shimmering on the twilight water.

The sound of hooves penetrated her thoughts and she swung her gaze to the carriage rumbling up the steep incline towards the tavern, pulled by two large, black carthorses. They swept onto the forecourt, snorting misty breath, and came to a halt at the tavern entrance. The carriage door opened and a tall man wrapped in a dark coat and hat stepped out into the dirt. The figure looked distantly familiar. Jo stiffened, then leaped from the window seat and hurried down the staircase and along a passage beside the main tavern. There was something she needed to protect. She darted through a door and raced down the stone steps into the great, cellars that were hollowed out of the rock beneath. It was almost too dark to see, and Jo struck a match and lit a lantern. Shadows fell between the many barrels of liquor. There were chambers spilling off the main cellar, an almost maze-like tangle of underground rooms and passages. Jo stopped outside a little wooden door with a softly glowing arched window. She hesitated, biting her lip. Then she felt on the barrel against the wall and grasped the key that was kept there. This was a visit she made often and in secret, and it was one that brought both sadness and joy. She let out a sigh, but as she was about to open the door she sensed someone behind her and she turned. Her stomach lurched as she saw a dark form silently towering above her. Jo threw her hand to her mouth to stifle a scream and as she moved, the light from the window fell upon the face of the figure.

It was, as she feared, John Cardinham.

He looked different; he had put on weight and was wearing a moustache. Yet, his features appeared somehow sharper. He had shadows beneath his eyes, eyes which, in the feeble light, were like deep pools of darkness that seemed to sink right into the jaws of the underworld. It was a countenance twisted with hate and jealousy.

He gave a spiteful grin, and Jo shook herself.

"You're back," she said, brushing past him. "How is Hell?"

"Oh, warmer than it is here." He gestured towards her chilly welcome, and peered through the window in the door. "I'll take you there sometime." But Jo was on her way upstairs, uninterested in the answer. Cardinham followed her. "How is the little spawn, by the way?" he asked as he caught her up.

Jo looked repulsed and didn't answer him. She wanted to distract him from the occupant of the locked room.

"What are you doing here? It's late."

"I've come to spend the night with you, my love."

"I don't think so."

Cardinham smiled and poured himself a cognac.

"Who's going to stop me?" Jo busied herself with collecting up a few empty tankards, glowering at him across the room. He smiled again. "You're exquisite when you scowl."

"Go back to Hell," replied Jo.

Cardinham laughed.

"Not without you, my treasure."

Jo placed the empty tankards on the bar and made to leave the room, but Cardinham intercepted her.

"Let me through," she demanded.

"Not until we've had a little talk."

Cardinham's tone was firm.

"*Let me through*," cried Jo, trying to push him away.

But he would not budge. He simply stood there, bellowing with laughter. Jo tried again in vain, then turned and went under the beams behind the bar to the back room. When she reappeared she was brandishing a flintlock rifle.

"Get out of my inn," she said.

Cardinham gave another laugh. Then he was closing in on her, paying no heed to the gun pointing at his head. He pressed his body close against her.

"Do not pretend you have the courage to kill a man," he hissed.

"It cannot take courage if a man such as you is capable of such feats," whispered Jo.

Incensed, he struck her across the jaw and sent her reeling.

"Well?" he laughed. "Come on then! Shoot me. *Kill* me."

His vile laugh echoed around the inn, around her head, deafening her.

"Come, Josephine! Is there no conviction to your threats? Pull the trigger!"

Jo repositioned the rifle and took aim, her heart pounding in her chest.

"That your father's gun?" Cardinham asked, strolling between the tables. Jo traced his steps with the barrel of the rifle. "He couldn't use it either. Didn't believe in killing, did he? How ironic that he paid for his belief with his life." He guffawed. "And you, you still follow his lead? You watched the yellow-bellied loon die because of his spinelessness and still, *still* you have not changed."

Jo let down the rifle and held her throbbing jaw in her hand.

"Indeed, my beliefs are stronger than ever because of his death," she retaliated. "And if only the bastard who killed him believed the same, my father would still be alive."

"He would have been alive if he had used *that gun*! There is no room left for saints in this world, Josephine. Only fools."

"You killed Lamorran," said Jo, taking aim again.

"So don't do me any favours," shrugged Cardinham indifferently.

"Use it. *Use that and kill me*, Jo. You hate me, remember? You *hate* me with *all your heart*. So *do it*, Jo. *Pull the trigger*."

For a few moments they stood staring at each other, Jo's finger poised on the trigger. Then her hand began to tremble, and she slowly lowered the gun.

Cardinham laughed.

"Well, I'm thankful, if not surprised," he said, "I wouldn't want to go without seeing MacBride die first."

"What a coincidence," said Jo. "I recall him confessing the same of you."

She regretted the words as soon as she said them.

In a flash Cardinham was beside her. He grabbed her by her hair, wrenching her head back to face him.

"So you've seen him then?"

"I've seen him but once," she replied, soberly. "When he came to demand the fate of his poor wife."

"I watched him sail," he breathed, his lips a whisper from the skin of her cheek. "He'll be back for the miners. I want to know where he'll be when he returns, Josephine."

"He won't talk to me now," said Jo firmly.

Cardinham shook her.

"*Make* him!" he ordered. "Gain his confidence and then send word to me. I want to know where the hoard will be stashed and when he and his men will be up to their tricks again."

"I will not betray him!" she cried.

Cardinham caught her jaw in his powerful fingers and forced her to look at him. She yelped out in pain.

"*Do it*," he said. "Or you know the consequences."

He kissed her brutally, his fingers digging into her face, before roughly releasing her and striding towards the door. Jo called after him, a hand on her stinging cheek.

"My father possessed valour and virtue, qualities you will never be capable of," she said as he was departing.

"Yet he is dead and I am alive," taunted Cardinham.

"I see the same traits in Martin MacBride," added Jo. "That is why I have always loved him."

Cardinham stopped and turned, his face a mixture of mockery and hate.

"Ironic, then, that you should become the catalyst in his destruction," he said, scornfully. He grinned, mockingly. When he saw the stout resolution in her eyes he added, "You know what I'll do, Josephine, if you don't do as I say. Remember, I 'possess no valour of virtue'. Do not make the mistake of thinking me incapable of such a deed. It will not be difficult." He turned and strode out into the night. "I await your news!"

Jo hurried across the flagstones and quickly drew the bolts after him.

CHAPTER THREE

MacBRIDE walked slowly across what was once the dining room of his home, his rain-heavy coat dripping and splattering patterns in the dust that covered the floor. He took a moment to look about him; the misty cobwebs that lingered in the corners, the abandoned table where many rich and happy dinners had been enjoyed. It was just a house now. Everything that had made it a home was gone. Returning from sea this time had been hard. While away, it was as if the death of his family had been nothing but a hideous dream, and this evening he had returned to Cornwall to waken and find it all true. The home that he had shared with his love and their precious daughter was as hollow and deserted as the chamber in his chest where his heart used to beat, as though the happy times it had harboured had never taken place, as if the people it had sheltered had never lived. Perhaps it would have been easier if he could have persuaded himself that this was indeed the case, but Lucy's woollen bonnet lay on the table, a cruel prompt to the inescapable truth, and MacBride's eyes filled with tears. But despair turned to anger and he hurled the table across the room before turning and kicking the broken door so hard that it landed with a clatter in the back alley.

It was late. Night had descended like a vast black cloud and surrounded the smuggler, who sat slumped in the corner of the room, a small candle flickering on a piece of old tin in front of him. Its flame tripped and twirled in the breeze which blew phantoms through the open doorway. MacBride stared at the dancing flame, his head slightly to one side, his eyes red from tears. He held his finger into it and watched as it bit into the skin. He felt so numb that it was almost a surprise to feel pain sear through him, giving him respite from his wholly-consuming grief.

The wounds were deep. Perhaps they were too deep. He took a swig from the bottle of French cognac that stood on the wooden boards beside the tobacco and cigarette ends. False warmth poured into his body. His Pa, back home in Sandgreen in Scotland, had warned him never to "take up with a lady". He had only been a boy at the time, recently bereft of his mother, and had timidly spoken of her one crisp morning while clambering down the meagre cliff path to the coast below with his turbulent father.

"Ach, make sure ye watch out for the wee lassies!" his father had said. "No such thing as love, my boy, ye just remember that. It's a lie. Ye pander to love, ye pander to the devil, laddie, and it'll rip yer livin' soul from yer body. Then ye'll be done for!"

"But you married Ma."

"Aye, and ye best do as I say, not as I did. I made the mistakes so ye could learn from 'em."

"Were marrying Ma a mistake, Father?"

Duncan MacBride gave a snort.

"Aye, it were a mistake. And I'll tell ye this, laddie, ye let your guard down and it *gets ye*! Ye've sold yer soul and ye'll never be a free man again." He had patted MacBride on the shoulder. "Keep away from them, Marty, my boy. Keep well away."

MacBride lit another crudely-rolled leaf cigarette – a new trick with tobacco that he'd seen once or twice in France. He lifted his flintlock pistol and studied it thoughtfully. Only now that it was too late did he understand. He'd do anything, even sell his soul, to get his wife and daughter back. He took another swig of Cousin Jackie.

"*Will you trade, Satan?*" he called, his voice echoing in the empty room. A mocking silence answered him. He leaned back against the stone wall, laughing. He took a drag on the cigarette.

Another swig of cognac. He held up the bottle as if toasting a spirit who might be present in the room with him. "To the grave," he said, and took a gulp. *What now?* The world was dark and bleak without his family. How much of him was even left alive anyway? He lifted the pistol again and stared at it. *Another swig.* Blinking, he took a deep gulp of air, a tear falling from each blue eye. Then, biting down on the cigarette in his mouth, he lifted the pistol so that the barrel rested against the underside of his chin. He gripped the trigger hard and closed his eyes. As he held his breath he could feel his heart pounding like waves crashing inside him and, screwing up his eyes, could almost see the great golden gates of Heaven waiting for him. The pounding became louder, as if desperately telling him he was still alive, begging him for mercy, filling his ears, and then his head. And before it snatched him from sweet release, MacBride pulled the trigger.

He screwed up his face in agony – not from the gunshot, but from the lack of it. The rain and the sea had dampened the gunpowder and rendered it useless. He gave a howl and hurled the pistol across the room. Throwing his head back against the wall, he wailed, "Oh God, free me!" He drew his hands over his face and prayed. "I ask of you not paradise or immortality, only numbness. Give me that at least. I don't want to see, I don't want to hear, I don't want to *feel*." He shuddered, and added in whisper, "I am not strong enough to endure your will. Save me."

Again, he was answered only with a mocking silence that echoed through his mind. He sat, his head in his hands. He stirred only to finish the bottle, and when it was dead he opened his eyes to find himself still alive. Duncan had come to sit at his feet and he ruffled the fur on the top of his head.

"Afraid you might have to fend for yourself again, eh?"

And he wrestled with him playfully.

CHAPTER FOUR

"**A**NOTHER round here, Miss Bryant!" called Bert Crocker, waving his glass in the air. A tin miner, he spoke with a voice choked with dust.

Tom Crycot, a fellow miner, nudged Eli Abe who was busy fanning out his hand of cards.

"Hear they're tightening up on the old smuggling rounds?"

"Aye," replied Abe, in a low voice. "We've had to dodge the bastards every time we've come back to port in the last three months. Now MacBride is back they're even hotter on our trail."

"He's got a bad reputation so far as they're concerned," nodded Crycot. "Shame. He's a good man."

Abe pooled some money into the pot at the centre of the table.

"That he is," he agreed. "He didn't deserve what they've done to him."

"Damn right," put in Doug Coby, as Jo leaned over from behind him to place a fresh ale on the table. "Damn fine lady, Morrie MacBride."

"You knew her well, Doug?" asked Crocker, adding his own coins to the pot.

"She lived next door. But she were one of the gang." He laughed. "Hanging out her red blouse on the line to warn us when Shanley or his father were about, then leading them on with those womanly looks of hers and distracting them while we moored the boat."

"She used to come out on *The Mevagissey* with us before Lucy was born," added Cattermole.

"Yeah, and she baffled the gaugers," laughed North. "You remember that time she stuffed some of the tea we'd brought back up her dress. She looked …" He stopped as he caught sight of MacBride standing in the doorway. MacBride strolled over and pulled up a chair.

"Bridie, I'm sorry …" North began.

MacBride appeared to ignore him. He took a good look around the bar, catching Jo's eye briefly as he did so. He smiled then turned back to the table. "On our own here tonight?" he asked.

"It would seem so," replied Doug. "You staying for a round of Pharo, boy?"

"No, I'm just here to take the orders," said MacBride, glancing over at the bar again.

"Well here's an order: stay for an ale. One at least."

"No," replied MacBride, firmly, "I'm not stopping."

For a moment or two they stared at each other stubbornly. Then Doug gave a sigh and, leaning back and balancing his chair on its hind legs, he whistled to the tables at the back. At once a man stood up and came over. He silently handed MacBride a tattered piece of rag paper.

"Usual code. Mops wrote it out for us." He gave Doug a quick nod, and retreated back to his table. MacBride glanced at the paper.

"These all miners' lodgings?" he asked.

"Aye, sir," answered the stranger.

There was a pause as MacBride read down the list.

"I don't have any cambric," he said shortly, "I can get that next time and get it to you. The rest I can do."

He turned to leave.

"There's a new lad," Crocker called after him, "Henry. Young

42

'un down at Ruan Major for the next couple of days. He'll make it worth your while."

"That's miles from Poldark!" cried Doug.

"It's no problem," said MacBride, calmly, and left the inn.

There was a pause.

"He seems OK," said Crycot, as the door swung shut behind him. "Just his normal nonchalant self."

"Nonchalant, aye," said Doug. "But I fear he's taking it a lot harder than he's letting show."

"You fear for him?" asked Crocker.

Doug pursed his lips.

"I fear for his sanity, maybe. I fear losing the man I know; a man I'm very fond of." He paused. "I remember when we met Lamorran. It was not long after I'd come down with him from Dumfries. His father had passed – a good friend of mine, Duncan was – and MacBride felt that Scotland had nothing more to offer him. But he was the only family Martha and I had ever had. He never told us he was leaving until he passed our door on his way; never invited us, the obstinate devil, but Martha had the horse saddled and the bags on the cart within moments." He laughed. "Pulled that cart all the way from Scotland, that horse."

"And I asked him what he could do," interrupted Crocker. "And he tells me he's a good fisherman. And I knows what that meant, course, and I knows it was of no good to him working down the tin mines when he is a lover of the open waves. So I tells him to go see the vicar – he knows all the fishermen."

"Aye, he did too," Doug said. "MacBride's father had been a free-trader, as had I, and it was all young Marty knew. We went to see old Malone and there was Lamorran at confession. Such a beauty, and she can have been no more than fifteen. And as soon as she caught sight of Martin that was it. She was on the boat with him the following day. I had to talk her father round, of course. He'd vowed to kill MacBride for involving his daughter in what he called 'such wicked immorality'. All this despite being one of our biggest customers in Newlyn!" He laughed. "He soon came round with the promise of a constant supply of cognac, but she would've followed MacBride to the ends of the world no matter what her father said. Dear Morrie."

Their mood had darkened.

"Cousin Jackie!" toasted Cattermole in a bid to lift their spirits. "Helped us out of many a tight spot!"

They raised their glasses.

"You think he'll pack up and move on again?" asked Crycot.

"Nothing would surprise me," replied Doug.

Jo came over to collect their glasses. She'd heard their conversation from behind the bar.

"I didn't mean to eavesdrop," she said. "But I'm sure you're wrong, Doug. Martin looks upon you as a father, and I cannot conceive that he would leave you and Martha now."

"Not in this world perhaps," agreed Doug softly.

He smiled sadly. Jo's face clouded with unease and she lowered herself into the chair next to him.

"No," she whispered. "He would never end it." When Doug did not answer she gripped his arm anxiously. "*Doug?* He would never do that, would he? You don't think he would do that?"

He smiled reassuringly.

"No," he said, covering her hand with his own. "No, I don't." He turned his gaze onto Cattermole and North. "But keep him going out to sea, boys. Keep him going out to sea. We have to keep him busy."

Jo excused herself and began wiping down the bar, her anxiety betrayed by the briskness of her movements. She collected a handful of empty glasses and disappeared into the kitchen.

A dark figure stood by the large iron sink.

"So he'll be going to Ruan Major, eh?" said Shanley.

"You just make sure you keep that to yourself," threatened Jo, crashing the glasses down on the side. "You promised me."

* * *

Sleep was still elusive for MacBride. Rest without sleep was no rest at all, bringing only purgatory and torture; nightmares far worse than any slumber could conjure up. He thanked the Lord that his trade meant he could work both day and night, and roaming the country as he was doing now was neither unusual nor unexpected, and provided a release from the confines of the place he once knew as home.

The wind was strong, sending the clouds scudding across the starry sky, the moonlight illuminating the trees clutching and clawing with bony fingers at the open countryside. MacBride slowed Morwellham at the fork in the road as a horse and cart approached from behind. It drew up beside him, with Doug and Abe at the reins.

"Well, that's the last of them here," said Doug softly.

All their goods had been sold to the miners.

"Good work," replied MacBride. "Take the cart back to the farm."

"Let me come with ye, eh laddie?"

But MacBride shook his head.

"You get back to Martha," he said. "Hide the cart and keep your head down. I'll draw less attention alone. I'll be back by morning."

Doug understood. He gave Abe a nod and, with a twitch of the reins, they set off westward.

The road south was long and straight but MacBride, engulfed by his own thoughts, took little heed of his surroundings. The rhythmic movement of the horse beneath him, together with the soft tread of the little terrier on the uneven road below him, was hypnotic. He didn't realise he was being followed until he had almost reached his destination. Roused from his thoughts by Duncan's growling, he wondered how long his pursuer had shadowed him. Not far, surely, or Duncan would have warned him earlier. MacBride frowned in surprise. Who did he know who could possibly be out in the middle of nowhere at this time of night? There was no chance he could have been followed from home – or even Poldark; it was too far. The only explanation was that somebody knew he would be travelling this way. But if somebody wanted to capture him selling smuggled goods to the miners then why not intercept him in the act at Poldark? Why follow him now, when he possessed so little on him that an arrest was hardly even a possibility? He directed the horse down a narrow rocky footpath and then stopped in the shadow of a great oak tree. There was silence, except for the sound of heavy breathing emanating from Morwellham's nostrils, but after a short while Martin heard the step of another horse as it turned into the footpath, and it was then he knew for certain they were being tracked. They proceeded along the footpath, now at a brisk trot, and at the first available opportunity made their way over a field and rejoined the main highway.

They could only have gone a quarter of a mile before they passed a large, thatched cottage set right on the road. MacBride glanced at it, then drew the horse to a halt. A lantern hung over the door, and in its illumination, MacBride could see that bottle ends were cemented under the eaves. The old sign. He would be safe here. The residents had shown themselves to be supporters of free trade and happy to provide a bed for the night or a hiding place for both smuggler and contraband if the revenue men were about. Without hesitation, MacBride dismounted and led the horse quietly around the back of the cottage. A brimming water trough waited for them and, behind it, an outhouse and a small barn full of new hay. Morwellham made himself at home and MacBride crept silently back to the front door. He took the lantern from its hook and blew out the flame, knocking gently on the door while looking furtively down the road in hope that nobody was in hearing distance. Duncan growled at his feet. Quickly, MacBride tried the handle. The door swung open and a dark hall greeted him. He immediately regretted extinguishing the lantern but, on closing the door softly behind him, he realised that there was a dim light coming from the crack in the doorway to his left. He swung open the door.

The light had come from a cosy fire crackling in the hearth. The room was sparsely furnished with a large dresser and two large, high-backed armchairs, one of which had its back to him and faced the fire. A man sat in this chair. MacBride could just see the very top of his head silhouetted against the firelight and his feet, crossed at the ankle, laid on the footrest.

He took a step into the room, and a voice floated up from the chair – a strangely jovial voice, a voice that MacBride knew all too well.

"Well, well, well! Martin MacBride! Fancy meeting you here!"

The man stood up and turned to face the smuggler, grinning widely.

MacBride gave a tired sigh and invited himself to slump in the other armchair.

"Cole Shanley," he said, kicking off his boots and putting his feet up on the footrest. Duncan sunk gratefully down onto the hearthrug. "What can I do for you?"

Shanley got up and took two glasses from the cabinet.

"It's more what I can do for you," he answered, taking down a bottle of brandy. "I was distressed you didn't come to see me when you arrived back in the bay. I'd quite missed you since your little holiday in Africa."

"I'm well aware you've been out of town, Cole. And I see you lured me here under false pretences. I do hope the poor, frost-bitten man you paid to follow me won't be joining us. It would be nice to have a romantic evening, just the two of us. Catch up on old times."

"You certainly haven't lost any of your charm."

Shanley held a glass of brandy out to his old adversary.

"It's not true what they say about me," grinned MacBride as he took the glass.

"Of course it isn't. I know that," said Shanley. "You entered a house with bottles under the eaves purely by chance."

"That's right. Nice little cottage you've got here. I'm guessing it's not really yours. It doesn't look quite your normal style; too few furnishings."

"Not very homely, is it?"

"Not very hospitable, no, but on the contrary to your remark it quite reminds me of home."

"It's been empty for months now," said Cole. "Customs House took it over as a trap for the 'free traders'. I must say I'm disappointed you walked into it so readily. Doesn't do much for your reputation – or for my confidence in you." He sank comfortably back into the chair. "Yes, a proper little smuggling haunt this used to be. There's a secret chamber under the floorboards in the kitchen, one above the hearth. Even that old dresser has a false back."

"Anything behind it?" MacBride enquired hopefully.

"'Fraid not," replied Shanley. "It's been moved, there's no hole in the wall. I don't know where it stood originally. You're welcome to take a look around. You'll have to give anything you find to me, of course."

He grinned.

"That would be a first," murmured MacBride.

"So what are you doing down here, Bridie? Bit far from home for a midnight stroll?"

"Given your presence, and mine, here in this house, I assume you already know the answer to that."

"You know I cannot allow you to proceed in selling smuggled goods from here."

"Oh, Cole! The same old lines." MacBride shrugged. "I've nothing on me anyway."

"No contraband? Or no silver to bribe the Customs Officer?"

"Depends on where your interests lie."

Cole sighed.

"With neither, as it happens. I'm here on a more personal matter. It would appear that somebody is concerned for your safety."

"And who might that be?"

"Josephine."

MacBride snorted with disbelief.

"You're here at her bidding?"

"It's Cardinham," continued Shanley. "Wants your head on a platter."

"He wants *my* head on a platter!" MacBride leapt from his chair. "The man as good as murdered my wife and daughter!"

"Careful, Bridie," warned Shanley, "he's come unhinged. He's crazy."

MacBride was furiously pacing the room, brandy still in hand.

"Well that makes two of us. We should be a good match for one another."

"But he has something on you," said Shanley. "In the eyes of the authorities you're committing a crime; he is upstanding in trying to prevent it."

"*Upstanding!* The spineless brute doesn't even have the guts to be here." He stopped suddenly, instinctively laying his hand on the pistol in his belt as though he might get his wish to shoot Cardinham at that very moment. "He *isn't* here, is he?"

"He is in London," said Shanley. "The Revenue Office have accepted his kind offer to become an Exciseman. He is training to be Exciseman in Chief, no less. And it's Jo's belief that as soon as he is able to leave the city he will be stationed down in Mounts Bay where he has claimed to know every inch of the land and has assured the Office that he is in no doubt of his abilities to control its spiralling smuggling situation."

MacBride stared.

"All this just to get at me?"

"Well that's certainly Jo's conviction. He's already informed them of your *merciless notoriety*."

"Why?" MacBride's voice was weak with incredulity. "I mean, I know he always had a thing for Morrie …"

"It would seem he became racked with jealousy over the friendship you and Josephine used to share."

MacBride shook his head. He sat down.

"Well, he's got nothing on me," he said, eventually, "*I* haven't murdered anyone."

"I don't believe he intended Morrie to do what she did. Perhaps he hoped if she'd give up on you, she'd go away with him."

"So if he couldn't have her, nobody could," said MacBride.

"It would seem so."

The two men fell silent. MacBride tried to make sense of what he'd heard.

"The fact remains, *I* haven't murdered anyone. They'll hardly give me the death penalty for smuggling. Hell, look how many times I've been summoned to court – every time I've been acquitted without charge! At worst they'll send me into the navy, but the local authorities wouldn't even stand for that. The judge at Penzance is a customer, for goodness' sake!"

"You're mistaking Cardinham for an honest man," Shanley said.

"He was an honest man when I knew him. A bastard, but an honest one. Morrie certainly believed all that he uttered, didn't she?"

"Well he's not honest now," said Shanley. "He's already taking great measures. He's moved me up the coast, suspecting I'd turn a blind eye to your activities. At any rate, I wasn't as stringent in the application of the law as he wanted. He's sending down more spies by the day to watch you and your men."

MacBride was incredulous.

"Come on, Cole! You know there's too many people on our side. I don't see how he'll ever be in any position to stop us."

"Neither do I. Yet," agreed Shanley. "But it seems he's not about to back down quietly. He's a clever swine, so watch your back."

MacBride snorted.

"If I thought I could get close enough to kill him in London, I would leave now."

"Then you'd be for it."

"So what do you suggest?" demanded MacBride. "I just lay back and let him get on with it?"

Cole shrugged.

"It's not my problem. I've warned you. I've done my bit. The rest is up to you."

"You're all heart!"

MacBride couldn't stop the corners of his mouth dragging into a grin. Cole grinned back sleepily.

"I'm offering you shelter for the night, aren't I? Shut up your bellyaching. Tomorrow we'll head back west. I stop at Porth Mellin."

He positioned a cushion comfortably behind his head and wriggled down into the chair.

MacBride scowled and poured himself another brandy.

Chapter Five

JOHN Cardinham took a long drag on his cigar. He was sitting behind a large desk littered with sheets of paper and a silver candelabra in need of a good polish. His legs were stretched out, his feet resting on another chair beside him, legs crossed at the ankles in exactly the same pose as his nemesis in Cole Shanley's borrowed cottage.

For a while, he simply eyed the man who sat uneasily opposite him.

"You know what your problem is, Pentlan?" he said. "You're not ruthless enough. In fact, I would contend your ability to be ruthless at all."

"Sir, I *am* making progress," replied Officer Pentlan. "Given a little more time we will have …"

But Cardinham cut him off.

"More time!" He was on his feet. "The tin miners are in Newlyn this very night, and where is MacBride? He's on velvet, that's where he is, and he's making a bloody fortune while he's at it! You should have him by now!"

"He's due in court next week, Sir! The locals have agreed …"

"The locals will take your money and deceive you!" spat Cardinham, kicking the chair angrily away. "Don't you understand! This man is a *hero* in their eyes. He brings them luxuries for a fraction of the price they should be paying. By virtue of this – this *sacrilegious vagabond* – these penniless saps can enjoy the indulgences of the rich, and you think that your payment of a few extra shillings will lead them to give up their extravagances? You are a fool, Pentlan!"

"They gave me their word."

"It is worth nothing," snarled Cardinham. "You underestimate the charm of the man. The locals would delight in fooling you and aiding his cause. He is their Robin Hood!" He paused, and lowered himself back into his chair, relaxing a little. "And you are a half-wit, Pentlan. I should have known, if I wanted to get the job done professionally I should have hired a professional." He rummaged through the piles of paper on his desk and held up a sheet. "See this? This is a statement declaring the services of a certain Jose Vaquero."

"*Sparky* Vaquero?" exclaimed Pentlan.

"Correct," replied Cardinham. "Infamous, isn't he? Know why? *Because he doesn't fail.*"

"But he's a pirate, sir."

"Indeed. This man captured three French men-o-war off Newfoundland with a crew of just fifty men. He's sacked and sunk more ships than anyone else; he's pillaged almost every town across the Caribbean, right down to Panama. He kills anyone who gets in his way: women, children, clergymen – he is a man with neither morals nor limitations. *That's* why people remember his name."

"But I thought this was exactly what we were standing against," said Pentlan, bewildered.

"Sometimes you have to use a sprat to catch a mackerel," said Cardinham. "Even the authorities have acknowledged his skills. He has the letter of the marque!"

Pentlan was shocked.

"He's a privateer?"

Cardinham nodded, grinning viciously.

"He's at the service of the state," he confirmed. "He's in *my* service."

* * *

Early the following morning, a horse was delivered to Cole Shanley at the little cottage outside Ruan Major. MacBride saddled Morwellham and they set off, Duncan trotting behind them. Upon leaving the cottage they came across a stout washerwoman from the village who took a liking to MacBride's rugged attractiveness, and curtsied shyly, bidding them a good morning.

"That's a heavy burden to be carrying for such a delicate lady as yourself," observed MacBride.

Shanley gave an impatient snort, but the washerwoman, captivated by the smuggler, appeared to notice nothing strange about the remark and smiled bashfully.

"Oh, I'm quite used to it," she replied. "Although you *could* carry it back to the village for me?"

"Well, madam, I'd love to," said MacBride. "But as hard luck would have it, I'm heading in just the opposite direction and it is vital I make haste – otherwise I would have been all too glad to oblige."

"Well now, never you mind, sir," said the washerwoman. "You have quite made my day as it is."

She turned to go and Shanley raised his hat to her as she did, but he and MacBride had only gone a few steps when MacBride swung back around.

"Hey there!" he called after her. She turned at once. "There *is* something you can do for me after all! You know young Henry Borden?"

She nodded eagerly.

"I do indeed," she cried. "Nice lad, lives just down here in the village."

"Would you be a beauty and tell him his wants are safely in the outhouse of that dear cottage over there?"

"Be a pleasure, sir! Be a pleasure!"

She turned and hurried off. Shanley stared at him.

"She didn't even offer to do anything for you in the first place!"

"Didn't she?" said MacBride, offhandedly.

He started off again, leaving the Customs Officer smiling. Cole knew he was watching a master at work. Many times he had witnessed just why the charming smuggler was so popular. And it would only be a matter of time before MacBride would need all the support he could muster.

* * *

The miners had gone back to work and the town was quiet and still.

The Anchor Inn, however, was noisy and busy, and filled with joviality. Sea-faring folk crowded around the bar in their heavy jerseys, puffing on pipes and supping their ales, talking and laughing heartily. A large boat had come into port and *The Anchor* was busier than usual. Lurret and his staff hurried between the ground and first floors to serve the common seamen below and the officers who drank in the bar above.

James Cattermole, Eli Abe, Jack North and Isaac Coby were sat at a large, round table at the back when MacBride and Doug came in.

"Here's Bridie," hailed a broad, white-haired man, who was sitting at the bar.

He raised his glass. Several others followed suit. MacBride grinned and the two embraced.

"It's been a long time, old friend," he said.

"Aye, that it has," agreed the man. He called over the bar. "Hey! A drink here for me ole matey," he cried. "And his aged companion!"

"Oy!" cried Doug. "Speak for yourself!"

"Now, now, don't let's start a brawl," the man said with a laugh. "Bit long in the tooth for that lark, aren't you?"

Doug made a lunge for him, but MacBride stepped between them, laughing.

"This is Sam Johnston, Doug," MacBride explained. "I used to work on his boat sometimes."

"Ah, you're the one they call 'Lost', eh?" Sam handed Doug an ale. "We met once, I believe, a long time ago. No hard feelings, Lost Doug Coby?"

Doug gave a snort. Was he ever going to be allowed to forget the time he went missing? He hadn't met with an accident at sea or encountered a blood-thirsty pirate as first believed; he had fallen into an open grave over at Talland, injured his leg and struck his head on a rogue rock, knocking himself silly. A local aristocratic lady had nursed him back to health and he had been back at Newlyn within a mere two weeks, but not before earning himself the enigmatic nickname 'Lost' and discovering several versions of exotic explanations for his sudden disappearance. MacBride grinned and turned to the barmaid.

"My cards down there?" he asked. The barmaid dutifully handed him a pack. "Joining us for a game?" he asked Sam, keen to get away before the conversation turned to tragic events.

"I'll be over in an ale or two," Sam called after them as they made their way to the others.

"Evening, Capt'n," said Cattermole as MacBride tossed him the cards and pulled up a chair. He began dealing them into six piles. "Cold one tonight."

"Aye, isn't it," Doug agreed, rubbing his hands to warm them. "Like midwinter out there."

"Feeling the cold, grandfather?" Sam shouted from the bar.

Doug scowled. MacBride chuckled and picked up his cards.

"How could he hear over all this racket?" muttered Doug, crossly.

Sam, guessing the old man was muttering about him, cupped his ear as if in answer.

"They call him 'The Bat'," explained MacBride, "What he's lost in sight he makes up for in ways not understood by man."

"He's blind?" Doug asked in surprise.

"Not totally," said MacBride. "But he can see only a little. You wouldn't know, would you?"

Doug stared in wonder at the large man holding forth at the bar, but his thoughts were interrupted by an exclamation from Jack North.

"Hey!" he cried. "I've got an ace of spades!"

At once, everybody sat up in surprise because there was only ever one pack of cards kept behind the bar in *The Anchor* and that pack had been supplied by MacBride himself – *without* the ace of spades. Cards were a luxury that few could afford. When smugglers brought them in, they took out the ace of spades, as the card itself carried the excise mark.

Doug grabbed North's card and examined it. He could see at once that it did not belong to the same pack as the others. The back was blood red with an emblem of some kind stamped onto the middle. Closer inspection revealed a skull over a cannon, and the initials: "*MM*".

Doug frowned, and then it dawned on him what he was holding. He looked up at MacBride, his eyes wide with fear.

"You all right there, Doug?" asked MacBride.

"It's a *Jolly Roger*," Doug said, breathlessly.

The table fell silent. MacBride put down his cards.

"A what?" asked Isaac.

"Death's head," Doug murmured.

He held out the card, but just as MacBride leaned across to take it, somebody else plucked it from Doug's grasp. It was Sam. He studied the card carefully.

"This is the flag of the pirate, Vaquero," he announced. "It is a warning. A sign. He is coming for you."

"Coming for who?" asked Doug.

Sam flicked the card across the table where it landed in front of MacBride. He pointed to the initials.

"Coming for you, MacBride."

There was a pause. Doug looked horrified.

"I'll rip it up," he said, decidedly, as though this act would make it go away. He lunged to grab it, but MacBride took it.

"No, don't," he said, "I could do with an ace."

"Hey! That card was mine," protested North.

"It's mine," quipped MacBride. "It's got my initials on."

"Have ye taken leave of your senses, laddie!" cried Doug. "Have you never heard of Vaquero?"

"Sparky," put in Sam, grinning horribly and showing his missing teeth. "For his love of blowing things up."

"He's a ruthless killer," said Doug. "He takes no keep of conscience!"

"They say he's mad, bad, and dangerous," grinned Sam.

"I heard he was a genius," shrugged MacBride. "A satirist. A *débauchée*. An extravagant rake capable only of living the high life. Sounds like fun to me. What have I to fear from a man such as that? God willing, he might even make me laugh."

"He's a *pirate!*" wailed Doug. "There must be a bounty on your head!"

"I've no doubt there is," replied MacBride. He appeared unaffected. "But this man has nothing he can take from me but pain. Good luck to the fellow, I say."

He placed a card down onto the centre of the table to signify the start of the game, but Doug clutched the arm of his shirt. He lowered his voice and looked around suspiciously.

"Somebody made sure you got that card," he said. "Somebody brought it in here."

"One of his merry gang, no doubt," whispered Sam. "Lot of

strangers in here tonight. *He might even be watching you at this very moment."*

He threw back his head and laughed. Doug tutted at him.

"He's gone mad," he said, inclining his head in Sam's direction.

But Sam misunderstood.

"Aye, that he is," he said, gravely. "Mad Sparky Vaquero. On your guard, Marty ole boy!" And with that he gave a nod and wandered away.

"Batty bat," growled Doug.

Nobody spoke. MacBride noticed Isaac looking furtively around the inn.

"He's not here," said MacBride.

"How do you know?" asked Isaac.

"A man such as Vaquero does not go unnoticed."

"Perhaps that's part of the genius?" suggested Cattermole. "He blends into the crowd, doesn't look anything out of the ordinary?"

But MacBride laughed.

"He's a pirate!" he said, "I assure you, he *revels* in looking 'out of the ordinary'!"

* * *

Not long after sunrise, a horse and carriage was sent to MacBride to escort him to the local court at Penzance. Just two hours later, the judge deemed MacBride *not guilty* and he was freed of all charges. Once the room had cleared of customs officers, the people in the court house dared to approach the smuggler one by one to put in their orders for the next landing of contraband. When the crowds had dispersed, MacBride departed the courtroom and made his way down the passage towards the sunlight.

A door opened and The Lord Justice came out and fell into step beside him.

"My jury placing orders?" he enquired, quietly.

"Yes, Your Honour."

The judge tutted and shook his head sadly.

"Miss Rathmore? The school ma'am?"

"Even Mr Rudder," nodded MacBride.

"Plaintiff's barrister? Well, well! What a melancholy world this is becoming! What was his want? Liquor of some form, I suppose?"

"And tobacco."

"And Miss Rathmore?"

"Tea."

"Should have guessed," nodded the judge. "A mighty tea drinker, that woman. Near cleaned us out here just waiting for your hearing. Can I at least rely on my good parish clerk not to have approached you with some fancy?"

"I am afraid not, Your Honour."

Once more the judge shook his head in dismay.

"What is the world coming to," he lamented.

They came out into the open and made ready to depart in different directions.

"And you, Your Honour?" asked MacBride.

The judge cleared his throat.

"Let us go and discuss it over some light refreshment," replied The Honourable Lord Justice briskly, turning and falling into step beside the smuggler. "I'm fair running out of tobacco myself and the drink cabinet's near run dry, not to mention my youngest daughter is due to be married next month. Oh, and my wife has asked if you are likely to encounter any fine silks? Her friend had one in a most delicate colour – a soft blue. And while I think on it, a little calico may be of use …"

* * *

Three weeks later, as MacBride and his crew headed home, the hold heavy with contraband, Isaac stood on the deck of *The*

Mevagissey and strained his eye as he looked through the spyglass.

"All looks clear, Capt'n," he called, his voice sharp and clear in the crisp, morning air.

"Head for the harbour!" ordered MacBride to the helmsman.

It had been a difficult voyage. The seas near the Channel Islands were rough, and a gale had ripped at the masts of *The Mevagissey* and damaged her topsail. Doug Coby had sailed with the crew, and despaired as he witnessed MacBride sinking into what he believed to be a deeper depression, cleverly disguised behind a veil of casual indifference and occasional witticisms. Doug had watched him, alone on the poop deck, looking over the rolling waves, a creature bound by torment.

"He troubles me," Doug said wearily to Martha when he returned to Hemlock Street.

"We'll invite him for dinner tonight, see if we can raise his spirits."

"He won't come," replied Doug, flatly.

"Yes he will," said Martha, refusing to let Doug's grim mood wear off onto her. "I'll cook his favourite and I won't take no for an answer. Where is he now? I'll go and tell him."

"They're down at The Anchor, unloading," he replied. Doug lowered himself into his armchair. "Ah! I never thought I'd make old bones, but Lord, they feel old today."

"Crock," said Martha, wiping her hands on her apron before whipping it off and putting on her coat. "I know how the boy is feeling. My, I felt it when I thought you were gone, Lost Coby! The heartbreak very near killed me!"

"Good," murmured Doug with a sleepy smile. He had his eyes closed and his feet resting on a stool, warm and contented in front of the hearth.

Martha chucked her apron at him.

* * *

Not a soul was to be seen at *The Anchor*. The tavern had only just opened its doors and the bar was deserted. Martha called to the innkeeper.

"Lurret?" There was silence. "Marty? James?" Still no answer. "Isaac? Anybody here?"

A door opened silently behind her and a dark figure crept in.

"Hello?" she said again, then felt a hand clasp tightly over her mouth. As she gasped, she heard a familiar voice in her ear.

"*Shush*," hissed Cattermole.

Lurret appeared, nodded an unspoken greeting and stationed himself behind the bar. He took a cloth from his belt and began wiping the glasses silently. Cattermole quickly led Martha through the door and down the passage into the cellars.

"The gaugers are about," he explained as they descended the cellar steps. "We thought it was too good to be true when we didn't see them at landing."

"Where are they?" asked Martha, taking in the scene around her. The cellars were filled with an array of barrels and kegs, boxes and nets. The crew were dotted here and there, smoking and joking, quite unperturbed.

"Don't know where they are," replied Cattermole, "waiting for us to come out, I imagine."

"Won't they come down here and check after a while?" said Martha.

"Not if you can create a diversion," said MacBride from the shadows.

He was sitting on a barrel, one leg arched, a bottle of brandy in his hand and a self-rolled cigarette hanging from the corner of his mouth.

"Only if I have your word you'll come for dinner tonight," said Martha.

MacBride grinned.

"I wouldn't miss your cooking for the world," he said.

"Then say no more. Lil Ferry is having a social morning. She'll help me lead them off. I'll be back soon."

Cattermole took her arm and guided her up the steep bottom step. Then, taking hold of her skirts, she quickly made her way up the rest and back through the door.

Isaac followed and flicked the key in the lock behind her.

MacBride grinned and closed his eyes.

* * *

Lil Ferry lived just a few doors down the street from *The Anchor* in a quaint, crooked little cottage squashed between two grand, tall town houses. It was remarkable how many people she could fit into this modest structure with its dark alcoves and hidden corners, but her social mornings always drew a fair crowd for she had the advantage of working for a distinguished local family – the Bolts of Newlyn – and gossip was plentiful.

Martha hurried in through the little black door without pausing to knock. Nobody would have heard a knock, she told herself. The parlour was full. Ivy Malone with her corn-coloured hair was there, as was Mary Rathmore who was perched as elegantly as possible on the edge of a rickety-looking chair. Sylvia Melthropp was sprawled over the chaise, her cheeks caked – as was her custom – with a crass blanket of rouge.

"Martha, dear friend," cried Lil, an ample lady who sat in the midst of her gathering rather as a spider would sit smugly in the centre of its fly-filled web. "How wonderful to see you!"

Everybody sat up, for Martha rarely attended social mornings, but when she did she often came bearing news of the heroic and handsome Martin MacBride and his gallant crew – a source of information far too wanting in supply, in Sylvia's opinion.

"How goes it with those rugged scoundrels?" asked Ivy, wasting no time.

"It is regarding that precise matter that I need your help, ladies," said Martha. "The customs officers are at this very moment awaiting their departure of *The Anchor* where they have been unloading. We must divert their attention."

Without further ado, like a scene rehearsed, the ladies removed themselves from the parlour and, chattering excitedly, hurried out through the front door, with only Sylvia pausing momentarily to check her countenance in the hall mirror.

* * *

Officer Pentlan, accompanied by twelve uniformed men, stood outside the doors of the tavern looking ready to pounce. As the women approached, Lil hailed him, waddling up the street towards him as fast as she could, her skirts in her hands.

Pentlan drew back in alarm.

"Stand back, men!" he ordered, taking a brave step forward. Women terrified him.

"Officer! Officer!" panted Martha.

"A ship! A ship run aground!" cut in Lil.

"Oh do *hurry*," begged Ivy as the women surrounded the officer. "They are drowning!"

Mary Rathmore began to weep.

"'Tis the reverend's wife," hissed one of the customs men to another. "This is no hoax!"

"Look lively, men!" bellowed Officer Pentlan. He held his stick aloft. "Lead the way, ladies!"

And the revenue men left for this new attraction, leaving MacBride and his gang to make good their escape.

* * *

It was dark. The secluded roads were veiled in a ghostly mist, which glowed like illuminated spirits in the cold moon. The two approaching horsemen made an eerie sight; the hooves of the beasts on which they rode – complete with heavy burdens – making no sound on the bleak track. The men themselves were silent and looked straight ahead.

Slowly, MacBride breathed in and out.

"Hear them?"

"Aye," whispered Doug. "They've followed us up from Heamoor."

MacBride shook his head.

"From Penzance," he corrected.

"But they tarry," whispered Doug. "They are no closer now than they were five miles back. Why do they not push for an arrest?"

"They are driving us somewhere," murmured MacBride.

"You do not think they are waiting to catch us make the delivery? Or hoping to stumble upon our stores?"

"What stores? We have two casks left – they've watched us deliver the others."

"They're afeard of us!" exclaimed Doug.

They continued in silence. All at once, the sound of approaching hooves grew louder.

"Looks as though you may be wrong, Doug," said MacBride in a low voice. "Split."

Without another word, Doug Coby took a right into a field out of sight. MacBride was about to follow but, instead, he jumped down from Morwellham and tugged hard at the gatepost to his side. Doug came back to help him, and within a moment they had it out of the ground. MacBride deftly untied the cask of brandy that hung from Doug's horse and slipped it into the socket before replacing the post.

"That was a stroke of luck," MacBride said. "Finding a smuggler's post close at hand. Now you can come out of the field and carry on with nothing to hide."

"What about you?" asked Doug, as the pursuers drew nearer.

"Hold them up for me," whispered MacBride, and he leapt back onto his horse and galloped off into the murky night.

"Look out for the demons!" Doug whispered after him.

Half a mile along the road, at the end of a long drive, stood a little, thatched cottage obscured by dark trees. A small, white rose grew by the back door.

MacBride cantered up the drive, led Morwellham around the back, and let himself in. No sooner had he done so than he experienced a terrible sensation of déjà-vu. An ominous silence hung in the air and, by comparison, his breathing seemed very loud. He gripped his pistol and moved stealthily into the hall, where he was grateful to encounter the family who lived there. But relief was immediately followed by dread when he noted the way their bodies were pressed up against the front door; the children facing inwards and hiding in the folds of their mother's skirts. Their father, lips pressed tightly together, had the look of a man about to receive an imminent death sentence. The mother, with wide, terrified eyes, gave the smallest of nods towards the parlour.

MacBride pressed himself up against the open sitting room door. Clearly this was no benign Shanley waiting to welcome him. He clasped his pistol more tightly and put his finger on the trigger, his eyes stony with rage for the man he thought might be on the other side of the door. Sweat began to bead on his forehead. He needed to concentrate, but the one fleeting vision of Lamorran and Lucy rushing into the sea to greet him was enough to put him off guard. He felt the sharp edge of a cold blade pressing against his throat.

"Surely such willing prey cannot be the great and elusive Martin MacBride?" said a strange voice.

MacBride opened his eyes. Before him stood a tall man dressed in fine clothes. A generous white shirt under a waistcoat of exotic animal hide billowed in the breeze that blew in through an open window. His breeches, also made from the skin of some foreign animal, vanished into great knee-length boots. A silver buckle fixed the leather strap he wore across his body and sheathed not one but two long knives, and a generous length of fabric was tied around his waist and left to hang down one side. Gold necklaces hung around his neck – a great jewel-studded medallion in their midst – several gold hoops dangled from his ears, and every finger clutching at the sword wore a ring. The man's skin was brown from a lifetime of sun; his eyes were dark and dangerous and twinkled almost maniacally. Not one hair grew from his smooth, golden-brown head.

MacBride breathed a sigh of relief and pushed the sword away.

"Surely a pirate with such renown as Jose Vaquero carries a greater sword than this?"

"I see my reputation precedes me," said Sparky, obviously pleased with the compliment. "As for you … you were not concentrating." Sparky turned and pointed towards MacBride with the tip of his sword. "I heard about your wife and child … their hauntings will be your undoing." Sparky flung the sword onto a large desk. "I wasn't planning on killing you as it turns out," he added in explanation.

"I wasn't thinking of my family," lied MacBride.

Sparky caught his eye momentarily and gave him the shadow of a grin in reply.

"No matter," he continued, unheeding of MacBride's words. "This," he said, drawing a magnificent, slender, shining sword from the corner of the room, "is *The Executioner*." He sliced the air with it a few times, its metal glinting and gleaming as he twisted it this way and that. He seemed to have glided off into another dimension, battling with some invisible foe. Then he came to and replaced the sword in its sheath. "But I only use it on special occasions," he added.

"And pray, what sort of special occasion would warrant the use of such a sword?" asked MacBride with an edge of sarcasm to his voice.

"I've had to run through several friends," replied Sparky, carelessly. "And a brother. It pricks my conscience so. I make the death as quick and painless as possible. I haven't the heart to see them suffer."

"I'm disappointed," said MacBride. "I was told you took no keep of conscience at all."

"And I was told that capturing you would be nigh impossible," quipped Sparky. "It would appear that we are both to be disappointed."

He poured himself a glass of rum which he downed in a single gulp before refilling the tumbler. MacBride plucked it from his grasp.

"Don't mind if I do," he said.

Sparky sighed.

"For a man in your current position, your manners seem rather lacking."

"On the contrary, it is yours that are to be questioned," replied MacBride, inviting himself to sit down.

He held up the glass in a silent toast before he too swallowed the draught in one.

"I see we both share a love for liquor," the pirate observed.

"I love nothing."

Sparky grinned, took another glass and filled it. He sat down.

"I assume you have had the fine pleasure of acquainting with Mr Cardinham?" said MacBride.

"Indeed. He was most informative. Martin MacBride – a Scotsman, he tells me," said Sparky. "Hence the white rose by the door, an old Scottish custom welcoming smugglers, I believe. For a man who hates you so completely, his demeanour betrays a great awe for you." He emptied his glass before adding, "Odd. I have seen nothing which warrants it."

MacBride looked untroubled and did not respond.

"I cannot see why a man such as he should have trouble seizing a man such as you," Sparky goaded further.

"If you had been Cardinham, I would have killed you," said MacBride, and catching Sparky's mocking look, added, "With my dying breath if necessary."

Sparky paused. His eye glinted.

"I believe you," he relented, "I glimpsed that lethal loathing in your eyes."

"So what will he have you do with me?"

Sparky sighed again.

"I am to take you to London," he said. "Unharmed – if possible. Although I'm still deciding about that …" He paused to frown at the empty glass in MacBride's hand. "Once in London I am to assist in sealing your, it must be said, gruesome fate." He grinned, but then shook his head sadly. "I much prefer to do the killing bit myself. It's little fun, this privateering business."

"Then why do it?" asked MacBride.

"It enables me to take what I want from other ships without punishment," grinned Sparky. "And your friend, Cardinham, pays very well."

"You could have more," said MacBride.

Sparky threw his head back and laughed.

"Even you could not match such a price. He pays from the King."

"But I can add to it," replied MacBride, calmly.

Sparky stopped laughing. He eyed MacBride cynically, then leaned forward in his chair.

"Speak of your mind."

"Cardinham cares only of seeing me hang. As you already know, he seems prepared to pay any price. I care only of seeing my family avenged. I want Cardinham dead. I, too, will pay any price. If *you* care only for wealth then you are in a position of ultimate power."

"I can exploit you both, you mean?" Sparky was first scornful, then thoughtful. "And if I am to receive Cardinham's money for your capture, what is it you will be paying me for? His murder?"

"Time. All I want from you is a little time."

"Why should I waste my time in order to allow you some of that precious commodity? They will think you are eluding me. I do not like that. My reputation is of great importance to me."

"Important, yes, but does it surpass your greed for wealth?" MacBride asked. "After all, my elusiveness is only what he already expects. I am not asking you to spare my life. Just give me the space to have my vengeance. That is all I want."

Sparky stared at the man before him in cynical bewilderment.

"The man as good as murdered my family," added MacBride. "Let me have my revenge. Then take me to London – receive your payment."

"And in return?" probed Sparky.

"Captain Vaquero, I am a rich man," answered MacBride. "I own six houses, two farms, several workhorses and many treasure stores. In return I shall leave you all that I own."

"You are a rich man indeed," he acceded. He paused, pouring himself another rum. "And I am a sick man." MacBride glanced up and Sparky nodded. "It is true. I may not look it, but my way of life is taking its toll." He held up the bottle of rum and laughed. "The good doctor, he tells me my liver is pickled! He tells me I am drinking myself to death." He took a swig. "That I have taken wenching and debauchery to such heights I am to expire through infection and self-abuse!" He roared with laughter. "*Self-abuse!* What a way to go! What a route! I'll make a handsome corpse, my friend!" He was rocking with mirth. Then he stopped, dropping his voice to a whisper. "Soon I shall not care for wealth." There was a short pause before he erupted with laughter again as though he had made a wonderful joke and was allowing MacBride time to get the punch line. "You should *pray* that you die before I do, lest I come for you from the grave to see you settle your debts!" He swallowed the rest of the rum and MacBride could see his body visibly relax and calm. He became quiet once more. "A lifetime of debauchery and self-abuse," he said. "That is what I am told I shall surely die from. And yet never, never have I seen a man with such a disregard for his own life as you."

He raised his eyes to meet MacBride's, who met his gaze directly.

'So do we have a deal?'

"Cardinham is too well protected in London. We will do well to bide our time and await his return to Cornwall. In the meantime, I feel we would make a good team in adding to these assets you claim to have." He bowed his head to signal he had made up his mind. "Show me these riches. If you have what you say, brother, then we have an accord."

And he leaned over the desk and gripped MacBride's hand solidly to seal the agreement.

CHAPTER SIX

"**B**UT Captain, this man isn't honourable," whispered Doug Coby urgently as they boarded the cutter. "Ye cannot trust him!" MacBride, untying the mooring ropes, did not answer. Doug persisted. "*Bad blood*, The Bat said, remember?!"

"Perhaps he has," shrugged MacBride, hauling the ropes in.

"I swear it, Captain, his word is worth nothing." Doug frowned, confused and impatient. "Ye cannae tell me ye are set on sailing out with the very man sent to kill ye?"

"What if I am?"

"But what of your crew?" Doug's agitation grew. "Care ye not for them? This man has no valour! He will kill you, Marty – he will kill us all! No doubt when we sleep in our bunks at night!"

They boarded the gangplank.

"I doubt that," said MacBride.

"And what is to become of us?" Doug cried. "Are we to become pirates?"

"We are fishermen, as we have always been. We're on *The Mevagissey*."

Doug came to a standstill when he saw Sparky, who was glugging at a bottle of liquor on the deck.

"So long as *he's* on board, it be a pirate ship,"

MacBride pointed at Sparky's schooner, *The Barentszee*, which was to accompany them.

"There are your pirates. That is the pirate ship. For the present, this is the vessel of a privateer." He boarded *The Mevagissey*. "And I assure you he's only borrowing it."

Sparky attempted to walk across the creaking deck, his palm clutching the neck of the bottle.

"Look at him!" hissed Doug,

"What about him?"

"The villain can't even stand up straight!"

"He has a rolling gait," shrugged MacBride, "Years of keeping balance on a heaving deck, that is."

Sparky rolled towards them and clapped Doug on the back with such force that he nearly toppled overboard.

"Aye there!" he bellowed cheerfully. "Ready to do our bit for King and Country!" He grinned at MacBride. "United in a common cause!"

"What common cause?" Doug asked.

Sparky grinned and slipped a scarred arm around the old man's shoulder.

"*Treasure, old boy!*" he whispered in his ear.

Then he cackled and teetered away. Doug turned to MacBride in rage.

"*That's* your common cause?"

"That's *his* cause," said MacBride. Doug continued to look angry. "You can't trust anything he says. He's a drunkard."

North and Cattermole came to join them with Isaac in tow.

"Capt'n?" said Cattermole. "Err … you *are* still Captain?"

"Not on this voyage," replied MacBride, shortly.

"What!" cried Doug Coby looking as though he was fit to burst.

"I want you to obey Captain Vaquero first and foremost on this voyage."

"We are done for, to be sure!" wailed Doug. "We are but dead men!"

"But no, Capt'n," broke in Abe.

MacBride cut him off. He was not prepared to debate the matter.

"We will be sailing seas this man knows better than I," he said. "He has the disposition to hold together both crews of unruly seamen."

"Unruly?" echoed Isaac. "His crew are all cut-throats."

"Right enough, son," smiled MacBride. "But rest assured, it won't be your throat they'll be cutting."

"How can ye be so sure?" demanded Doug. "There might be a bounty on all our heads! I say we are mad to take our chances."

"You do not trust me?"

Anger flickered across MacBride's face. Doug saw the warning signs and hesitated.

"You are not of usual mind."

"Because I will not hide from a man who is out to have me butchered? Cardinham has declared this war – I shall stand my ground and fight him, and by God I shall win! The man we sail with may be a ruthless vagabond, and yes, there is room for my faith in him to grow – my faith in anyone at present is limited – but I am *not* insane! The cold fact of the matter is that this man can use me, and I can use him. Pirate or not, I assure you, he will not have the better of me! We work together. And we," – he indicated to his crew around him – "work together. If any of you find you are lacking confidence in your captain, then you may leave before we set sail."

And tossing the rope angrily to one side, he turned and walked away.

* * *

Nobody left. They set sail and encountered their first merchant ship five days later.

"You have a favoured method in the capturing of ships?" enquired MacBride, his eye glued to the spyglass.

"I have many methods," grinned Sparky. "I love them all. You see the rigging? That there is a ship from Vigo."

"Are you authorised to capture any ship?" asked Isaac from the helm.

"So long as they ain't Allermayne nor Hollander," replied Sparky. "Nor English, course." He winked and peered back over the water. "But he likes us to catch the Spaniards best."

Then, with a nod, he roared an order which thundered from sailor to sailor down the ship, and a flag was hoisted up the main mast. MacBride expected to see Sparky's Jolly Roger unravel, the skull and cannon, but instead the cloth unwound to reveal the Spanish flag, flapping in the wind.

"Why warn them?" shrugged Sparky. "I've never understood it."

MacBride felt Doug nudge him roughly.

"No valour," he reminded him.

Sparky overheard him and laughed.

"Load the cannons! Chain shot!" He turned to the pirate in the ratlines. "Slow match and fire pots!"

And echoes of *"Slow match and fire pots!"* were carried up to the fighting top.

"Make ready the boarding planks!" he roared. "Release the topsail! Full attack!"

The ship quivered as the cannons were fired. Swivel guns mounted on pivots sprayed the enemy decks with fire. All hands were on deck. MacBride could see that young Isaac was terrified, yet it was a fear that made him smile. A cannon ball crashed onto the deck behind them, sending deadly wooden shards through the air. There was shouting. Smoke. Men running. Some throwing tar grenades into the enemy ship's rigging. One of Sparky's pirates dropped a box of caltrops made up of pointed nails at Isaac's feet and, shouting over the noise in some foreign dialect, waved in the direction of the merchant vessel before lifting his feet and patting the soles of his boots.

"Throw them over!" MacBride yelled. "It will stop them boarding. They're barefoot!"

Isaac, wild and impassioned, began lobbing the spiked metal weapons onto the deck as the irons drew the ship closer to *The Mevagissey.*

The boarding planks came down and Vaquero's crew swarmed up the steep wooden sides of the merchant ship armed with swords, pistols, muskets, daggers, axes and cutlasses – anything they could lay their hands on. MacBride swiftly drew his sword and took his pistol in the other hand. Isaac tried to follow his lead and his hand flicked to his scabbard, but MacBride reached out and stayed it, shaking his head. Undeterred, Isaac drew his sword and pushed forward, but MacBride threw him back, launching him a foot or so across the deck. Isaac was too young to fight.

But MacBride turned and ran overboard across the plank to the merchant vessel.

* * *

By nightfall the ship had been taken.

The majority of the Spanish had escaped in rowing boats. The remainder, those who had surrendered in favour of being shot, were now prisoners on board *The Mevagissey* and would make up the numbers – seven of MacBride's crew members had been lost and three more injured.

Sparky, although unperturbed over the dead, was annoyed that he had to deal with the injured. Sitting at the table in the Great Cabin, he begrudgingly counted out one hundred pieces of gold to be given to each of the sailors; one who had lost a finger, another who had lost an eye. For the sailor who lost his right arm, Sparky groaned as he counted out six hundred pieces.

MacBride, who watched Sparky from the opposite side of the

cabin, caught the pirate's eye and shook his head at him.

'A little charity,' he said.

"Bloody charity," yelled Sparky, grabbing a bottle of rum. "Wish they'd finished the job for me. Don't have to compensate the dead!"

He left the cabin, slamming the door behind him. MacBride followed him along the wood-panelled passageway.

"So where's my share?"

"Your share? The last week of your life is your share!"

"And what about the use of my ship?"

"I use your ship because your 'crew' are familiar with it. Mine could sail any ship blindfolded."

"I'll have you know, Captain, that my crew are the most able-bodied in the country," said MacBride. "You won't find fighters like them anywhere else in England!"

"So that is why your English ships are such easy bait for me!" scoffed Sparky, still irritated by having to pay out compensation to some of the crew.

"We had a deal," said MacBride.

Sparky picked up his pace. At the far end of the corridor, he threw open a cabin door.

"Doctor Cottle!" he roared to the surgeon who sat inside in the company of two friendly bottles of spirits. "The injured are below deck! Sort them out, I don't want to lose any more specie today!" He removed his dagger and held it to Dr Cottle's throat as the surgeon shuffled past. "You understand?" he said. "I want them with all their attachments. For every man who loses something I shall personally remove the same piece from your body." Dr Cottle began to sweat. Sparky held the point of the blade dangerously close to the surgeon's eyeball and twisted it quickly between his fingers. "Do you understand?"

Dr Cottle nodded violently and scurried off.

Sparky retrieved the bottles from the table.

"Captain, at least pay my crew," said MacBride, his tone serious now. "They have lost a lot today. They don't understand why I am doing this."

"*I* don't understand why you are doing this!" cried Vaquero, spinning around. "But we had a deal. You get your time, I get your service. It is you who jeopardised your crew, brother. Do not trouble me with your conscience."

He turned to walk away, but MacBride pulled him back roughly.

"Do not make the mistake of thinking you can do this without me," he growled. "I know Cornwall like the back of my hand. When we return there, you will need my guidance. If they see you have acquainted yourself with the likes of me you will be covered in tar and hung from the gibbet before nightfall!"

Sparky shrugged.

"I am of far too great a use to the authorities for them to resort to that."

"You are of no use to the authorities if you do not carry out your tasks," MacBride replied. Sparky spun round to find MacBride pointing a pistol into his side. "What is to stop me from killing you now and saving myself all this aggravation?"

Sparky pushed the barrel down gently.

"*You care only for seeing Cardinham die and you will pay any price,*" he quoted. "Besides, it would not be possible to kill me." MacBride turned to see three pirates clutching cutlasses or muskets had silently surrounded him. "You need me," continued Sparky. "You need me to get close to Cardinham."

MacBride reluctantly slid his pistol back into his belt. He caught sight of Doug Coby standing below on the main deck, eyeing him furiously. He turned back to Sparky.

"There are twelve coffers of doubloons in your cabin. They will only be swallowed by gambling and drinking once we're ashore. I have cellars still full of French cognac. You can have it. All of it. Just pay the crew."

Sparky looked duly thoughtful but before he could answer, Doug, having overheard the conversation, came puffing up the steps.

"Don't ye bring Josephine into this," he cried, "That there liquor is hers!"

"Josephine?" Sparky arched an eyebrow. "You have a wench, brother?"

"No," snapped MacBride. "I don't.' He turned to Doug. "And I owe her nothing."

"Ye can't offer what is hers in settlement."

Sparky frowned at him. He coughed politely and stepped forward so that he was standing between the two smugglers.

"I have decided to accept your offer," he announced.

"Martin!" raged Doug. "What are ye doing? Do you not care? T'isn't right."

Something seemed to snap inside MacBride and he turned and slung a right hook at his first mate. Doug struggled to stay upright, clutching at his bleeding nose.

"First I care not for my crew, then I care not for Jo. What would you have me do, Doug?"

"I would have you do what the boy I used to know would do," replied Doug, bitterly. "Not be a merciless brigand who drinks poison from the mouth of this, this barbarous miscreant!"

MacBride caught him by the collar and drew him swiftly within a breath of his own face. When he spoke, his voice was deep and ragged.

"We are *all* brigands! Me *and* you. We always were!" He released him roughly. Doug staggered back a step or two. "You want to know where the boy you knew is? You want to know? He is in *Hell.*" The word came out as a guttural roar, but behind his viciously glinting eyes there laid an unspeakable pain. "So, father-to-me, when each beat of your heart pumps agony into every tiny corner of your body, when you loathe your very soul and you would do anything for the sweet release of death but you have the devil breathing down your neck, then – *then* you can tell me where I can find the capacity to care for others."

There was a pause. Sparky raised his brow and looked to Doug in anticipation.

"You still be here," said Doug quietly. "Ye still care for something."

"I care for my wife. My daughter," said MacBride, "I won't rest until their deaths are avenged."

Doug shook his head.

"Then ye put the dead before the living," he said. "It is a dream that cannot be conquered, Martin. Nothing will bring them back."

"I do not need them back," snapped MacBride, "I need to be with them."

Doug wiped the blood from his nose onto his sleeve.

"Mercy me. Well may God permit me to enjoy the time I have left with ye."

And he turned and went down the steps, pushing a pirate out of his path with surprising force.

* * *

They had been at sea for almost a month, landing in France and Spain only when they needed to pick up extra goods and supplies, which for Sparky, consisted solely of rum.

Four ships had been captured, the last of which belonged to a Spanish pirate who had been waiting off the Devon coast for the West Country fishing fleets to return. Sparky had taken over all but one of the ships, and now their fleet had swelled from two to five.

The Mevagissey had a vast treasure aboard, as well as a stash of contraband they had picked up when they docked in Guernsey at MacBride's insistence. Now they were heading for home via the mighty contraband markets of Plymouth and Cawsand.

MacBride sat up on the fighting top with the spyglass, keeping a lookout for customs vessels.

He ran his eye over the ship. Isaac, who had been bitterly disappointed to learn they were not to sail with Sparky to some exotic Caribbean pirate haunt, stood at the helm, his eyes still filled with stars from the excitement of the battles they had fought, the earth-shattering boom of cannon fire still ringing in his young ears.

It was MacBride's conscience that troubled him now as he watched Isaac steer them towards home. The intrigue and fascination was still plain to read upon his face; his muscles still taut with trepidation. It was infatuation such as this, MacBride thought, which led to an itching for infinitely greater thrills. And he, Martin MacBride, had infected Isaac with his first taste of that danger; he had started him on that path that may well lead to his death.

He glanced over at Doug Coby, Isaac's uncle, who stared back at him from the deck, a cold frown shadowing his kindly features. MacBride's heart sank a little further. He and Doug had hardly spoken for a week now and, after observing Isaac over the last few days, MacBride had to admit he could understand why. Doug hadn't brought Isaac aboard to have him turned him into a pirate any more than he had expected MacBride to let Sparky captain the ship. MacBride felt a wave of shame, and, not for the first time, questioned whether he was doing the right thing.

Sparky stood at the helm with Isaac, chewing on a piece of leather. He caught Isaac staring at him in fascination, and offered him a piece, already half chewed. Isaac declined politely. MacBride gleaned some hope for his future that he did so.

Ahead of them, the rugged coast of Cornwall appeared out of the mist.

"We're coming close to land," said MacBride shortly. He made his way down the ratlines onto deck. "There's a sheltered inlet of water at Wembury. We head for there and wait until nightfall, then we'll sail over to Cawsand. I want the other ships to unload and sail straight into Plymouth. I've arranged for the shore fraternity to signal us in if it's all clear. Tomorrow night we make for Newlyn."

Without waiting for an answer he turned and stalked away, leaving Sparky staring after him quizzically. "Abe! Start slinging the kegs to the bar!" MacBride shouted. "And Mole! Furl the topsail and hide the brandy!"

As thunder rumbled, they began throwing the barrels overboard.

* * *

On land, a man standing close to the edge of a cliff peered through the storm-filled darkness at a horse trotting swiftly along the coast road below him. He waited for the rider to pass.

"Aye, all's clear down there," he muttered to his companion. And then he raised his voice and called, "Spout lantern!"

"Spout lantern!" echoed another man into the shadows.

A small twinkle of light emerged from the spout on the iron lamp and cut through the falling night. The beam could only be seen from one direction and was carefully passed up to the man at the front. Taking it and holding it up in front of him, the man uncovered the spout opening briefly, sending a direct beam of light out into the inky blackness of the ocean.

* * *

"Make for the light!" MacBride cried aboard *The Mevagissey*. "Mole – go help Isaac. It's a watery grave for us all if he calls it wrong!"

Slowly and silently, like a prowling sea giant, the ship made its way through the gloom towards the signal, followed at some distance by the second vessel.

MacBride studied his compass meticulously before hauling more tubs and casks overboard. Then he joined Isaac and Cattermole at the helm, expertly steering the cutter between the rocky reefs into the cove.

"Lower the rower!" he yelled, as the anker was thrown over the side.

Two of Sparky's crew who stood beside the rowing boat regarded Sparky, their captain, questioningly. He caught their eyes and took the bottle from his mouth.

"Lower the rower!" he repeated irritably, waving his hand and scowling. At once the boat was lowered for MacBride to row over to Sparky's ship to give further orders and lower the ankers.

* * *

The shore fraternity were now all gathered on the beach, innocently armed with stout grapnels and a few fishing lines.

"Who in hell *is* that?" one of them asked as Sparky thrust his way through the surf from billow to billow.

He waded ashore, his bottle still somehow is his grasp. He lifted it to his mouth and took a swig, then growled and spat it out, tossing the bottle into the sea. Striding assuredly up to the watching crowd, his head shiny with brine in the lamplight, he drew his sword in annoyance and shouted,

"Drink! Drink! Drink!"

The shore fraternity drew back in alarm, appalled that none of them had any liquor upon their persons to give him. One pointed to a large, rambling house that stood on the cliff top.

"Plenty to drink in there," he said, speaking slowly and clearly, suspecting the strange man before him didn't speak good English.

The others nodded eagerly.

The corsair's eyes followed his finger to the house, shrewdly taking in the overhanging cliffs and the steep rocky sides broken here and there by tortuous pathways. It would be madness to try to negotiate these tracks after drinking anything stronger than water, but to Sparky, anything that led to a keg of brandy or a bottle of rum was a worthy risk. He shrugged his shoulders and headed to the cliff.

Just then the rower pulled ashore and North vaulted out.

"Captain Vaquero!" he cried. "The wind is keen! The cliff paths will kill you!"

"Not I!" called back Sparky.

"There is an easier way," cried North, and he pointed to a cave near the headland. "Rame Hole. Leads right up to the house! But don't turn off the main tunnel. The cliff is riddled with caves, you'll be lost forever if you go roamin'."

"Lost! Not I!" scoffed Sparky, trudging towards the cave. "You have forgotten who you are talking to." He stopped and grinned, sniffing the air. "Smell that? On the wind?"

North regarded Sparky suspiciously before cautiously sniffing the air. To him it was full only of sea salt.

"Smell what?"

"Moonshine and firewater!" laughed Sparky, heartily. "Fear not, my boy! My nose leads me the true route."

He laughed again and kicked his way over the beach to the cave, followed by the eyes of those waiting for their orders on shore. They stared as he entered the open mouth of the cave and melted into the shadows.

"It's a long story," explained North to one of the shore fraternity who turned to him, his eyebrows raised in question.

"What happened to Bridie?"

As if in answer to his question, Sparky's ship came into view around the headland. North pointed to it and grinned. Several men shuffled on their feet uncomfortably, but the man who had signalled the spout lantern stepped forward and turned to them.

"Look lively, lads! Marty MacBride's a-comin'! There's free goods for us all!"

* * *

The crews of *The Mevagissey* and *The Barentszee* spent the night on the cliff-top at Rame House. It was a substantial abode boasting seventeen bedrooms and owned by a rather paunchy old fellow who went by the name of Talfryn. Talfryn was very fond of his comforts and made no argument against putting up the smugglers. He didn't flinch when Sparky strode in and demanded to know where the rum was, but waved in the direction of the pantry and informed the Barbary pirate that if he'd be good enough to bring in a bottle or three then he would join him for a nightcap.

The men were tired after their voyage and slept soundly, most of them lying on blankets and mats in the bedrooms. Sparky and Talfryn, who had become the best of friends by the bottom of the second bottle, slumped drunkenly on the parlour chairs, Sparky still grasping the neck of the bottle and Talfryn snoring loudly, his mouth wide open.

Only MacBride did not sleep. He spent the night, heavily disguised and hooded, aiding the fishermen in the retrieval of the ankers, after re-investigating the whole area for snooping revenue men.

The great wealth of contraband was lugged safely through the caves to the passage under the house and stored in the secret chambers there. In the past it had often been left in Rame Hole, but MacBride had insisted that no corners were to be cut that night and all the stores were to be well hidden, much to the disgruntlement of the weary shore fraternity.

"This is the biggest load I've brought in," he said. "There are two substantial ships anchored offshore, and the Plymouth market is tomorrow. The gaugers are bound to be about, and it would be nothing short of foolish to take chances with such a lot at stake."

And so he worked with his comrades through the night, lugging contraband into the secret chambers underneath Rame House, until the first hues of dawn touched the skyline.

CHAPTER SEVEN

MacBRIDE and Sparky left Plymouth several days later; MacBride supremely rich and Sparky, typically, less so.

"T'as been a splendid weekend," sighed Sparky. He languished on the poop deck, enjoying watching MacBride do all the work. "I must confess, I find it somewhat gratifying to be able to spend what I like in the secure knowledge that all the specie you have earned will soon be mine."

"Much more of your debauchery and I'll be tempted to wager on your dying before me," said MacBride before shouting orders to the quartermaster.

Sparky closed his eyes lazily against the sharp sunlight.

"Wealth is an addictive thing. You have some, and then you want more."

"It doesn't seem to work that way for you."

"Ah! It does, it does. I want more drink, more women! For such things, a man needs more riches." He turned his head and opened one eye. "Not tempted to go back on our agreement?"

"By no means," replied MacBride. "Wealth only serves one purpose for me now. I take no pleasure in anything else it can provide."

Sparky seemed content with this answer and shut his eye again.

"It sometimes troubles me to know that the man I journey with is barely of this world."

"That's rich," muttered MacBride.

"No partialities, no loves … Then I savvy I care not."

"Wealth has never made life easy for me," said the smuggler. "Once you're rich, you're a target for black-hearted, cold-blooded devils."

"It is not in your interests to deter me of my love of money," said Sparky.

"I rest assured it would be an impossible task. But had I not been sailing a laden ship into the Mediterranean, I would never have been marked, captured and sold."

"You need to learn to kill," mumbled Sparky. Then he sat up. Sheltering his eyes with his hand, he regarded MacBride curiously. "Algiers?" he asked.

"What of it?"

Sparky settled back down and closed his eyes again.

"My homeland."

"You're from Algiers?"

Something twisted sickeningly in MacBride's stomach.

"Moroccan port of Sallee. Bought a lot of slaves in Algiers though."

He grinned wickedly.

The twisting inside MacBride's stomach turned to anger and bubbled up inside of him. Gritting his teeth, he grabbed his flintlock and cocked the trigger. Sparky heard, but did not flinch. He didn't even open an eye.

"We both know you won't do it," he said languidly. "But it's reassuring to know there are some passions still running beneath the stone."

"I lost cherished friends at Algiers."

"Have you checked my ship? I may have purchased them."

MacBride kicked over a barrel, and was rewarded with witnessing Sparky start.

"They died!" he bellowed. "Horribly."

"Dealing slaves is no crime," grinned Sparky, aggravatingly. "There's a lot of value in black ivory."

He stopped the barrel that was rolling towards him with the sole of his boot.

"You miserable, heartless bastard!" MacBride was beside himself. "I watched mothers torn from their children, children torn from their mothers, imprisoned by monsters who took such unearthly pleasure in pain. They cut off their ears! I saw women and children hanged! Impaled!"

Sparky did not answer. He twisted his dagger into the side of the barrel, his thoughts apparently elsewhere.

"People went mad with hunger and fear," MacBride said. He stared out over the ocean, his voice a little quieter now. *"People."*

Sparky was unmoved.

"I must say, you did well to come out in one piece," he said, picking a long shaft of straw from the deck and inserting it carefully through the little hole he'd made in the barrel. "Rough treatment for you." He looked up, squinting in the sun. "Rough hands, rough treatment. Shows you're poor. Smooth hands and they treat you better. Hold you for ransom." He began to suck raw, undiluted spirit through the straw. He licked his lips. "You could smell the cells from Sallee," he added.

MacBride gripped the leather strap that lay across the pirate's chest and pulled him sharply towards him so that their eyes met.

"And how did you treat the people *you* bought?" he breathed, dangerously.

"I didn't buy women or children," the pirate said. "They were too weak for my uses. But I had men and I treated them well – if they rowed well, that is. If they collapsed I tried to revive them, of course I did. Flogging brings them round. But if that didn't work, I'd chuck them overboard. Let them walk home!"

He chuckled.

"You are truly of evil blood," said MacBride. "There is surely not an honourable bone in your body."

"But you already knew that," replied Sparky. "I am renowned for it. You want honourable bones, you visit a bone-yard. That's where they all end up."

"That's where we all end up, eventually."

"Some get there quicker than others," grinned Sparky. "Besides, they won't bury my bones in a bone-yard. He paused.

"Anyway, I don't know what you're objecting to. The way I treat people is no different to the way they are treated ashore. The land is the King's empire. The sea is ours."

"Do not include me in your empire. I set out only to make a good living for my family. My veins do not consist of the ice that runs through yours."

"That from a man who casts no shadow of emotion but anger? A man whose only ambition in life is to kill?"

"I am nothing like you, heathen pirate."

Sparky flicked out the straw and got to his feet. He pointed it at MacBride.

"You are *just* like me! Robber of the sea! The only difference between you and me is that *you* think there is one! You're hardly a patriot." Once again, MacBride went for his pistol. Sparky smiled. "I know what you think. You think I am a pirate and you are a hero." He sat down again. "Well let me tell you this, my friend. The difference between a pirate and a hero is merely a question of politics. The way your friend, Mr Cardinham, sees it, it is *you* who is the pirate whereas *I* serve to be the hero … which brings me to remember that the only thing you care for is seeing Mr Cardinham die. I would advise you to remove your hand from your pistol and *honour* our accord." MacBride growled again, his hand still stubbornly clutching at the flintlock. Sparky smiled. "An accord which included, as I recall, cellars full of French cognac, did it not?"

MacBride clenched his jaw.

'It did,' he conceded.

"And where do I find this 'Cousin Jackie' as you call it?"

There was a moment's pause.

"Pensilva Cellars," muttered MacBride, at last removing his hand reluctantly from the pistol.

"Then let us go there!"

Sparky grasped the top of MacBride's boot as he turned to walk away. "My good friend," he added, his voice almost gentle, "I can see you are in pain. I venture that Cardinham can be an even worthier antagonist than I am known to be. It would be a shame to let your wrath get the better of you when you have managed so admirably to suppress every other human sentiment."

MacBride regarded him angrily.

"My patience wears thin," he said.

"It is not one of my greatest attributes either," admitted Sparky. "But patience is what our strategy requires, so patience is what we must have. Cardinham is a clever man. His supreme strength is his lack of morals." He grinned. "*I* should know. It will take more than honour to overcome such a man. You will have to see the world through his eyes – through *my* eyes. It is a graceless age. Say goodbye to the hero you once were, for there is no place for him here." With that, he turned to face down ship, raised his arm, and in a staggeringly loud voice bellowed, "*To Pensilva!*"

* * *

It was raining in Newlyn again.

Cole Shanley opened the door of the watch house on Bessy's Cove and walked in, his overcoat wrapped tightly around him to keep out the biting night wind. He found the look-out already occupied by four young revenue men, all heavily armed with pistols and cudgels.

"What are you doing here?"

"Our duty, Sir."

"Then I will relieve you. You may leave."

"But we're under orders," protested Officer Roberts. "Strict orders."

"Orders from whom?" enquired Shanley.

"From Mr Cardinham, Sir."

"Mr Cardinham – while he might like to think it – is not in charge down here yet. And when he is, he will be in charge of excise, *not* customs. That is my post. May I suggest that you make your way up to Miss Josephine Bryant's and ensure she is paying the appropriate taxes."

But Roberts was troubled.

"But, Sir, Mr Cardinham has been tipped off that Mr MacBride will be landing here tonight."

Shanley stared at him.

"Aye, he'll be right," he said, forming his word slowly to give them gravitas. "That is precisely the reason I am here."

"But won't you want some support?" asked Roberts, straightening his back and making himself as tall as possible.

"Do you want a night off or not?" asked Shanley in exasperation. "Be off with you!"

And the men, despite their better judgement, left.

* * *

Sparky glanced anxiously at the precarious reefs and rocks that lay between *The Barentszee* and the mainland.

"I know the location of every rock as I know the back of my hand," MacBride reassured him.

"HAVE AN ANKER TO WINDWARD!" yelled Sparky. Then he turned to MacBride. "Wreck my ship and I'll be taking you straight to London," he added quietly.

MacBride had no intention of wrecking his ship. There was too much at stake to make mistakes now.

* * *

"I don't think Mr Cardinham is going to be too pleased about us leaving our post," said one of the revenue men as they crunched along the shingle in the darkness towards the pathway that led up the cliff.

"Who cares?" said another. "As Mr Shanley said, he's still in charge down here. We need to follow his orders. Let Cardinham get angry with him."

"Do you think we ought to do as he says and go to Pensilva?"

"Definitely! A pint of her best ale for me!"

"I certainly wouldn't pass up any opportunity to see the fine Miss Bryant!"

Suddenly Officer Roberts stopped and gripped the man beside him in fear. He raised a shaking hand to the cliff top. The others followed his gaze and there, looking down on them, stood an illuminated spectre, its ghostly white rags blowing eerily in the wind.

"Good Lord!"

Roberts fell to his knees and began to pray.

"That's that smuggler, Broomsworth!" gasped another. "The one they hanged! I know it! He's come back to haunt us!"

"They didn't hang him for smuggling – they hanged him for murder! And it weren't in these parts anyway!" yelled the first.

"But I assisted in capturing him!" wailed the second. "And he told us when we took him, he said he'd be back as a plague on our very souls!" He howled. "It's him! It is! I see it!"

"I can't see his face."

"He hasn't got a face!"

"Then how can you be sure 'tis him?"

Just as hysteria threatened to take over, Officer Roberts felt something touch him lightly on the shoulder. Letting out a high pitched scream, he flipped around.

"Oh! Mr Coby, sir!" he exhaled.

"Aye?" said Doug through the darkness, "Ye appear to have been expecting another?"

Roberts pointed to the cliff top in terror. Doug peered through the gloom, straining his eyes.

"I see nothing."

Sure enough, the figure had vanished.

"But it was there," squeaked Roberts. "Wasn't it, men?"

"What was there?" frowned Doug.

"T'was a spirit!" answered one of the others. "A ghost! As sure as I am standing here! Risen straight up through the gates of Hell itself."

"Smuggler Broomsworth it was, I'm sure of it!"

"A ghoulish, satanic wraith," Roberts said.

"With rotting skin and bleeding eyes!"

The four men stared desperately at Doug, imploring him to believe them. Doug frowned and peered back up at the cliff-top. Then he looked back at the revenue men. He turned and ran his canny gaze over the night shore behind him. When he turned back there was a wicked glint in his eye.

"Aye, 'tis a fine night for the dead to walk." He made his way up the beach, leaving the men looking at each other in horror. His voice floated back over the shingle. "If I were you, I'd get yourselves home. Lock ye doors and fasten ye windows. Leave the spirits to the night!"

* * *

Cole Shanley left the watch house and clambered up over the rocks to a small, craggy cavity in the cliff. He bent down and lifted a small boulder, revealing a hollow in the rock beneath. He crouched and lowered his hand into the darkness and felt for a small bag made of sackcloth. As he pulled it out it dripped with icy water. Loosening the drawstring, he tipped several coins into his palm.

He grinned, poured them back into his bag and, being a reasonable officer, slipped the bag into his overcoat. As he made his way back to the watch house, he caught sight of dark shadows coming up the beach towards him, but was unable to make out who they belonged to until they were almost upon him.

"Evening, gentlemen," said Shanley.

MacBride nodded amicably, looking rather portly due to being padded out with body bags beneath his waistcoat, which were stuffed with tea.

"You put on weight, MacBride?" he said as the smugger trudged past him.

Not wanting to stop for a late night chat, MacBride kept walking.

"Sir, your pocket is unbuttoned," he called over his shoulder.

Shanley smiled.

"Aye, but never mind, my man, my money's safe enough!"

And he turned and walked towards the sea.

"Take roller!" he heard Cattermole call to the men in the rower.

Shanley caught up with Doug Coby near the top of the cliff.

"A word, sir?"

Doug turned to regard him warily.

"Aye. What is it?"

"I've just heard. Cardinham's returned," said Shanley shortly.

Doug winced as the customs officer brushed past him and disappeared into the darkness.

* * *

"Ghosts!" Cardinham sent all the glasses on the table smashing to the floor with one swipe of his arm. "There are no such things!"

He stood in the back room of Pensilva, the four revenue men before him.

"We all saw it, sir," said Roberts, sounding more defiant than he felt. "As clear as day."

"Yet at night," he spat, lividly. "You stupid, spineless idiots! Cornwall is filled with ghosts! There are funerals of men that are not yet dead, there are phantom huntsmen on the roads across the moors, there are witches in the valleys. Talland churchyard is filled with devils! I can assure you, you vacuous fools, that what you saw was nothing more spiritual than good French brandy on its way to some inn or farmer or squire unwilling to pay the duties! You had my orders, and you disobeyed them because you had been hoodwinked into believing you saw some … some spirit from the deep!"

He grabbed Roberts by the scruff of the neck and held him roughly against the wall.

"Actually, sir, you were overruled," spluttered Roberts.

Cardinham dropped him in surprise. He landed heavily on his feet.

"*Overruled?*" he shouted. "By whom?"

"By Mr Shanley, sir."

"Shanley!" Cardinham's eyes were burning. "What is Shanley doing down here? He should be covering Tintagel and Port Isaac." The three officers had the good sense to stay silent. "Damn the bloody turncoat!" He turned back to Roberts who had rejoined his comrades. "And damn you, you vapid halfwits! Where's Shanley now?"

"At the watch house," muttered Roberts, looking both ashamed and embarrassed.

"I'll have to sort this shambles out myself!" cried Cardinham, charging out of the door.

He collided with a figure walking down the passage towards him. He raised his fist, ready to vent his rage on any man who dared, intentionally or otherwise, get in his way. But then he caught sight of the face of the man he had crashed into, stopped dead in his tracks and dropped his arm.

"*You!*" he cried.

"John," acknowledged Sparky.

"What in God's name? Have you caught MacBride?"

"It was on that very note that I was seeking you," said Sparky. "Is there somewhere we can speak plainly?"

"Yes, yes, of course," muttered Cardinham, looking bewildered. He turned and entered the back room again, shooing Roberts and his officers out like children from under him. He pulled out a chair and motioned to Sparky to sit down. "What news?"

"You don't happen to have a good rum on your person?" said Sparky.

Cardinham was smart enough to recognise this was not an enquiry, and he opened the door and yelled after Roberts. Jo entered the room some minutes later, looking harassed. She set the decanter down on the table, unable to hide a brief flash of surprise as Sparky caught her eye. He smiled at her, touching his hat and looking unapologetically lecherous.

"And you can take your eyes off her," snapped Cardinham as Jo quietly left the room.

"Belongs to you, does she?" asked Sparky, innocently.

"That's no concern of yours," said Cardinham.

"If you're paying me to stay celibate as well as to snare MacBride then I am afraid our agreement will have to end now."

"Look Jose …"

"Captain Vaquero."

Cardinham gritted his teeth.

"*Captain* Vaquero, was there something in particular you wanted to discuss?"

"MacBride," replied Sparky, taking a swig of rum.

"Yes? What of him?" said Cardinham impatiently.

"He's offered me a small fortune should I agree to spare him the time to kill you," Sparky said, casually.

"The fool! He thought you'd agree to that?"

"I did."

Cardinham stopped and stared in amazement. For a moment he was speechless.

"And I suppose you think I will increase your prize in order to prevent that?" he snarled.

"Well, that's up to you," conceded Sparky. "Obviously the bidding now lies with you, and needless to say I have successfully procured MacBride's trust. I still intend to escort him to London and receive my reward from Georgy-Porgy, but if I am to gain by taking my time to do so, then I of course will."

"And MacBride tells you he is willing to suffer London even after I have been disposed of?" Cardinham scoffed, regarding Sparky with the scornful air he usually kept for the revenue officers.

Sparky smiled slowly in response.

"I think he harbours quite an appetite for it."

"For the gallows? Don't be absurd! Every man fears death."

"On the contrary, some men invite it," said Sparky. "And if death is wished for, what better than a hero's death at the gibbet?"

"What, that light-fingered free-booter?" Cardinham's face grew red. "He will be no martyr! The man is a robber. A highwayman!"

"And yet he is known as 'The Knight of the Road'?" mused Sparky, thoughtfully.

Cardinham was boiling with anger.

"I tell you, he is a dirty little picaroon and the country will revel in watching him hang!"

Sparky took exception to the slur on picaroons; he was, after all, one himself.

"Remember who you are talking to," he said. "It would not do to offend me."

Cardinham waved his hand dismissively, but wisely chose not to pursue the matter.

"MacBride is a villain and must pay the price for his wrong-doings."

"I don't dispute that," said Sparky. "But my experience lends me to the belief that it is not always the villain who is looked upon unfavourably. Take my good self for example."

"You're no hero," snapped Cardinham.

"Not in the eyes of the law, perhaps."

"You think a lot of yourself!"

"As must you, to employ me on such an 'arduous mission'. If I recall correctly, it seemed a task 'elusive to all the customs officers and excise men of Cornwall' that you were asking of me."

"The officers are simpletons destitute of both brain and brawn." He paused, frowning as he turned to Sparky. "The trouble with Cornwall is that the whole coast is inhabited principally by smugglers, under the denomination of *fishermen*, of course, and those who are not smugglers are the smugglers' customers. The officers risk their lives to make arrests and then the magistrates simply let the bastards go free again. MacBride knows this, and I have seen him anchor two wherries full of men and guns within the limits of this port, and I watched him lay there four whole days in open defiance, discharging contraband goods. I want the weasel brought down." He paused again. "And besides, I knew admiration was a weakness of yours, so I used it in order to secure your services."

"Ha!" laughed Sparky. "If that were the case you would not have felt pressed into offering me such a grand sum. We all know what my true weakness is, John, and admiration is not it. I simply do not see the point in modesty for modesty's sake."

He took another slug of rum.

"So, Captain Vaquero, you have told me of MacBride's plans," said Cardinham, after a moment's thought. "Why?"

Sparky lifted his chin.

"Because my allegiance lies with the man who holds my honorarium."

"Why should I trust you?"

"Take it from me; trust no man. Especially a pirate. I have found that my total lack of trust has kept me alive to this day."

"But you trust me?"

"My dear man, you are positively the *last* person I would depend on. You would not know honour if it crawled up your arse." Cardinham jumped to his feet, knocking over his chair. "Now, now, don't be angry. It takes one to know one. The point is, I am here to give you a sporting chance. I can take MacBride any time I like. He has already documented that all is mine in the event of his death, and if you make it worth my while, I will take him prisoner and leave for London before the week is out."

"You are playing us off against one another!"

Sparky reflected on the suggestion as if the idea was new to him.

"I must admit it all works very well in my favour, but that's the game. You should be glad, John, that I, like you, am not a moral man. If I had been, I would have taken the smuggler's offer and done as I was asked – by both of you. I do not believe the sparing of life came into our accord, and therefore I would not be breaking it."

Cardinham scrutinised the man in front of him, a frown on his face. Then he dropped his shoulders and sighed.

"What are your terms?"

"I want half the money now, plus another 2500 ounces of silver."

Cardinham made a choking noise.

"You're insane," he said. "Where do you think I am going to find that kind of money?"

"Rob the authorities?" shrugged Sparky. "Oh come, come! Do not take the trouble of pretending to be an honest protector of the law. I am not a fool. I can see that your hatred of MacBride is born out of something far more powerful than a simple felony. This passion is not about bringing a man to justice."

"Nevertheless, the fact that I am on the side of the law is my protection as well as my opportunity to have the man lawfully killed. So long as I abide by the law they cannot bring this murder home to me."

"All right then, I'll take the girl."

"What girl?"

"You know what girl."

"I don't know what you're talking about."

"Have it your way," shrugged Sparky, standing to leave. "But take my advice; watch your back. The man is thirsty for your blood. He's probably already aware of your return."

As he reached the door he heard the sound of footsteps hurrying down the passage beyond. Someone had been eavesdropping.

"Wait!" commanded Cardinham, getting to his feet. "Wait," he repeated, weakly.

Sparky turned to face him, hand still on the handle of the door.

"I'll find the money. Just give me a few days."

Sparky said no more and left the room. He walked down the passage and into the tavern, where he caught Jo's eye as she stretched to reach a tankard hanging from the top of the bar. He grinned wilfully and she stared back at him, her eyes cold as stone.

Chapter Eight

A S the tavern door opened and the crew of *The Mevagissey* entered, Jo busied herself lining up tankards and glasses along the bar and pouring their favourite drinks. She sensed MacBride's presence without lifting her head.

"I was quite prepared never to see you in here again," she said.

"I promised Sparky the cognac in your cellars," replied MacBride.

Jo looked up and met his eye.

"Of course."

"It's not like that, Jo."

"No, it's all right," she said. "I understand. You've come to pick the bones clean."

"Jo … "

"Just give me a moment."

She poured the last of the ale before unwrapping the apron from around her slim waist and dropping it lightly onto the counter. MacBride's eyes followed her as she disappeared through the swing door into the passage, her posture as proud and composed as always.

Once she heard the door shut behind her, she quickened her step and hurried down into the cellars, unhooking the ring of keys from her belt as she did so. A stout, old woman sat on a chair, darning. As she heard footsteps approaching, she anxiously placed her sewing on the table beside her.

"Quick, Hetty, we have to move our charge upstairs for a while," said Jo.

"What's the black-hearted beggar doing now?"

"It's not him," Jo whispered. "It's MacBride."

A moment later and Jo stalked back into the bar.

"Jackie's just where you left him," she said, dropping a key into MacBride's palm.

"Jo," he began, catching her arm as she made her way back behind the bar. She turned to him, her face blank so that it was impossible to see what she was feeling.

"Yes?" she said, patiently.

"I'm not doing this to hurt you."

"I know. You promised your pirate friend."

"Josephine!"

"I know, Bridie. I know *you*. This is not your style of revenge. Taking Jackie doesn't hurt. Your indifference does. I'd rather you hated me. I'd rather you *were* taking revenge."

She slipped her hand from his grip, leaving MacBride to look on as she began taking orders from the rabble at the bar. He turned and went through the swing door. Jo lifted her eyes as the sound of the door banging reached her ears and she stared after him uncomfortably. Pouring out a measure of brandy she looked over to where Sparky was sitting, a rum in one hand, a feather of cards in the other. He was laughing with his fellow pirates, seemingly oblivious to what was going on in the rest of the tavern. They crashed their blackjacks together in toasts.

Jo's eyes narrowed and she absent-mindedly placed the bottle onto the bar.

"Hey, Josie love!" cried Sam, breaking into her thoughts. "My brandy?"

She turned her head to look at him, her eyes thoughtful.

"Here, help yourself," she murmured, and, after sliding the bottle and the glass over to him, she slipped out through the swing door.

The moment she moved, Sparky lifted his eyes and watched her go. Then, raising the rum to the quiet smile that played upon his lips, he joined in with the revelries again.

* * *

It was cool in the cellars. Soft candles flickered in the corner where MacBride was laboriously shifting barrels. Jo went up to him and touched him lightly on the elbow. He started and spun around.

"Jumpy, aren't you?" said Jo.

"I am when people creep up on me," he said, curtly.

"I didn't creep up on you!"

"What is it? I thought the bar was busy?"

She regarded him with a combination of hurt and surprise.

"I'm sorry," she said, her tone slow and purposeful. "I'll go." But as she turned her back on him, she heard the soft thud of the cellar door closing. She darted to see who was there, but the stairwell was empty; whoever had been listening had gone. In that instant she made up her mind and, pushing MacBride right into the corner, she lifted her lips to his ear and whispered, "*Don't trust the pirate.*"

MacBride's forehead creased. For a brief moment, he found it difficult to take in what she was saying. He could feel her breath on his face, her delicate scent somehow overwhelming him, sending his head spinning and his thoughts with it. Old, secret emotions, latterly too faint to need suppressing, now bubbled within his belly as he fought with a new need for restraint, and his muscles tensed as he looked into her eyes.

Jo misunderstood his confusion.

"I heard him talking to John," she urged him. "He told him of your agreement – inheritance for time?" He stared at her as though he hadn't heard what she had said. She shook him by the shoulders and pulled him closer. "With Heaven as my witness – it's true! I swear it, by bell, book and candle – he is John's servant!"

MacBride's eyes flicked over her face. He blinked tightly, and pushed her away.

"Sparky is no man's servant," he said, brushing past her.

She caught his arm and pulled him back.

"You can't buy his loyalty," she said, forgetting to whisper.

"I wouldn't have to, if you would tell me where Cardinham is."

Jo's shoulders sagged.

"I don't know," she said, weakly. "He left when he heard you were on your way." She glimpsed the spark of anger in his eye. "He knows your wrath; your vow of vengeance."

MacBride reeled.

"He cannot know it. Not even he has suffered hate such as this. My loathing for that man would have me tear him from limb to limb with my bare hands."

"To what purpose?"

Jo could not keep the bitterness from her voice.

"Peace of mind!"

She shook her head. A fear lay behind her eyes.

"You cannot die," she whispered, her head pounding with the constraints of Cardinham's threats.

"I want justice for my family," replied MacBride, bluntly.

Once more he turned to go, but Jo intercepted him.

"Don't trust anyone," she pleaded. She looked down at the floor. *"Anyone."*

MacBride stared at her.

"When did I wrong you, Jo?" he asked.

She didn't know how to reply.

"Apart from relieving me of all my best French cognac for your pirate friend?" she said.

A smile crossed her lips. MacBride laughed in return.

"I trust you, Jo," he said. "Don't let me down."

She stood aside and let him pass, her heart sinking to her feet.

* * *

"The keys, brother," said MacBride, handing over Jo's keys to the cellars. "He's there when you want him."

Sparky winked.

"You keep your promises," he said, with a slight nod of his head. "That is good to know. I thought that fine Flossie might have swayed your good judgement."

He looked past MacBride to the swing door and Jo, who had just come back into the room. MacBride followed his gaze.

"She is nothing to me."

"Nay, of course not." Sparky leaned forward, grinning. "But few can resist Venus herself." He leaned back in his chair again and, lifting his rum, inclined his neck in the direction of the bar. "And she is surely her."

"She is not for the likes of you," MacBride said, sharply.

Sparky grinned his manic grin and his eyes sparked.

"So I've been told," he acknowledged, mysteriously.

CHAPTER NINE

A T last, summer had broken through.

From the shore, MacBride's eyes passed lazily over the flurry of activity that was taking place aboard *The Barentszee* and a captured sloop, *The Manzana Silvestre,* as they bobbed in the harbour. Horse-drawn wagons and caravans rolled up to water's edge, and men aboard were busy caulking before they set out to sea.

It was pleasant to sit on the warm, sandy bank, a leaf cigarette held between his fingers. To his side sat Sparky with a bottle of Jo's cognac in his hand.

"I have a feeling, comrade, that this will be our last voyage together," he said.

"That gives me good heart," replied MacBride. "It means that I will at last succeed in cornering that slippery whoreson. Or, perchance, this is your subtle way of telling me my time is running out?"

"Aye, the sands are falling," said Sparky, amiably. "For all three of us. Least you'll be able to experience the proper life before your hour is up."

"How's that?"

"We're going home, brother."

MacBride stirred.

"To Sallee?"

"Aye. And Algiers."

MacBride winced.

"Oh good,' he said. "I was beginning to miss the place."

Sparky laughed.

"I thought as much. Nevertheless, I go for my own good reasons; to pay homage to the pirate empire. I make my fortune each time I return to the Barbary States."

"Why didn't you stay there?"

"Ah, it's hot. And I, like you, have not the fondest memories of the place." MacBride regarded him with piqued interest. "They kidnapped me as a boy and demanded a large price from me." He nodded at the smuggler and smiled. "Ah yes, we have more in common that you thought. That's the trouble with an empire ruled by pirate kings; piracy is the only law. Each man for himself."

"So England's a comfortable option?"

MacBride laid back and closed his eyes.

"Indeed. Why spend your life watching your back when a healthy living can be earned more smoothly elsewhere? I had a good education – I could speak English well. The corsairs are brave and daring; they are to be respected and honoured … but never trusted."

"I am well aware."

The sun beat down upon them. MacBride watched the gulls wheel in the sky through half closed lids.

"I'll have him, you know," he said, "Cardinham. I'll find him. And I'll take him down with me."

"I don't doubt you for a moment, brother."

* * *

Cardinham flashed his identity tag at the guard of the Somerset gaol.

"Mr Cardinham, Excise Officer in Chief. I would like a word with the prisoner."

The guard inclined his head and stepped aside, allowing the officer to enter the cell.

"Hallows!" said Cardinham, inviting himself to sit down opposite the stout, sullen-looking prisoner who was sitting at the table.

He stretched out his arm and shook the smuggler's reluctant hand.

Cardinham ran his eyes around the cold grey walls, turning his head from the smell of urine that emanated from the iron bucket in the corner.

"Nice in here, isn't it?"

"What do you want?" demanded Hallows, his face still stony.

"I have an offer for you that, should you be willing to co-operate, will prove beneficial to us both."

"Oh aye?"

"You are aware that giving the name of an accomplice is rewarded with five hundred guineas or a free pardon?"

"I am not interested, Officer. My associates and I have strong loyalties."

"I don't care about your associates," interrupted Cardinham. "I am going to give you the name of a man I want you to claim was with you on the Lyme Landing."

"You want me to lie?"

"That's right," he replied, without hesitation. He removed a piece of parchment and a quill from his bag. "This is the testimony. All you have to do is sign it."

"Who is this man?"

"His name is MacBride."

"Never heard of him."

"That's because he's never worked in these parts."

"And for signing your declaration you will let me go free?"

"You have my word."

"Why?"

Cardinham sighed wearily.

"Let's just say he has offended me, personally. Once you have stated that he was an accomplice his name will be gazetted, and if he does not surrender within forty days he will be appointed the death penalty."

"And if he surrenders? If someone turns him in?"

"Impossible," replied Cardinham with a smirk. "He's not even in the country. You will be signing his death warrant. You walk, I get my man. Do we have an understanding?"

Hallows nodded and picked up the quill.

* * *

Coby and the rest of the crew had stayed in Cornwall, with Cattermole overseeing the building of a new vessel at Polperro. MacBride had accompanied Sparky's crew alone, and for the last few weeks, had become a pirate.

The days had been busy on the schooner. MacBride quietly observed Sparky's skill in navigation – his cabin in the quarter deck was a shrine to magnetic compasses, backstaffs, sundials and lodestones. His bunk was strewn with telescopes and waggoners, and a large ornate globe rested on the footlocker, yet he did not seem to possess one book of maps or charts.

Several rules were observed on board, of which Sparky was rigorous in the upkeep. Lights were to be out at eight o'clock precisely. All weapons were to be kept meticulously clean and ready for use. The need for this had been demonstrated numerous times off the coast of Spain, where several ships had been captured: two brigantines, a sloop, a caravel, and even a junk.

Each seizure seemed a game to Sparky. He had many different means of capturing and plundering, and strived never to use the same method twice in a row.

Sometimes he would release a red banner known as the "No Quarter" from the mast – a sign that they were going to attack. On another occasion he might raise a friendly flag. But he never raised his own Jolly Roger.

The jamming of the rudder captured the caravel, and the air had soon filled with the crackling of rifles and blunderbuss, musket, flintlock and cannon. Each seized ship was submitted to a ritual known as "Strike Colours" – the practice of pulling down the ship's flag to symbolise its surrender. When one of the crew, a marauder known only as "Mantis", failed to clean the blood from his cutlass, he was made to "kiss the gunner's daughter", which everyone knew meant being bent over a cannon and flogged raw and had nothing to do with pleasure at all.

The reason for Vaquero's notoriety became plain to see as each vessel was taken with apparent ease, and with few pirates badly injured. Only one had lost a limb when he suffered an injury which required amputation by the ship's cook; Dr Cottle had been quite overcome with liquor at the crucial time.

It was dawn when they reached the Mediterranean and spotted the galley. MacBride had just reached the sloop and was climbing the boarding ropes when he heard Cyprian Bezique, the first pirate mate, give a shout.

"What is it?" MacBride asked as he reached the forecastle.

"Christian trading ship," answered Cyprian, handing him the spyglass and pointing across the water.

MacBride lifted the spyglass to his eye and found the ship on the horizon. The very sight of it made his blood run cold.

"You think Sparky's seen it?" he asked.

"Most certainly," nodded Cyprian at once. "He has the sight of a man with seven earrings."

MacBride grinned inwardly. Cyprian took up a biscuit and tapped it against the wood to knock the weevils out.

"Captain can get much for such a ship in Algiers," he said as he took a bite out of his biscuit.

"And not just the ship …" MacBride muttered.

Sure enough, *The Barentszee* changed its course in order to pursue the Christian vessel and the sloop, *The Manzana Silvestre,* followed.

The take was easy, too easy for Sparky. The gaining of a galley with over a hundred "slaves" ensured a rather jovial mood on board. The pirate crew had been thinly dispersed over the three ships; the Christians kept prisoner aboard their own vessel. MacBride, suspecting trouble, kept a close eye on both Sparky's ship and the captive galley, glancing up into the sails of the sloop at the sail-maker who hung from the ratlines, repairing a rip with a large needle. Eventually, he cut his way through the pirates to the helmsman.

"Steer in close to the Christians," he ordered, and at the helmsman's protest, he pushed a pistol into his side. "While I am on this ship, I am Captain. You will do as I say."

Cyprian arrived as soon as he detected the change of course.

"What are you doing?" he demanded the of helmsman. "I gave no order!"

The helmsman indicated uncomfortably to the barrel of the pistol that rested just below his ribs.

"I wish to board the Christian ship," announced MacBride.

His words were greeted with a look of intense suspicion.

"To what purpose?" Cyprian asked.

MacBride smile, cordially.

"My good man, as Vaquero is captaining *The Barentszee* and with the superior skills of you and I both here on the sloop, I fear there is a substantial lack of experienced captaincy aboard the vessel of the Christians. The likelihood of rebellion is high."

Bezique frowned, struggling between the desire to accept this lavish compliment and feeling obligated to keep MacBride away from the Christian vessel.

"Thank you," he said, at last. "But I shall go."

"As you wish," replied MacBride, amicably.

However, as soon as they had drawn to boarding distance, and the grappling irons had pulled the two ships together, MacBride swung over to the captured ship using one of the boarding ropes.

Cyprian stared furiously from the deck, torn between following him and not wishing to leave *The Manzana Silvestre* without a captain. It was a decision he did not have to make. MacBride ordered the surprised pirates to abandon ship and the Christians, now freed from their manacles below deck, began pulling at the oars. Before anybody knew what had happened the pirates had left the galley and boarded the sloop and the Christian ship began to move away.

From the deck of *The Manzana Silvestre*, Cyprian could do nothing. Furious, he punched the innocent quartermaster before turning back to see MacBride row the sender to *The Barentszee*.

"Captain will acquaint you with the nine tails for that," a grim pirate informed the smuggler as he heaved himself up onto deck.

And already, Sparky was pacing the deck, wheeling the cat o' nine tails. As MacBride approached him from behind, Sparky swung round, his arm outstretched, and striking MacBride across the mouth sent him flying to the ground. He pulled at his lash to flog him, but it wouldn't come. Spinning around, he saw a pirate standing on it.

"Get off my wuddy blip!" he shouted, yanking it from under the pirate's boots.

MacBride, touching his oozing lip briefly, slowly got to his feet and aimed a solid blow back at the pirate. As Vaquero hit the deck, MacBride found himself surrounded by cutlasses and pistols. But Sparky, to everyone's surprise, waved them away, his eyes resting darkly on MacBride.

"What makes you think you have the licence to captain my men?" he yelled. "You set free my slaves!"

"I don't approve of slave snatching," said MacBride.

"I don't care. They were valuable goods."

"They are not animals, and they are not yours. Algiers is full of slaves. You would have been lucky to get an onion each for them."

Sparky drew close, his face twisted with rage.

"I *like* onions," he sneered. "And there were women on that ship I could have sold as a harem. I have the perfect customer in Tripoli."

"We're not going to Tripoli."

"We go where *I* say!" bellowed Sparky. "Me! Your captain!"

MacBride wiped away the blood that was trickling down his chin.

"I thought you said it was bad luck having a woman on board."

"It's bad luck having *you* on board! I like women. I like them on board best." He turned to the Arab pirate who stood beside him. "Tell them to load the cannons," he ordered.

But as soon as the words were out, MacBride seized him by the collar of his shirt.

"You dare!" he shouted. "I've been on a slave ship! I will not let you have them just to satisfy your thrill!"

"It's not for thrill, it's for opulence!"

"For how long? You are already a wealthy man! You told me yourself you might be dead tomorrow. You can't take it with you!"

Sparky glowered.

"That's very direct," he muttered uncomfortably.

"Afraid *you'll* go to Hell?"

Sparky grunted and waved down the Arab he had given the order to. MacBride followed him as he stalked into his cabin. "You're right," he said, closing the door behind him. "This isn't about thrill. But it's not about opulence either. This is about your need to leave behind a legacy of barbarity. Your infamous reputation."

"When you've earned notoriety like me, it becomes necessary to protect it in order to secure a fast surrender," Sparky said. "In order that your name be remembered."

"And you think that the release of one ship will change that?"

"My reputation is such that I have never shown mercy."

"How nice for you."

"Yes, I like it."

"And I thought you were a free man – ruled by nobody."

"Get to your point, MacBride."

"You are governed by every man who has ever heard of your brutal reputation and believes it must be nothing short of inexorable. *You*, yourself, are nothing more than a slave to your prestige and whatever it demands from you."

The two men stared bitterly at each other.

"I wanted a galley," scowled Sparky, petulantly, pulling a bottle of dark rum from his cabinet. MacBride, infuriated by the constant drinking, swiped the bottle from his grasp. Sparky snatched the bottle back and brought it down heavily on the smuggler's head, causing it to shatter in all directions. MacBride lost consciousness and sunk to the floor. Sparky pulled another bottle from the cabinet.

"Forgive me, brother," said the pirate, between gulps. "But I wish to ensure the demise of my life … before that of my *prestige*."

CHAPTER TEN

"HOW are you finding life as a pirate, Bridie?" asked Sparky, through the crisp darkness. "Learned anything?"

It was some time since MacBride and the pirates had seen land, yet the peace that the smuggler had once found at sea began to wane. He watched as Sparky slightly adjusted the astrolabe he was looking through.

"I've learned to appreciate Martha's cooking," replied MacBride, biting into a lime.

A sleepy hen wandered past, pecking here and there at the deck, but the flash of clashing swords caught MacBride's eye some way down deck near the mainmast. Sparky continued to study the constellations.

"Take no heed, brother," said Sparky. His tone was dismissive. "They're just settling their differences."

There came a cry, followed by a splash.

"Looks like they settled them," said MacBride. "Who was it?"

"It is not important. I'll look into it later."

When Sparky had satisfied himself that all was right with the night sky, he took a rare chance to sit down beside MacBride amidst the boarding pikes, ruffling the fur on the top of Duncan's head. He'd taken a shine to the dog.

MacBride was twisting a thick stalk of maquis between his fingers.

"Missing home, brother?"

"Home?"

A faint smile played about MacBride's lips.

"Your homeland of myth and warrior kings?"

MacBride laughed and shook his head.

"The lowlands of Scotland were my homeland once. I have no home now. It is of no matter. But Cardinham is eating me. I'll wait no longer."

Sparky produced a bottle of brandy out of nowhere and pulled the cork with his teeth.

"To carve the gizzard of the crafty Cardinham? In that case, on our return, what is the plan?"

"He thinks he is meeting you. I appear. I kill him."

"If you don't mind me saying, I believe the odds of you getting close to the man are stacked against you. He seems solely focussed on you. You won't catch him unaware."

"Thanks for pointing that out."

Sparky raised his eyes and studied the stars again.

"If I am correct, we are about thirty miles from the Gibraltar Straits," he said.

"What of it?"

Sparky frowned with concentration, then called to the quartermaster, Gibbon.

"I could produce a small distraction for your nemesis to occupy his mind."

Gibbon approached and Sparky addressed him.

"Take the rower to Zedekiah. Tell him to take a message to *The Aida Alada*. I'd like her to meet me at Cape Cornwall. You will find her somewhere about the Canaries. Tell her the course is North North East and to land at Mounts Bay."

"*Aida Alada*?" echoed MacBride.

"Old ship of mine," explained Sparky.

"Shall I take the message that you are in need of her assistance?" enquired Gibbon.

Sparky roared with laughter.

"That will not make the little cimarron come! Tell her – ha! – tell her that I am to be married. At Newlyn." Sparky looked extremely pleased with himself and rubbed his hands together. "*Ahora! Ahora!*" he cried, waving Gibbon away. Then he threw his arms into the air and, grinning widely, cried, "Retribution, amormio! Retribution!"

And he slung his brandy to his mouth. MacBride studied him closely.

"I don't get the impression that you are doing this solely to help me," he said, watching as Gibbon made ready to sail to Zedekiah, who had been put in charge of one of the brigantines they had seized and was following them at some distance.

"Ah, I would like to see her just once more before I go," acknowledged Sparky, his smile, for once, a genuine one.

* * *

MacBride could not get out of Algiers quick enough, but Sparky, who lived up to his merciless name and had not forgotten about MacBride's assistance with the escape of his slaves, delighted in taking a painful amount of time over all his affairs. The silver lining came when their extended stay revealed the death of the patroon who had enslaved MacBride. He had been shot in the back by another of his former slaves, tidings which almost made the trip worthwhile.

At last, when the seized ships had been sold, *The Manzana Silvestre* exchanged for a galley, and Sparky's lust sufficiently satisfied with rum and the company of beautiful, young Algerian women, they set sail for Cornwall, stopping only once at Cherbourg to pick up extra contraband, and meet *The Mevagissey* which had sailed out to meet them.

Yet, despite having being desperate to leave Algiers, MacBride's spirits ebbed as they drew closer to home. Sparky watched him as he sat on deck, looking sadly out into the waves.

"My droll, quick-witted friend tarries off shore again," Sparky said to nobody in particular.

"All his troubles wait for him at home," said Doug, who was working nearby. "At sea, nothing has changed. The ocean is his freedom."

Sparky went over to Doug and slapped him hard on the back.

"Lighten up, comrade!" he cried. "The man shall learn to live again!" He paused, grinning. "Of course, by that time he'll be on his way to the gallows."

"I can't see how you can take a man you have become so close to, to be killed," said Doug, crossly. "Oh, I know what you're going to say. You had an arrangement. An *accord*. No doubt you are too business-minded to let your compassion interfere … No, I forget. You have no compassion. You slew your own brother, I heard."

"Yes, he was an ass."

Doug shook his head.

"So you will honour your accord, and yet your substantial lack of morals will prevent any pricking of conscience!" Sparky opened his mouth to protest, but Doug stepped in, pleading. "Do you really *want* Marty to die?"

"I want his dog," shrugged Sparky. "I've become attached."

* * *

"Word has it that MacBride and his cronies will be in around noon," Cardinham said as he carefully loaded bullets into his pistol. He was sitting at the desk in the study at Pensilva. "I want you to watch out for them, my darling, and ride your horse along the coast road when they are in sight."

Jo knew that a rider on the coast path was a sign to the smugglers that there was no danger in coming to landing and off-loading, but she did not let her anger show.

"I'm sure even your dopiest assistants could manage that," she said.

"Yes, but I doubt the free-booters would trust one of them," Cardinham said, glancing up and shooting her a patronising glare.

"I doubt the 'free-booters' would be able to recognise the figure on the horse," retaliated Jo.

"Hmmm." Cardinham was unconvinced. "You underestimate the man." He looked up again briefly, adding, "*Both* of them."

Jo frowned.

"You want him to hate me."

Cardinham smiled a crooked smile.

"Oh! Would that be so tragic?" he mocked.

Jo pulled out a chair and sat down opposite him

"Have I been wrong from the start?" she implored, softly appealing to the better nature she hoped Cardinham still possessed somewhere. "Were you ever principled?"

But the man was unaffected.

"It's my principles that want to see the vermin brought to justice," he said.

"No it's not," said Jo. "It's your pathetic jealousy. Your insecurity. Because you think you're inferior to him." She got up and paced the room. "And you *are* less of a man."

"We all know how you feel about MacBride," said Cardinham, smirking. "Oh. Except him, of course."

Jo placed her hands on the table and leaned over to him.

"It is not my feelings for Martin which makes me think you are a lesser man," she said. "It is plainly obvious that you are inferior to any man, you are such a poor excuse for one."

Cardinham's face did not move, but as he lifted his eyes to hers she was rewarded to see the familiar flash of anger.

"Your opinions are hardly of consequence," he said, levelly. "You either do as I say, Josephine, or you will be responsible for my actions. The choice is yours. I have little preference. But I know which would make him hate you more."

"I never thought you had the capability," said Jo, sadly.

"I never thought you did. There was never much selflessness about you; you were hardly brimming with motherly love." He flinched, as though expecting a blow for this, but it did not come.

"I suppose I wasn't with a man virile enough to bring those qualities out in me," quipped Jo, simply. "You were hardly my hero. And now, I see, hardly a man."

Cardinham gritted his teeth.

"Your insults may make you feel better in the short term, but in less than two hours you're still going to be out there giving your lover the all-clear." He slid his pistol into his belt and walked towards the door. "And please don't let our captive out of the cellar again. I saw her as I came up the path. You know I don't like her having the roam of the place."

"And where are you going to go?" asked Jo, choosing to ignore this last comment. She was not prepared to discuss the secret she had been forced to share with him. "I assume you don't have the mettle to stick around and face him?"

"On the contrary, there is nothing I'd like more than to see MacBride captured," he replied.

As Cardinham disappeared into the hall, Jo made ready to leave for the coast road with a heavy heart.

* * *

"Land ahoy!" Isaac's voice rang out over the ship.

Sparky frowned, squinting out over the sea. He scowled and called to Cyprian Bezique.

"Quick!" he ordered. "Another earring!"

MacBride, now standing beside him, looked amused.

"Earrings don't improve your eyesight," he said, trying not to grin.

Sparky stared at him incredulously.

"Of course they do. Gold ones, at any rate."

Cyprian hurried up with a needle and a gold ring, and MacBride winced as he watched the pirate first mate draw the point through Sparky's lobe.

'Now I can see if there are enemies waiting for me,' Sparky said.

MacBride looked on, astounded at the power of belief.

* * *

Rider on the coast path!"

Sparky darted up to the helm where he snatched the spyglass from the boy. He was suspicious of tricks.

"It's your fine Flossie from the inn," he said as MacBride joined him.

He passed the spyglass over.

"All is well then."

Sparky regarded him thoughtfully.

MacBride frowned.

"What?"

"I am thinking …" said Sparky, taking time to choose his words carefully. "I am thinking what if this lovely lassie is not as trustworthy as you so believe, savvy?"

"I have known Josephine ever since I arrived in Cornwall," MacBride said, firmly. "I assure you she has only ever done right by me."

"That's odd," said Sparky. "I'm certain I picked up on some tension between the two of you."

"She was John Cardinham's fiancée," said MacBride, shortly.

"Really?" remarked Sparky. Although his tone sounded surprised his face did not show it. "He did well for himself ... Still, my instincts tell me that this is not the moment to have your faith in her tested."

"Your instincts? And what do you use to improve them? Tattoos?" MacBride raised a brow. "I know Jo," he insisted. "She has a strong and just heart. She won't be bribed."

* * *

They sailed into an ambush. Cardinham's men were lying in wait for them, and when the crew landed, the men emerged, pistols drawn.

"Take care that eight trusty officers be placed on board to prevent any goods from being unshipped," Cardinham ordered.

He grinned at MacBride as the authorities battled to restrain him. Then he turned and walked away with the air of a contented man. MacBride fought off the three officers that tried to hold him and bolted towards the gangplank, only to be met by Sparky, his own pistol in his hand.

MacBride stared in confusion.

"So this is how it is!" said the smuggler. "You want to make up your mind whose side you're on!"

He pushed past, expecting the pirate to block his way, but Sparky merely called after him.

"This is neither the time nor the place, my friend," he shouted.

The smuggler walked purposefully back to him. *The Mevagissey* was crawling with revenue men, and many had surrounded the duo, pistols drawn.

"I trust you no more than I am likely to listen to you," said MacBride.

Sparky stepped out of the line of fire.

"That may be so, but I only confirm your doubts," he replied, striding away, his job done. He turned and added, "We both learned the moment we met that if you let your vengeful emotions guide you, you will only fail in your task."

Several officers leaped upon MacBride armed with handcuffs, but Sparky waved them aside.

"Come, come, friends!" he said. "Can you not see that this man is under my control?" He pulled a piece of paper from somewhere inside his waistcoat. "The Letter of the Marque," he announced. "And it says that I, Captain Vaquero, am hereby commanded by His Majesty King George to chase, capture and seize enemy ships, and am employed directly from John Cardinham. I think I can handle it from here, gentlemen. Back off please."

The revenue men loosened their grips, staring at Sparky in a mixture of awe and bewilderment.

"Let us see that document," demanded one of the officers, but another pulled him back.

"It's true! I heard Cardinham say so!"

"But Cardinham is in charge of excise, not customs. Vaquero's services have nothing to do with us."

"If Shanley had his way we wouldn't even be here."

"But Shanley's not in control any more down here."

"Oh? Since when?"

Doug Coby hurried onto the scene and MacBride, seizing the opportunity provided by the confusion, whipped the hat from Coby's head and quick as a flash tossed it over the side of the ship.

"MAN OVERBOARD!" bellowed Sparky before Doug had even realised his hat had gone.

He clutched at the air on top of his head where it had been.

There was a stampede starboard as crew and officers alike threw themselves to the sides in order to glimpse who had fallen, and more cries of "Man overboard!" rang out.

"Throw the rope!" ordered MacBride, his hands framing his mouth. He began to take steps steadily backwards, away from the fracas, and the echoes of "Throw the rope!" thundered from sailor to sailor along the ship.

Amidst the chaos, and with the officers backs turned, MacBride dived swiftly over port side, the whoosh of icy cold water filling his ears as the ocean closed silently over his head.

And he swam powerfully towards the headland.

* * *

Cardinham's face was white, but he said nothing.

"We tried to catch him, sir," said the officer, rather crestfallen. "But once he reached the cliff he was up it like a goat! I've never seen a man climb a sheer rock face as he did. Extraordinary! He's quite a …"

Cardinham's hand grabbed his throat and prevented him from completing his sentence. The assisting officer looked on, gasping.

"Next time just shoot the bastard," said Cardinham, quietly.

The revenue officer looked alarmed.

"We can't do that!" he said. "It's against the law."

"Not if it is in defence of your life," replied Cardinham.

The revenue officer failed to pick up on the danger behind the smoothness of his reply.

"But Cardinham, sir, the man has never murdered and our lives did not appear to be in danger. It would be perjury if we were to claim otherwise."

Cardinham hurled over a box of tobacco.

"If you fail me again I WILL KILL YOU MYSELF!" he shouted. "Thus you may vow you would be acting in DEFENCE OF YOUR LIFE!"

His voice ricocheted off the cliffs surrounding the harbour and nearby officers and captured crew turned to stare. He lowered his voice once more and, struggling to keep it steady, he said, "Now collect the loot and gauge the duty." He paused, scanning the shore. "And bring Vaquero to me." The officers turned to do his bidding. "And that boat," added Cardinham through gritted teeth, "that *bloody* boat! Saw it into three!"

* * *

"I hope, for your sake, you were not assisting in MacBride's escape?" said Cardinham, menacingly advancing over the pebbles towards the privateer.

"I was," replied Sparky, matter-of-factly.

"Whose side are you on!"

"I don't think it would be fair for me to take sides," replied Sparky. "Although until you find me my money I am buying MacBride his time."

"You side only with yourself," spat Cardinham. "You view every situation from the angle of how you can benefit most."

"I find it odd that I am expected to act differently from the reputation which I am renowned for."

Cardinham flicked his dagger to Sparky's chest.

"You obey *me* or I shall have you hung for treason!"

"*You* would threaten *me* with treason?" Sparky laughed.

A look of amazement fell across Cardinham's face as he felt the barrel of a pistol resting against his temple, and the blade of *The Executioner* next to his throat. He stared at Sparky, who had apparently produced the two without moving. He was about to call for help when Pentlan appeared beside him. Sparky withdrew his weapons. He had made his point.

"The ship is empty, sir," announced Pentlan, importantly.

"What have we got?" asked Cardinham, not taking his eyes from Sparky.

Pentlan drew a long, curling piece of parchment from his pocket.

"There's a lot, sir. Eight hundred pounds of tobacco, one hundred and eighty-nine kegs of brandy, sugar in quantities unknown, fifty stalks of snuff, twenty hundred weight of fullers earth, numerous bottles of claret, seventy casks of wine, thirty oilskin bags of fine tea, six thousand gallons of spirits, twenty-four dozen packs of playing cards, green tea valued at approximately thirteen pounds, sixteen shillings and ten pence, one hundred and seventy two pieces of cambric, and several dozen crates of figs, nutshells, silk and lace, pepper, coffee, calico and china." There was a long pause. "And one parrot."

"Popinjay," corrected Sparky. "Mine."

And he gave a high whistle, which brought the parrot soaring over to land on his shoulder. He tickled it under its chin and muttered something lovingly in Spanish. Then he gave Cardinham a polite nod and turned to go.

"I'll have your money soon," said Cardinham. "Then I want MacBride brought down."

"As soon as the bargain has been completed I shall do just that," replied Sparky. "Until then, MacBride and all he earns is mine. Therefore, all the goods you have there on the beach by rights belong to me. You could further your case by passing them onto their rightful owner."

"Impossible," said Cardinham at once. "It is out of my hands. And that is contraband. You're hardly the rightful owner."

Sparky shrugged and walked off, but as he passed Pentlan he plucked the contraband list from his hand.

"Oh, and Cardinham?" He grinned and winked. "I hope your hiding place is a good one ..."

* * *

It was silent in the woods; an unnatural, deathly silence which permeated through the trees. Not a twitch nor a breath escaped the place that characteristically pulsed with the very heartbeat of life. There was no birdsong, and the air itself seemed frozen as though time itself had stopped.

The silence was cracked by a low whistle, then shattered immediately afterwards by the explosion of a rifle as the rabbits pelted from the undergrowth.

Before Jo had lowered the gun, there was a sound of twigs

cracking behind her, and, she spun, the rifle still pointing in front of her.

Hetty let out a piercing scream and Jo lowered the gun at once.

"I'm fast at reloading – but not that fast," Jo reassured her. She caught the look on the elderly woman's face. "What is it?" she demanded.

Hetty drew in a deep breath, her hand resting on her heaving chest.

"Mr Cardinham, Miss," she puffed, sucking in another deep breath as she produced a handkerchief from her apron pocket and proceeded to mop her brow. "On his way to the tavern."

Without a moment's hesitation, Jo picked up her skirts and hurried away.

* * *

Jo stood in front of the oval mirror in her bedroom. She ran a brush through her long, dark hair.

"I'm really not sure it's a good idea that you stay here," said a dark voice. Jo was wise enough not to answer. "As Excise Officer in Chief, I request the production of your license, please."

Jo addressed the dark shape on the landing.

"You know perfectly well that my license is quite official."

The light from the oil lamp on her dressing table fell on him as he emerged from the hall and stepped into her bedroom.

"Nevertheless, my position dictates that I must check these things from time to time." He lifted his hand to smooth Jo's hair. "It has also come to light to the authorities that you have been accepting smuggled goods into your inn … selling under the counter, shall we say, thus failing in paying the correct excise duty."

Jo stared at him.

"You're wrong there," she said, pulling away from him. She began dividing her hair up in order to tie it into its usual plait. "As it happens I have no contraband on my premises at all. Feel free to take a look."

"Oh, I always feel free to take a look," he smirked, inserting his finger down the top of her loose smock and pulling her to him.

She hit him hard with a swing of her right hand that sent him flying to the ground. Clutching his cheek, he glowered up at her from the floorboards.

"You would do much better to play by my rules," he snarled.

"I couldn't think of anything worse," replied Jo, turning back to the mirror and dividing her locks again.

Cardinham leapt to his feet and pulled her hair back so that she was forced to look at him, one hand clutching roughly at her arm.

"If I hear you have been out in Wistmans Wood with our hostage, or if you have taken her anywhere outside of the confines of that cellar, I shall personally remove you from this place, even if that means I have to kill you first!"

Jo gripped his wrist and twisted her arm out of his grasp.

"You cannot keep a human being locked in a cellar."

"She is no human being to me. She is a parasite, and a mere pawn. If she is discovered, and MacBride finds out, I shall kill all three of you."

"And hang for your trouble," added Jo, cuttingly.

"Don't be so sure. The authorities want MacBride as much as I do."

"They hardly encourage personal vendettas."

"They do if it serves their purpose. I can see being on your own has not cured you of your ignorance."

"Get out please."

"Gladly, after I've seen her."

"You can see her through the window."

Cardinham drew up close.

"I will be leaving my carriage on the forecourt," he muttered. "Now that MacBride is aware of what an untrustworthy, scurvy little scrap you are, I think he will keep his distance, especially if he happens to see my coach and thinks that I am living back under this roof, that you were fighting my side all along." He leered at her, smugly. "In the meantime, you can assist me by using the carriage at night to patrol the so-called haunted highways. We both know the stories are mere subterfuge; now I want them proved." Jo gave him an icy glare, but Cardinham simply laughed. "Come, come! We live in days of supernatural belief, but that is not to say that all that passes is true. You will come to no harm. The devils are merely the local villains, and I am sure they would not harm a lady. Rob and rape one, maybe, but then that's no more than a little whore like you deserves."

Jo ignored the insult.

"The locals hardly need their eyes opened to what goes on. The whole of Newlyn takes part in it."

"Now I don't believe that for a moment. There are still some noble, upstanding members of this community who are waiting to see the outlaws brought to justice."

"Am I to assume that by noble and upstanding, you mean like yourself?" interrupted Jo.

"Indeed – although even if what you say is true, then your removing their smoke screen will, if nothing else, lead to the whole of Newlyn loathing you, possibly abandoning your inn, and frankly, right now, little would give me more pleasure."

* * *

All was dark and silent in the street until Isaac stumbled on a stray hen and sent it clucking in terror.

"Shush," scolded MacBride. "You wanna feel the darbies on you?"

"First time I've been to Penzance, in the dark like," Isaac whispered.

"Any more of that and it could well be your last."

The procession of seven smugglers fell silent again as they crept around the corner of the alley.

"They'll be expecting us, Marty," warned Doug.

MacBride drew his hand to hold the line while he checked it was safe to continue. One solitary figure, illuminated by the glow of his pipe, stood several feet away, leaning against a shop door. He glimpsed MacBride and turned pointedly to face the wall.

"Shoulda left it a week, methinks," added Doug.

"They'll be selling tomorrow," whispered MacBride. "I'm not letting the entire last trip go to waste. I've already lost my boat. They're not having the loot as well."

He gave a nod, but as the gang proceeded up to the customs house, the doors of the house burst open and a terrible figure with wild, unruly hair spiralling from her head like the serpents of Medusa, emerged. Her face was in shadow as she picked up her skirts and made straight towards them, wailing like a harrowed banshee.

"Lord preserve our souls!" cried Doug, recoiling in horror. "It be Black Joan herself!"

But as the figure drew near, and the wailing turned out to be cackling, the men's fear dissolved into stifled laughter.

"Sparky!" exclaimed MacBride. "What the hell are you doing here?"

Sparky moved towards them, reeking of liquor.

"Been *dreshing* up, haven't I?" slurred Sparky, lifting up his various layers of voluminous calico and lace skirts.

"You said you'd be down *The Anchor*!"

"Been there all afternoon. Ran aground on the specie front."

"Where's the guard?"

"Turned up his *toesh*." MacBride gave him a quizzical look. "Hopped a twig," Sparky elaborated. "Dead as a herring! Beyond the grave!"

"*You killed him?* Lord, Sparky, they'll hang me for this!"

"*Washn't* you?" frowned Sparky.

"I don't think they're likely to come to any other conclusion after we steal *my* loot back!"

Sparky thought hard for a moment or two, his brow creased with concentration. He was finding coherent thought difficult. Eventually he shook his head. Rifling through his petticoats he produced a small leather flask.

"Can't think right without a drink," he muttered. He took a swig and lowered the flask, a painful look on his face. MacBride regarded him in a somewhat grudging humour. "You …" Sparky began. He paused a little longer, before drawing the flask thoughtfully to his lips again and taking another gulp. There was murmuring in the ranks. "Quiet in the cavalcade! I'm having a moment of cognit – *shay* – *cognay*." Unable to get the words out, he gave up. "He mightn't have done it yet," he started, heading back to the customs house.

MacBride was at his heels, exasperated by the pirate's apparent lack of urgency.

"Who mightn't have done what?"

Sparky slowed his leisurely sway in order to take another swig from the flask. MacBride indicated to the others to follow. They found the guard of the customs house pressed up against the wall in the foyer, Cyprian Bezique poised to slit his throat with his cutlass.

"*Shprian*, better not do that, I is thinking on *reflectshon*," said Sparky. The guard nodded furiously. Sparky picked a pistol up from the floor. "May I have this?" There was more furious nodding from the guard as the pirate began to examine it.

MacBride shook his head.

"Leave him to it," he told his men. "Check the carts are out back. Let's load up."

* * *

The carts were loaded and almost ready to leave when gunshot sounded and the front-facing windowpane shattered. MacBride sprinted back to the foyer, expecting to see a troop of revenue men arriving.

Sparky was standing there alone, staring in puzzlement from the pistol to the window, and back again.

"I don't know how I did that," he said, innocently. He paused and looked back at the gun, turning it over in his hands. "An odd *contrapshun*," he decided, profoundly.

"Anyone would think you'd never used a gun!" cried MacBride. "Well, that'll have brought them running! Come on, let's get out of here."

"I thought it was all getting too easy," said Sparky as the smuggler grasped his arm and guided him out into the wind.

"And it's no fun for you, is it, when there's no danger of getting caught?' said MacBride. "Still, I know where we can hide the booty until the coast is clear. Come on … let's get out of here."

Less than ten minutes later, MacBride hammered on the window of a prosperous Penzance house.

After some time, a man in a nightcap opened it. It was the Lord Justice.

"Life and death, Your Honour," winked MacBride.

CHAPTER ELEVEN

VERGIL Sommerby, local squire and Justice of the Peace, entered *The Anchor* the following lunchtime, looking grave. He waved away Lurret's offer of a light and friendly tipple and proceeded straight to the back of the tavern where MacBride and Sparky sat amidst their crews.

Mr Sommerby dragged out a chair and sat down opposite them, nodding at each of them in turn.

"What can we do for you, sir?" MacBride asked, politely.

"I would like to know what you were up to last night," said Sommerby, coming straight to the point.

Sparky raised his blackjack, undisturbed. MacBride held Vergil's gaze intently.

"Can I ask what this is in reference to?" he said after a beat.

Sommerby scowled.

"A ship – a merchant lugger – was wrecked on the rocks somewhere off Cribba Head last night," he informed them.

MacBride looked momentarily taken aback.

"And you're looking for the bounty?" he asked.

"It was taken. Pretty quick, too. Ship was stripped of cargo, sails and rigging – any moveable object – before the majority of the locals even arrived." He surveyed the smuggler sternly. "You are aware, MacBride, of the law that has now been passed, demanding that the specific wrecking of ships with lights will result in the death penalty?"

"You believe the ship was wrecked purposely?"

"Sadly, I am left in no doubt at all. The lights were noticed. I am told the locals who arrived on the scene first were beaten away by masked men with such barbarity that three were left dead, and nobody dared save even one cask for fear of losing their lives in the attempt."

Sparky raised an eyebrow in interest.

"I have never in my life wrecked a ship, nor killed a man," assured MacBride, looking directly at Sommerby.

"I am aware of that, Martin," said Sommerby. He looked pointedly at Sparky. "But I am not quite so well-acquainted with the quirks of your colleague here." Sparky pursed his lips but did not attempt to join the conversation. "Does your friend not speak English?"

"Not when in the company of liquor," replied MacBride, apologetically.

Looking frustrated, Sommerby opened his mouth to interrogate further when he felt a tap on his shoulder and turned to find Officer Roberts standing beside him with a scroll of parchment.

The squire took it impatiently, lifting his pince-nez from the chain around his neck. He read the letter before fixing MacBride with a mystified stare over the top of the parchment.

"This is from Officer Shanley," he said. "It seems Penzance Customs House was robbed last night. Apparently he is quite convinced that you were behind it."

"Oh? Why is that, sir?"

"I will tell you. His words are as follows." He cleared his throat and began to read. "'I believe this to be the work of MacBride as he is an upright man, and has taken nothing which did not belong to him.'" He scoffed at the last part. "Belong to him! I ask you."

Sparky stared at MacBride accusingly.

"We only took what belonged to us!" he cried. "Why didn't we take it all?"

"That wouldn't be ethical," MacBride protested.

"Ethical! I'm not going to get rich while you're being *ethical*."

"If you wanted more perhaps you should have refrained from getting drunk and organised it yourself. We couldn't have fitted any more into the carts as it was."

"Whose carts, gentlemen?" Sommerby interrupted.

"A local farmer's," replied Sparky, irritably waving the squire's words away. He turned to MacBride again. "Why did we not take more carts?"

"I didn't want more and he doesn't have more."

"How ridiculous!"

"I checked the lanes to the farm this morning," Sommerby cut in again, "There were no cart tracks."

"I expect they would have got someone to drive a herd of sheep over them," said Sparky, dismissively.

MacBride glared at him.

"You're giving away my secrets here!"

"You're giving away my goods! My money! *My women!*"

"If you wanted it all, you should have taken it all."

"I would have if I'd known you weren't going to. At least then they wouldn't have been able to track it back to us!"

MacBride sighed.

"What can I say? I'm an honest man. That's why Mr Sommerby here knew he'd get a straight answer from me and we can't be accused of a worse crime."

Both turned to Sommerby, who was frowning hard. He appeared not to be listening to them.

"But if it wasn't you at Cribba Head …" he mused. "Then who was it?"

* * *

Cardinham sat at the desk in the Excise Office, staring up at Pentlan with a look of resentment on his face.

"They take it all?"

"Everything that was aboard their ship, Sir."

Cardinham glowered at the desk.

"Shanley said it was MacBride," continued Pentlan. "There were no tracks but the horses at Sanmoor were most weary this morning."

"Of course it was him," breathed Cardinham, scratching at the desk with the point of his dagger. "Damn Shanley!"

"But, as I said, 'twas Shanley who reported it. Why would he do that if he was a friend of MacBride as you say he is?"

"Not a friend, an acquaintance. Obviously he had heard of the wrecking. *Damn.*" He sat heavily back in the chair and sighed. "No matter. They may have got themselves out of the frame for Cribba Head, but this gives me grounds for reinforcements."

"Sir?"

Cardinham smiled.

"Bring me the quill, Pentlan."

It was some time before the Excise Officer in Chief replaced his quill. Pentlan, who had been sitting opposite him in an uncomfortable silence, obediently took the letter that Cardinham slid across the desk to him and began to read.

My Lord,

It saddens me to tell you that, despite my greatest efforts, the smuggling situation in south-western Cornwall is spiralling out of control. I fear too many forces strive against the King's Law and against myself, not least from the inside. Complete cargoes are being landed at the harbours of Penzance, Newlyn, Porthleven and Coverack, which must be with the connivance of the local superior and inferior officers. The inhabitants of these ports are described as being proud in what they term "The Smuggling Service", and The Penzance Collector and I are in agreement that it is almost impossible to convict an offender by Cornish Jury.

It shocks me to report that this last night bore both the shameless robbery of the Penzance Customs House, and a brutal wrecking at Porthcurno resulting in the total loss of crew and the death of three locals at the hands of barbaric sea plunderers.

However, these, My Lord, are the facts. So long as my men struggle to carry out their duties, their lives are in danger.

It is with good mind, by the powers granted by the late Act of Indemnity, that I urge you to excite your officers and get help from the soldiers.

With the assistance of a party of dragoons, I am confident I can overcome these Owlers and the lowest of low, the footpads who steal from those out walking, and have them brought to justice.

I wait in trust of their arrival.

Your sincere servant,

Cardinham

Excise Officer in Chief

"We shall have the heathen," said Cardinham, taking back the parchment. He folded it and pressed in the wax seal. "In the meantime, I want you to go back to St. Levan and meet with Abner, my associate there. At the sunken road in the woods there are sixty-eight tuns of wine. Load them up and proceed with the revenue towards Truro, stopping at Carnkie on the way, where Morgan will have thirty five tons of coffee."

"Sir?" Pentlan looked bewildered.

"From there, you will travel to Sunset Creek, where the remaining sixteen casks of indigo and forty-two and a half pieces of brandy should by now have arrived. Take it to Devon. Sell it. I want you back in five days' time with the money."

There was silence. Pentlan stared, aghast.

"What's the matter with you?" snapped Cardinham, "Pirate cut out your tongue?" Pentlan hastily got to his feet. "Oh, and Pentlan?" called Cardinham as the officer hurried to the door, "Don't dare return with less than five hundred guineas."

* * *

Meanwhile, many miles out on a turbulent sea, the Christian vessel that MacBride had set free was spotted by another ship; *The Aida Alada.*

"*Cesario! Perseguir!*" came a voice on the wind.

Cesario looked up from the spyglass to see his captain on the forecastle. She stood with her back against him, her hair tossed by the gale, highlighted, untamed and beautiful against the stormy sky.

* * *

It was quiet and dark, but the courtyard behind the Lord Justice's house in Penzance was a hive of activity. Seven carts were loaded. The first drew silently out of the courtyard onto the street. MacBride, at the reins, wore a heavy overcoat and a brooding look. At his side sat Sparky, cutting chunks out of an apple and eating them off the blade of his knife.

'What's wrong with you?' he asked. MacBride did not answer. 'Ah, I see. Your lady getting you down?'

'None of your business,' MacBride replied.

"Get over it, man. You're a loner, like me."

Still there was silence, except for the muted trundle of cart wheels.

"It is wrong to trust a woman," Sparky continued. "They are complicated creatures who lead only to the mouth of Hell. I don't get involved." He paused to see whether this would gain any form of reaction from the troubled MacBride. "I'm right, aren't I? She floated every boat in your harbour? Even the sunken sender?" He was rewarded with a reluctant laugh. Sparky chuckled too. "She's a hot-spring, though," he added. "Never looked like she needed you."

"She always did very well on her own," nodded the smuggler. "Her pride saw to that." He looked thoughtful. "I used to go out hunting game with her," he continued. "She'd give a whistle a second before she pulled the trigger. Said it helped perfect her aim. It was too easy otherwise." He leaned back, visibly relaxing at the memory. "Before she inherited Pensilva, she lived in a … a kind of chicken shack, it was. Covered in weeds, and the roof wouldn't hold the rain. I went there one night trying to escape Shanley. Hid my wagon full of wool in the wood. But she didn't know it was me and hit me over the head with a shovel."

Sparky threw back his head and laughed.

"What divine assistance when you needed it! Proves my point really."

"She was never a bad girl."

"Ha! You defend her even now! I'll wager she didn't beg your forgiveness and tenderly bathe your wounds?"

"No, she told me that that was what you got for prowling around a lady's house in the dead of night." He shrugged. "She let me stay, though. I hid under the bed when Cole came knocking and she soon sent him on his way."

"Knocked him on the head with a shovel too, did she?"

MacBride smiled.

"She did."

"Mouth of Hell," Sparky reminded him.

MacBride shook his head sadly.

"I don't understand why she betrayed me on the coast path," he said.

Sparky gave him a scornful look.

"If you wear your heart like a weapon it's going to take some wounding."

"My heart?" echoed MacBride. He shook his head. "I don't love her."

"Your wife is dead. You weren't going to return home to find she'd come back with angel dust in her hair."

MacBride was taken aback at the mention of his wife. He had not spoken of his loss for many months; his friends knew better than to mention it. Yet, oddly, he found himself surprised that the words had not escaped Sparky's lips before, for the man held no guard over his tongue. Now his lack of subtlety brought MacBride's mind to an abrupt start. He recalled the feelings Jo had aroused in him when they were together in the cellar on the day he went to get the brandy. He had thought he would never feel that way again.

"Well, I hate her now," he said.

Sparky looked unconvinced.

"On the subject of women … she'll be here any day."

He was looking up at the moon peeking out from behind the branches of trees that reached across the lane.

"She?"

"Craven."

"Craven? Who is Craven?"

"Craven LaFayette. My wife."

"Your *wife*! What happened to not getting involved!"

"I'm not involved."

"Mouth of Hell, you said!"

"Well, where do you think I learned that? The woman's a witch!"

"Then why marry her?"

"She's a very pretty witch," shrugged Sparky. Then he grinned. "Spicy."

The pirate suddenly leaned over and took the reins from the smuggler, pulling the horses to a stop.

"What is it?" asked MacBride.

Sparky nodded towards a rambling, long house on their path, its windows spilling welcoming candlelight onto the road, a soft hum of merriment escaping from inside. A sign protruding from the wall near the door creaked in the breeze. It read: *The Merry Maidens.*

"I am in much need of refreshment," announced Sparky, and with two leaps he sprang from the cart and bounded in through the door, leaving MacBride no choice but to signal to the convoy to stop and follow him in.

They crowded into the already busy inn.

"Well, if it isn't old Marty back from the dead!" cried a voice from the dark depths of the tavern. A tall, dark-haired man emerged from the shadows, grinning. Clearly, he had not been back from sea for long; his scruffy hair was filled with salt and his jerkin was rugged and torn. "The ale here is strong, right enough, and my mind flighty, for I've faith I see the shadow of a ghost before me!" He shook MacBride warmly by the hand. "I heard you were dead, my friend."

"Give me a chance," muttered Sparky.

MacBride stepped back and introduced the pirate to his long-lost friend.

"And this is John Clements," he said to Sparky. "He is a very long way from home."

"Aye," nodded Clements. "I am to marry Miss Quiller this coming August. Business has been busy and the endless stream of nuisance gaugers now at Talland have made travel necessary." He took Sparky's hand in a firm handshake. "One look at this man tells me I am right in thinking I am looking at none other than the infamous Captain Vaquero of *The Barentszee*?"

Sparky glowed in response to this statement and caught Clements' hand in a tight grip.

"Your instincts do not betray you, amigo."

Clements turned back to MacBride.

"And I recognise your loyal crew," said Clements. "Although you are missing one or two … James and Jack?"

"In the courtyard," said MacBride. "Keeping an eye on things."

"You have trade?" asked Clements, his eyes sparkling.

"Seven carts of it," replied MacBride.

"Lord above! Nought's a-changed! And only two men guarding?"

"Twelve men guarding."

"Lord above!" said Clements again, this time with a laugh. Then he stopped as something over MacBride's shoulder caught his eye. When he spoke again it was very slowly. "In the courtyard? Out the back?"

"What is it?" asked MacBride, warily, not wanting to look behind him.

Clements remained focussed on the entrance to the tavern.

"I hate to be the hole in one's coat, but it appears the God-forsaken gaugers have followed me down."

MacBride turned instinctively to catch the look of smug surprise as it settled on the faces of three excise men who'd recognised him and realised they had found two notorious smugglers together. He grimaced and turned back to Clements.

"You have goods with you, John?" MacBride asked softly.

Clements shook his head regretfully.

"Not I. Not here. My men work back at Polperro. The idea was to lead the revenue down here to enable my crew to land in peace. It would appear that our plan is to cost you dearly, my friend."

Sparky, irritated at the prospect of losing more goods, ordered another rum. MacBride tried to hide his annoyance.

"You weren't to know," he said to Clements. "And if they've come in through the front then there's a chance they mayn't have seen the carts in the courtyard." He spoke in a low voice to the men gathered around him. "Look shifty and keep them busy."

The three excise men, who had been making their way through the unhelpful drinkers, reached the smugglers at last, wearing looks of satisfaction on their faces.

"Well, well, well!" said the first, resting his arm on the bar and leaning into it a little. The rowdy inn fell silent. "Mr Clements *and* Mr MacBride! How unexpected! Now what can you two possibly be up to?"

MacBride did not answer, but leaned back to reveal Sparky propping up the bar behind him. He jerked his head anxiously in his direction.

"Shush," he whispered almost inaudibly. "I think he's after me."

The gaugers stared in astonishment.

"Who's that?" whispered the second excise man to the first.

The first shook his head in answer.

"Some kind of … pirate … or privateer?"

The word 'privateer', though spoken exceedingly softly, seemed to reach Sparky's ears, and he raised his head slowly, stretched his neck, and turned to the men beside him, squinting a little.

"Yes?" he sighed, in a suffering tone of voice.

"Will you be so good as to tell us your name?" asked excise man number one.

"I have many names," said Sparky, "but am best known as Captain Jose Vaquero." He took a gulp of his rum and began to sway. "I am looking for a certain Mister MacBride. I seem to have lost him." MacBride shook his head in despair at his comrade then turned to the officers and raised a finger to his lips to keep them from telling on him. Sparky would not be deterred. "Any *ashishtance*, gentlemen, will be greatly, and I mean *greatly* rewarded."

He smiled crookedly and, still tightly gripping the rum, lowered the upper part of his body over the bar and closed his eyes.

The three excise men stared at each other, baffled. MacBride put his arm around one of the men and patted his shoulder. Clements offered them a seat at the table. Both smugglers were excellent charmers and in no time at all the excise men, secure in the knowledge that their prey was in their sights and could cause no further trouble, allowed themselves to be captivated by their wit, charisma and camaraderie, almost regretting they would have to expose the certain dark deeds taking place in the tavern that night.

When they pulled themselves together and made ready to make arrests, Captain Vaquero chose to come round from his stupor and join them at the table, still apparently unaware that the smuggler he was supposed to be capturing was sat right beside him. He reintroduced himself and proceeded to tell the excise men about his great adventures on the seven high seas. As the men listened, mesmerised, James Cattermole peered through the thick, leaded window into the inn to see what was keeping MacBride. He spotted the revenue men at once, and gave the order that the carts were to leave, one by one, and make their way on to Newlyn following different routes so as not to attract attention.

When at last Sparky finished a full account of his adventures, the spellbound excise men rallied each other, and informed the smugglers that they would have to make a full search of the whereabouts.

"Oh," said MacBride.

"It's the law, you see," said the third excise man, apologetically.

"Well … if it's the law," murmured MacBride.

He turned to Clements, who nodded.

"If it's the *law* …" he agreed. He turned to the excise man. "But we've only come here for a quiet drink – just two long-lost friends catching up. You won't find nothing."

"Yes, but if it's the *law*," MacBride broke in. "And they feel they must …"

"It's our duty, you see," said the officer.

"It's their duty," nodded MacBride to Clements.

"Duty," echoed Clements, nodding placidly.

* * *

The search proved utterly fruitless, with all but one of the carts long gone and the last cart left behind filled only with simple provisions. The amazed excise men apologised for the inconvenience, and MacBride and Clements proved very understanding. They shook their heads shamefully in the direction of the inebriated privateer, carefully helping him to his feet and loading him onto the cart.

Clements and MacBride exchanged a few quiet words and parted ways. Sparky, seemingly fast recovering from his drunken stupor, was sat up in the front of the wagon. Abe, who had been left behind, climbed up next to the pirate and flicked the reins, and the cart rumbled away down the dusty track. MacBride mounted Morwellham and followed at a leisurely pace.

* * *

The roads outside Newlyn were quiet and dark, still draped in the delicate mist that had made sailing into the harbour so tricky. MacBride was content to let Morwellham fall into a laggard amble and some distance had opened up between him and the wagon when he spotted the carriage.

At first he could not see it clearly – the distant trundling of wheels he had vaguely assumed was coming from the smugglers' cart ahead. But presently, his ears picked up the sound of hooves thudding, unmuffled, coming not from in front of him, but away to his right. Whoever they belonged to, they were hidden somewhere on the track that led through the pine trees on the other side of the valley. He slowed Morwellham to a stop beside a large oak, and watched silently.

The shadow of a carriage came into sight here and there through the breaks in the trees, a swinging lantern glowing eerily from the front.

MacBride did not move. He crouched a moment or two longer in thought. The path through the trees was one used often by himself and his crew. It led to a large manor house where their goods were sometimes secreted. The tall, dark pines provided excellent concealment if the revenue were on their tail. Few people dared to walk that path, for the legends of ghosts were rife, and many of the rich who had taken the road unaware of the danger had lost their goods to the fine-fingered highwayman – MacBride's alter ego. It was an enterprise which not only succeeded in providing the smuggler with more wealth, but also served to ensure the rumours of the road being a dangerous route to travel were kept alive, leaving MacBride and his crew to conduct their business in peace.

MacBride strained his eyes, trying to catch a better glimpse of the carriage through the trees. He was able to determine it was large and rich in luxury, and he needed no further persuasion to draw the flintlock, vault back onto Morwellham, and gallop swiftly down the steep slope into the valley.

A wide stream gargled at the bottom. As the horse galloped through the clear, bubbling water towards the forest bank on the far side, it kicked up plumes of spray. It was only after MacBride negotiated the horse skilfully through the thick trees that ran parallel to the road and drew near to the carriage did he recognise the stage. He was in pursuit of none other than John Cardinham. He felt adrenalin and hatred rise together like a tidal wave from his belly to this throat. He hollered to Morwellham to go faster to catch the carriage which was trying to pull away from him and, as he drew level, he dropped the reins and cocked his flintlock, drawing a knife from his belt with his free hand.

"Halt there, bastard, or lose your life!"

The horses were immediately pulled to a halt with a cry, and the carriage was stayed, the coachman just out of view. MacBride's expert fingers rested on the trigger, poised to move like lightening to shoot the man he expected to see with his gun at the ready at the front of the stage. It was destined to be a test of who could shoot quickest, and the smuggler would be damned if it wasn't him.

But the figure that came into view was not the one he expected. Huddled in a dark cloak, he caught a glimpse of long, dark hair hanging from inside the hood At the same second he was about to shoot, he realised who it was.

"*Josephine!*" he cried, dropping the pistol to the ground. "Dammit, Jo, what the hell are you doing? I could have killed you!"

CHAPTER TWELVE

JOSEPHINE took down her hood and lifted her head to look at him with dark, steady eyes. Her composure appeared as calm as ever.

"They will kill you for this, Martin," she said.

"They'd have to catch me at it first."

"That's a mighty chance you take, and you don't look as if you are being too careful from where I'm sitting."

"What's to chance?" shrugged MacBride, his adrenalin only ebbing slightly. "But you! You ride in Cardinham's carriage? On these roads? It is you who take a mighty chance, Josephine. You must have a death wish."

"Not I," she said, pointedly.

"You side with him. You set me up!" MacBride drew his flintlock again. But Jo shook her head firmly.

"No," she said with such feeling that it was plain to see she was telling the truth.

MacBride stepped from Morwellham onto the stage and sat down beside her. Taking her hands in his, he looked hard at her.

"Please, Jo," he said, softly, "I don't understand. Tell me what's going on. Why are you doing this?"

He held her gaze, his eyes searching hers for an answer, then feeling her hesitate, her hands trembling in his.

Jo didn't know what to say. Everything within her wanted to tell him the truth, to tell him how much she hated Cardinham, how much she feared him and despised all that he had done to her. Martin would know what to do. He would have the answer, and everything would be all right.

But fear stirred in her heart when she remembered Cardinham's malevolent threats. This would be all he would need to carry them out. So she uttered not a word, but lifted her chin defiantly, and willed herself not to cry.

"Please, Jo," MacBride whispered. "I don't want to hate you."

It was true. Here, with Josephine Bryant, he suddenly found himself feeling at home for the first time since he had first sailed back into harbour. He sensed Jo knew it, too.

"And I don't want you to die."

"Then give me something to live for."

She gazed at him. Her eyes dropped to his lips, and she fought the urge to kiss him. A look of pain crossed her face, and she turned away, pulling her hands from his.

"You don't understand," she said, swallowing heavily.

"God, I know I don't. Tell me, Jo. Tell me what's happening. Tell me you're not working with him."

She lifted her face to look at him again, but her look was now one of regret. She felt weak.

"I hate him," she said, unable to keep her voice from quivering. "With every bone in my body, I hate him."

"What has he done to you?" demanded MacBride at once.

But Jo lifted her hand to cup his face.

"Oh, Martin," she whispered. "I hate him for what he's done to *you.*"

MacBride stared at her for a moment, then his face clouded.

"But you tricked me. I trusted you."

"I warned you not to trust anybody."

"I didn't know that included you."

"It had to."

"What hold can he have over you?"

Jo looked pleadingly at him, but did not answer.

"Just, *please*, Jo, just tell me where he is. I'll sort it. It'll be over."

"It won't be over. You'll die for it."

MacBride lost his patience.

"What the hell do you care! You had me captured!"

Jo shook her head at him.

"Cornwall will not hang you for smuggling – and you are no murderer."

"But Jo …"

But she put her fingers to his mouth.

"Shush."

Then she let her hand fall and flicked the reins. The carriage rumbled into motion again, with Morwellham following obediently in their wake.

MacBride was aware that he would get no more from Jo. He closed his eyes and leaned back against the stage, inhaling her sweet scent, and pushing away the pricks of guilt as he savoured each moment of peace that being in her presence brought him.

There was silence. The rhythmic trundling of the carriage over the dirt track pulsed through the smuggler like waves of calm, and he allowed himself to look up at her from the corner of his eye, at the outline of her sculpted, oval face highlighted against the swinging lantern, her long lashes, the tiniest glint of moisture on her honeyed lips.

She fixed her gaze on the road ahead, his feelings unheeded, the sparkle of moonlight in her eyes. But their glazed stare told him that she was a thousand miles away, and MacBride felt his heart flush as he realised, for the first time in his life, that this was one situation he had no idea how to handle. He felt confused, and the only thing he was sure of was that he never wanted the stage to reach Newlyn.

He opened his mouth to speak. To tell her he wanted her. To tell of the healing she brought him. The side of his face tingled where she had touched it and his fingers twitched where he had clasped her hand. He opened his mouth to tell her that she lightened his soul, and made him want to live again, but he couldn't bring himself to say the words. He let out a sigh and forced himself to think of the real world.

The moon burned brightly above him.

"Can we use your cellars?" he asked. "My men are unloading at the cave but it will be a full moon in a couple of days and the tide will be high." Keeping her eyes forward, Jo smiled and nodded. It was only afterwards that it occurred to her what problems it might cause if Cardinham returned before the contraband was moved on. She frowned and drew in a deep breath.

"All right?" MacBride asked.

"Yes," she said. "Just try not to leave it too long." MacBride looked uncertain, but nodded. "How much did you bring this time?" asked Jo, lightly.

"Too much," admitted MacBride. "Loads and loads. Everything imaginable. And two hundred unstamped ingots hidden under the pilchards. Surprised we didn't sink."

He caught her eye and grinned. She grinned back.

"They have a new cutter?" Jo said. "*The Spider*, I hear she's called. Did she not intercept you?"

"We landed up the coast," replied MacBride. "And Cardinham's messed up the whole business anyway. The revenue don't know whether to attack or obey Sparky, knowing who he's employed by."

Jo's face broke into a wide smile. She sparkled. MacBride watched her, unable to resist grinning back.

"You're like sunlight," he said, "after a very long time in the dark."

And she smiled again.

* * *

The rest of the journey passed in a light-hearted manner – MacBride his old nonchalant, witty self and Jo joining in. By the time the carriage trundled up the steep road to Pensilva, any tension had all but evaporated, and it was almost like old times. But as they drew to a halt on the forecourt and MacBride jumped to the ground, he turned back to her soberly, and the tension returned.

"So, Jo, what do I do? I see Cardinham's carriage – do I give chase? And if I see you there, do I trust you?"

Jo looked torn and troubled, but she shook her head.

"No," she whispered, and ached at the hurt which was plain to read upon his face. "And don't give chase. If it is Cardinham, and you hesitate thinking it might be me, he will kill you." MacBride opened his mouth to speak, but again she stayed him. "Understand this. The day will come where we shall have John Cardinham, and justice will be done," she said, dropping her voice as she caught sight of Cattermole emerging from the gloom behind them. "And despite what I may do, I will always be allied to you. Always."

There was a pause. The curtains in one of the upper rooms twitched, and Hetty's face appeared at the window.

"Come on, Jo," said MacBride, shaking his head. "You got me in a right mess here …"

Jo bit her lip in frustration, but when she spoke her voice was as cool as usual.

"Then you'd best treat me as your adversary, Martin," she said, curtly.

Then, quickly planting a chaste kiss on his cheek, she released the horses, took the lantern from the carriage, and disappeared through the tavern door without looking back.

MacBride thumped the wall in frustration, skinning his knuckles. He turned to see Cattermole standing beside him.

"Dammit!" he growled, before brushing past him and striding away.

Cattermole made to follow, calling Duncan, who was scratching at the tavern door and whining. The dog did not follow.

"Duncan!" hissed Cattermole. "Come!"

* * *

MacBride was in the graveyard, kneeling at the stone commemorating his wife and child. The inscription on the tombstone read:

Here lies Lamorran, wife of Martin MacBride,
who departed this life Jan 2nd 1789 aged 24 years.
Now at peace.
And in loving memory of Lucy MacBride,
taken by the sea on the same day, aged 3 years.
On tranquil land or stormy sea, but always together.

MacBride prayed he might be reunited with them.

"There are ways of raising the dead, brother," came Sparky's jovial voice from behind him. MacBride jumped, and stirred from his troubles. "Although I hear they do not always look as you remember them," Sparky added. "Especially when their flesh has been eaten by brine."

"Thanks for that," acknowledged MacBride, straightening up and pulling his belt tight.

"I mean, I've never done it, personally," Sparky continued, unperturbed. "I suppose if you can call upon their ghost and not stir their corpse ..."

"There's a saying in Scotland," interrupted MacBride, his eyes still resting on the gravestone. "That no man can be a fisherman without a wife."

"Lucky you're not a fishermen, then," said Sparky, absent-mindedly pulling a jewel from his overcoat pocket and holding it up to the sun. He turned it this way and that to see how many fissures ran through it.

"They wore long leather boots that were soaked in oil, and had to be kept dry for the voyage," explained MacBride. "When my father set sail, my mother and the other wives took off their shoes and stockings, tucked up their skirts, and carried the men on their backs to the boats offshore." Sparky turned from his gem and regarded MacBride with interest. "They waded through freezing water to pick mussels and shell them for bait," he continued. "And when the fish were landed they had to bind their fingers and thumbs with rags to stop them nicking themselves when gutting the fish. My mother took scars to the grave."

"And did your wife do the same for you?" asked the pirate.

"She would have done anything for me."

"Hmmm. Pity she's not still here, she could have taught Craven a lesson or two. Hallowed be the day when she becomes my little skentskivvy."

"Morrie was hardly my skivvy," grinned MacBride. He paused, glancing at the jewel between Sparky's fingers. "But everything had meaning when she was here. Mending the nets, splicing the ropes, out on wave and wind to win a living from the unforgiving sea …"

"Very poetic," observed Sparky. "Pity you weren't here when they died, you could have had that inscribed on their bonestone."

"If I had been here, they would not have died," said MacBride, churlishly.

"Peace, brother," began Sparky, but he was interrupted as Doug Coby hurried up.

"Well boy?" he called, angrily. "What were ye up to last night, may I ask?"

"Pardon?"

"Ye left us and went galloping down the valley." He drew close and whispered, "I saw you, you know. Ye and 'er, like Dick Turpin and Moll Cutpurse! Ye all but had your tricorn hat and mask and your long capes!"

MacBride looked amused at this exaggeration.

"What's he talking about?" broke in Sparky, fervently. "Who were you with? Not your fine Flossie from the inn!"

"Looting and foot padding!" bristled Doug.

"Ooh, I like the sound of this!" chimed in Sparky, rubbing his hands.

"I had Morwellham. I was hardly foot padding," grinned MacBride.

"Aye, but the meaning's still the same! They'll hang you for it!"

"You were road robbing, Bride?" Sparky asked, eagerly. "Good on you, *hermano*! What did you get?"

"I wasn't road robbing," said MacBride, patiently.

"I've told him time and time again," cried Doug, turning to the pirate. "He used to tie his wretches to a tree! Bad enough then, but to be seen without a mask!"

"Everyone knew it was me, anyway," shrugged MacBride.

"Maybe, but they could nae prove it, could they? And that's what matters!" Doug was really getting worked up. He directed his words at Sparky again. "I thought he'd stopped it! He promised he wouldn't do it no more once Lucy was here!"

"Well, Lucy's not here now, is she," said MacBride, sharply.

"Gah!" cried Doug, flinging his arm furiously. Sparky ducked to avoid being hit. "He wants to die and he doesn't give a damn about anyone around him."

He went to storm off.

"I was with Jo," MacBride said. "I thought she was Cardinham."

"Easy mistake to make," said Sparky with irony.

"And we stole from no one," he added.

"No one?" echoed Sparky, morosely. "No one at all?"

"No-one at all," replied MacBride, firmly, to the pirate. Doug growled and stalked off. Sparky caught up with him and placed a weather-beaten hand on his shoulder.

"Have a heart, old man. The boy is a tortured soul."

"Don't you talk to me of having heart!" cried Doug, and he tossed Sparky's hand aside and strode out of the gate.

* * *

"Now don't you go and get your knickers in a twist over that voyager, Mr MacBride," advised Hetty, wisely. Jo sat in the rocking chair in one of the comfortably furnished cellar rooms, gently rocking to and fro and darning, while Hetty fussed around her like a mother hen. "I agree he's a fair 'andsome man, and his courage is certainly undaunted, but the man is a drifter now, who only looks out for himself. He'll spend all his life out on the ocean, and you will be spending all yours sitting here, waiting for his return."

Jo continued rocking, gently.

"He's become reckless," continued Hetty. "And if he's reckless with his own life, he's reckless with the lives of everybody around him. Oh yes – it's true! Mark my words, my girl! He's dangerous to know. I quite believe he's well on the road to madness! He's star-crossed you know – brings ill luck."

Jo smiled.

"With all due respect, Hetty, I do not think you have the faintest idea what you are talking about."

"Oh, don't I now!" Hetty said indignantly, her hands flying to her hips.

"The man is hardly ill-fated. Apart from the obvious tragedy of losing his wife, he has come out of even the most treacherous of adventures in one piece. The revenue cannot catch him, even Algiers could not hold him. On the contrary, I quite believe I have never met a man more charmed."

"Charm*ing*, you mean," corrected Hetty. "Now, the pilferer he's taken to roam with, *he* lives a charmed life, or so I am told."

161

"No, Hetty, you are quite confused. It is he who is mad."

"And he'll not be the only one, right enough, if you can't get Mr MacBride outta your head, my girl!"

Jo carried on with her darning.

"I don't know where you've got it all from," she said, good-naturedly. "You really shouldn't believe idle gossip. I expect you've been down to Lil Ferry's again?"

"Not at all, ma'am," said Hetty stoutly, drawing herself up to her full height of four feet ten. "Don't think I can't see when a woman is in love. It's the oldest feeling on the earth! I saw you draw up with him on Mr Cardinham's carriage and when you came in through that door you had a wild and wanton look in your eyes, oh yes you did, though you may look at me like that! I could feel the heat from it burning inside you when you walked past! You were all maggoty-headed, yes, yes, and you only came down from it this morning. Now why is that, I'd like to know? He's broken your heart already, I'll wager!"

"You're very much on the wrong track," said Jo, placidly. "Cole came to see me this morning."

"Ah! Now there's a fine and dependable fellow! And what did he tell you about that rogue?"

"He told me that John is at Ruddlemoor and on his way back. We are to expect him by dusk."

Hetty was silent at last. She slowly lowered herself into the armchair.

"But ... all Mr MacBride's contraband!" she muttered, unable to hide the panic in her voice. "What will you do?"

"The only thing I can do," replied Jo, matter-of-factly. "I'm going to tell him it's here."

Hetty leapt to her feet, wringing her hands in her pinny.

"But ma'am! Mr MacBride?"

"Mr MacBride can look after himself. I have other priorities."

"But ma'am! They will have them, sure as eggs are eggs!"

Jo at last looked up from her sewing.

"I told you that you were on the wrong track," she said, quietly.

"I most certainly was!" cried Hetty. "But … but *Mr MacBride!*" Now Jo appeared to be in no need of curing from her lovesickness, Hetty switched tack. "He is a good man. My darling, he *trusts* you!"

"Then he is a fool," said Jo, carelessly. "I have warned him in no uncertain terms not to."

Hetty stared at the woman before her in disbelief as she continued earnestly with her darning. Then she lowered her eyes and sadly left the room.

As soon as the door had shut behind her, Jo's finger quivered and she pricked her finger. Then her composure cracked, and she sobbed silently into the blood-spotted linen.

* * *

Cardinham arrived in good time, sweeping into Pensilva with his dark cloak billowing out behind him. The first thing he saw was Jo, sitting at one of the tables in the empty tavern, her head in her hands. Her eyes were dry, but red from weeping. Rather than it stirring his compassion, however, it incensed him to see her heart so tortured over another. Especially when that other was Martin MacBride.

"Downstairs?" he demanded.

She lowered her head in shame and nodded. Hetty stood in the shadows, her palm pressed tightly over her mouth and tears welling in her eyes as she watched the evil man storm off into the cellar.

Within minutes he had reappeared and marched back out through the great tavern door to his carriage without a word. Jo leaped from the chair and ran after him, but his stage was already pulling away down the hill. Losing no time, Jo hitched up her skirts and ran down the cliff path that led to the beach. Looking back over her shoulder at the departing carriage, she promptly collided with James Cattermole.

"Jo?" he said, catching her by the shoulders. "You all right?"

"Where's Martin?" she gasped, the distress plain to see upon her face.

"I don't know," shrugged Cattermole. "Off on his own somewhere. Why?"

"John's coming for him!" cried Jo. "Him and all of you! He's gathering reinforcements as we speak! He's got the dragoons down here!"

"What! How …?"

"I told him about the loot in the cellars," she wept.

"You *told* him! *Why*?"

"There's no time to explain now, James," said Jo, unable to keep the shame from her voice. "We've got to find him. We'll spilt up. I'll go down to the beach and up through the town, you head out towards the church and the farm."

* * *

It was Cattermole who found MacBride first. He had been taking the evening air with Mops Malone in the church garden. MacBride saw Cattermole approaching and stopped in his tracks when he saw the look of concern on his face.

"It's Jo," he panted, urgently.

Fear became etched on MacBride's face.

"What? Is she all right? What's happened to her?"

Cattermole tried to catch his breath.

"I'm sorry, Bridie," he said, grimly. "She told Cardinham about the stores in her cellars. We're all to be arrested."

The smuggler's shoulders sank in disbelief.

"No," he croaked, shaking his head. "That's a lie. Who told you this?"

Cattermole looked regretful.

"She did."

"I don't believe you." MacBride spoke through clenched teeth. "She wouldn't. She wouldn't, James, not now. She wouldn't do this to me now." He paused, waiting for Cattermole, Mops, anybody, to suggest some kind of reprieve; some justifiable reason behind her actions.

Nobody spoke.

"*Damn* her!" he cried, "Damn the evil bitch!" He reached for Cattermole and shook him. "Where is she? *Where?* Tell me, God damn me or I swear I'll kill you!"

"There's no time!" Cattermole pushed him off. "The dragoons are coming! We have to leave!"

But MacBride would not be side-tracked.

"*WHERE?*" he shouted.

"He's right, my son," said Father Malone, catching his arm. "I told you – about the Milton gang? Your name was gazetted. Yours will be a sentence of death. You must leave here. Do not tarry further!"

"I will not go!" bellowed MacBride, shaking Cattermole again. "Not until I find her and kill her!"

Cattermole knew MacBride well enough to realise his attempts at persuasion would be fruitless.

"She took the beach road towards town," he sighed.

MacBride released him and was gone. Then he turned.

"Get the boys out of town, James!" he ordered through the darkness. "They will not trouble to follow you. It's me they want."

* * *

The streets of Newlyn were empty and cool, despite the heat of the evening, and the very air that followed in the smuggler's wake was icy. The few people out under the early moonlight who had the misfortune to encounter him were as taken aback by his uncharacteristic silence as they were by his narrowed eyes staring straight ahead, his clenched fists and pounding stride.

Josephine had been seen and had asked for him, they had confirmed, but nobody, not even Lurret at *The Anchor*, could tell him where she had gone.

"She came in about twenty minutes ago …"

"What direction did she leave in?" interrupted MacBride.

"I'm sorry, Marty, I didn't see."

The door slammed shut.

As a last resort, MacBride made for Pensilva Cellars itself. And there, on the sands of the cove below the tavern, where an abandoned bonfire smouldered in the mouth of a cave, he saw her.

She had her back to him, her hands clutching at her tangled hair in anguish as she waded through the dark shallows. So fierce was the fury within him that he did not even feel his heart stir at the sight of her earthy beauty, and he heard himself roar out her name as he sprinted up to her.

She whipped around to face him, valiantly.

"What was it, Jo?" he cried. "What made you do it? Was it the blood money? What did you get? Five hundred? For turning me in? That was what I was worth?"

"I didn't do it for money!" cried Jo, furiously snatching her arm from his grasp.

"For love then. For John Cardinham." The words sickened him. "You're still with him."

"I am *not*!" She twisted round and began to stride back across the shore towards the crooked little cliff path up to her inn.

"After everything you said!" MacBride shouted after her.

She turned back.

"I *meant* everything I said," she cried. "Including telling you not to trust anyone!"

"Well I'm sorry, but I never believed *you'd* let me down!"

"Well, by your leave, Mr MacBride, let me tell you that I am sick of being bullied by men!"

"Bullied! When have *I* ever bullied you?"

"Every thought of you bullies me," she cried, bitterly. "I fight you, every day! And all I've struggled to do is the *right thing*!"

"Oh, you *must* be working with Cardinham!"

Jo was so contorted with rage she could hardly answer him.

"Yes!" she said. "I *am* working for him! Happy? There, I've said it!"

"You've a heart of stone," said MacBride, resentfully. "You've severed every bond that ever was between us."

"Maybe I'm just not the woman you thought I was," said Jo, her voice hard.

She walked away, but MacBride caught her arm again.

"Don't you walk away from me!" he yelled, his voice rasping slightly.

"Don't *touch* me!" she cried, pulling her arm back once more.

MacBride flexed his fingers. They tingled where they had touched her skin. He shook his head and looked up from his hand.

"I just want to understand, Jo," he said, his voice mellowing.

Her eyes met his. She thought she saw the sea reflected in them, and her fury was washed away.

"What are you doing here?" she pleaded, softly. "Why aren't you running?" He held her gaze but did not answer. "You're not afraid?" she whispered. "You're not afraid of losing? Of being alone? Of dying?"

He placed his hand on the side of her shoulder, his eyes scouring her face for a flicker of something that might make some sense to him.

"How can you play brave when there is nothing that frightens you?" she said. She bit her lip and her eyes filled with tears. "But *I'm* afraid. I'm afraid when I close my eyes and all I see is you. I sit and watch you sail away and I'm afraid you'll never return – that every moment I have with you might be the last. I'm scared because I know you'll leave me here. I have suffered torture of the cruelest kind these past months. Inside I am bleeding. But you can't see it. You don't know." MacBride tilted his head as he tried to take this in. "You will never know how much this hurts," she continued. "I don't want to see you, I don't want to *touch* you!"

She pulled away from him angrily.

MacBride was staggered to hear the echo of his own words in hers; the words he had spoken alone in his empty home. *I don't want to see, I don't want to hear, I don't want to feel.* But he realised now he had missed a word when he had spoken them. *Alone.* Because, more than anything, he didn't want to feel alone. He was not the loner Sparky had deemed him, then.

And here, before him, was a woman speaking those same words, with the same fear in her eyes. And he felt alone no more.

Jo sensed what he was thinking.

"You are everywhere I go, everything I do, you are eternal in me," she whispered. "I want you so much I want your very breath in my lungs. For you to breathe through me. But I can never have you."

"Jo," he said huskily, taking her hand, "Jo, tell me. Tell me why you did it."

There was barely a whisper between their faces. She could feel his hot breath on her mouth. She squirmed and pulled away again.

"Don't touch me," she murmured, and her voice held a note of warning. "Please don't touch me, Martin."

But MacBride ignored her. He did not loosen his grasp, instead pulling her back to face him.

"I have to know," he pleaded. "This is breaking me. I … I don't know what to do."

He struggled to find the rage and hurt that had burned so

ferociously in him just minutes earlier, feeling vulnerable without it, a gladiator without his shield. He wanted to shake her, to demand she tell him what in hell she was playing at, why she'd betrayed him. To give him a reason to hate her, or a reason to forgive her.

"Let *go*!"

She was wheeling like a wild thing, trying to free her arm from his grasp. MacBride lifted his other hand to cup her face, to calm her, but his thumb brushed her lips lightly, sending those familiar sparks through him, and before he knew what was happening he had tossed her wrist aside allowing him to move his hand to the back of her head, where he gripped her hair in his fist to pull her to him and he was kissing her; a fierce kiss, as though his fury had returned and moved to his mouth. He felt her body rise as she kissed him back with the same passion, her hands at his neck, her body pressed into his.

In the second his resolve was broken, Jo's fight was lost. Her mouth was hungry, raw. Her skin prickled wherever his hands touched her, and as she slid her fingers into the hair at the back of his neck, he moved his to her waist and effortlessly lifted her. She curled her legs around him as, without taking his mouth from hers, he carried her over the beach to the cave, where he moved one hand to her head and gently lowered her onto the cool sand.

He was kneeling over her, his knees either side of her thighs, as she ripped the shirt from his body. The colour of his skin was warm and soft against the dying firelight of the bonfire, and she ran her hands up over his chest, twisting them around his neck again as she pulled his lips down to meet hers. Again her body rose to meet him as he lowered himself onto her.

That warm summer night in the cave under Pensilva they reached a place they had been yet to touch. For several sacred hours they, and all around them, were at peace, the fears and fury forgotten.

The night was quiet, with only the soft lapping of the sea creeping steadily away from them as the tide retreated.

The final flickers in the fire died, and still the lovers were passionately entwined. The flecked white moon glided gracefully across the sky. The distant glow of dawn was slowly approaching, just an hour or so away over the horizon when at last MacBride fell back onto the sand, exhausted. His arm lay beneath Jo's neck, and she turned onto her side and cuddled into his hot body. She sighed deeply, desperate to savour every blessed movement.

But they were both drained, and within moments they were asleep.

Chapter Thirteen

"COME on, Dougie, man!" begged Cattermole. "There's no time!"

"I'm not leavin' without me laddie!" insisted Doug, stubbornly.

He charged out of MacBride's cottage with Cattermole closely behind.

"He knows how the cards lie, Doug. He'll do what he wants."

Doug Coby was out in the middle of Hemlock Street looking furtively up and down through the darkness.

"Doug," said Cattermole, trying a different tack, "I'm not leaving you. You stay – I stay."

"Don't you dare, James," cried Doug, marching back to him. "This is not your battle."

"I'm not leaving you," repeated Cattermole, challenging Doug in a battle of obstinacy.

"And *I* said I'm not leavin' me laddie!"

"Then I'm not leaving either," said a voice.

Doug spun around to see Isaac stood in the doorway of his cottage. Martha was with him, her arm around his shoulder, her pleading eyes upon her husband.

"Oh yes you will, me laddie! You'll do exactly what I tell ye!"

But Isaac was as stubborn as his uncle, and shook his head defiantly.

Cattermole rested a hand on Doug's shoulder and spoke to him gently.

"We won't find him if he doesn't want to be found. And even if we do, nothing you or I can say will make him come if he doesn't want to."

"You're abandoning him!" cried Isaac, lunging at Cattermole. "After all he's done for you."

But Cattermole caught his punch swiftly in his fist.

"Bridie only needs saving from himself," he growled, releasing Isaac's wrist. He turned to Doug and added, "And if he wants to die there is nothing any of us can do to stop him. To remain here would only ensure capture, and we will be of no use to the man locked away or serving the neighbour. Now, I received an order from my captain and I intend to see that it is carried out. Come! We must all leave now, and have trust in our good captain that his dexterity for outfoxing will once again spare him the darbies." Doug, clearly torn, looked to Martha for guidance, but she was biding her time. "He is a grown man," continued Cattermole, encouraged that he was at last getting through. "And a wise one at that. It is Isaac who needs your protection now."

"Don't you leave because of me!" piped up Isaac. "I'm staying no matter."

Martha lifted her hand and silenced them.

"There is another," she said. "One who needn't leave."

Cattermole and Doug stared at each other in realisation.

"The pirate!" they called in unison.

* * *

Farmer Rogers' cries of rage went unheeded as Morwellham was quietly led out of his stable by two dragoons, forfeited for being used to carry spirits and other contraband.

The roads at Sanmoor Farm were black as ink, and once the farmer's cries had been left behind, the air was still and silent, the remaining horses grateful for the peace.

And still MacBride slept, peacefully for the first time since his return from Algiers. His friends were the waves that swept the shore soothingly outside the sanctuary where he and Jo lay, reaching his sleeping ears like a lullaby to balm the soul. The air was breathless, the night long, the rumblings of the coming storm far, far over the horizon.

* * *

"We shall have a fine job persuading that slubberdegullion of a pirate to help," grumbled Doug as he, Cattermole and Isaac marched down Hemlock Street towards *The Anchor*. "He cares for no one but himself!"

But to their surprise, Sparky proved unexpectedly willing – once they had managed to awaken him, that is. He had been easy to find, his snores erupting loudly from the outhouse behind the inn, and there he was, slumped over some bales of hay, his mouth open and his fingers, as usual, grasping the leather neck of his bottle. Bringing him round from his slumber proved more difficult, and for some time it seemed that he was happy to conduct a conversation with them in his sleep. But once Doug had given him a sharp slap across the face and yelled that MacBride was about to be captured and hanged, he sat up at once.

"What? *Now*?" he stuttered, irritably, as though it couldn't have come at a more inconvenient time. "Where is he?"

Cattermole shrugged and shook his head.

"He said he was killing Jo Bryant."

"Well we can't be having that!" said the pirate, unsteadily getting to his feet and heading out of the door.

The three fishermen stared after him in surprise.

"Hey!" cried Doug, hurrying in his wake. "You'll help him then?"

Sparky stopped and placed a hand on the old man's head.

"There is a large sum of money waiting for me when I reach London with *el proscrito*," he answered. "But only if it is *I* who conveys him."

"Why, ye devil!" stormed Doug, furiously, but Cattermole stayed him.

"It works in our favour for now," he said, as the pirate ambled into the half-light. "Let him be."

* * *

A rough kick to the sole of his foot brought MacBride rudely out of his dreams. He sat up, blinking in the light of the pirate's lantern. Shading his eyes, he looked up in the direction of the lamp and saw Sparky standing over him, grinning.

"Kill her, you said," grinned the pirate, but he kept his voice soft, so as not to wake her.

MacBride gazed at Jo, still lying peacefully beside him, doll-like. He allowed himself a few precious moments to take his fill of her, imprint the image forever in his memory. Then he reached for his shirt.

* * *

The Barentszee was anchored offshore. MacBride obediently stood with Sparky at the water's edge as the rowing boat approached.

"You act strangely when you are angry with a woman," chuckled Sparky, unable to let the matter drop. "What happened?"

"I just wanted to see straight," shrugged MacBride. "But being in her presence makes thinking difficult."

"Ha! You should have got an earring! Sleeping with a woman is no way to see straight, brother!"

The rower reached wading distance and the oars were pulled in. Sparky placed a hand on MacBride's shoulder.

"I leave you in the capable hands of my finest men. Your father – what isn't - tells me of the Isle of Lundy off the Devon coast where you will be safe?"

"Tell Jo I love her," said MacBride, wading through the shallows.

"I'll tell Jo *I* love her," said Sparky. "Ha! Ensnared well and good by the women's voodoo!"

MacBride gazed sadly back at the cave as they rowed closer and closer to the ship. But his heart was content, and he drew in a deep breath of new air. As he exhaled, however, something on the shore caught his eye. Sparky had staggered and fallen. At once, one of his crew appeared from nowhere, running across the shore to assist him. The pirate allowed himself to be helped to his feet, leaning heavily against his companion, who put a stolid arm tightly around his waist and supported him as they made their way to the cliff back.

"Captain's sick," the rower informed him. "Pickled liver's my guess," he added with a wise nod.

* * *

John Cardinham's fist slammed down on the table top with a crash.

"Where is he?" he shouted.

Sparky appeared quite recovered from his fall on the beach thanks to a short period of time at Pensilva and a measure of Jo's best spirits. He sat lazily by the fireplace with his feet on the footstool, looking unabashed.

"Where is the rest of my money?" asked the privateer.

"You won't get your bloody money if you don't tell me *where he is!*"

The locals, drinking in the main tavern, stared uncertainly at each other as the bellowing emanating from across the passage grew louder. Jo, wiping glasses behind the bar, glanced anxiously at the swing door.

"You won't get to know where he is if you don't pay me what you owe me," replied Sparky.

"You shameless conniving …" began Cardinham.

"Pay me," Sparky cut in, sitting up and looking directly at the excise officer. "Pay me, and I shall go with you to make good his capture and ensure his journey to London to receive the rest of my prize."

* * *

It was early. Dawn was breaking and the clear, pale skies were alive with the chorus of birds over *The Anchor*.

Sparky was woken by an urgent shaking. Blinking in the morning light, he could see Lurret crouched over him, an excited spark dancing in his eyes.

Sparky groaned and laid his head back down upon the straw.

"You been 'ere all night then?" asked the innkeeper.

"Whassit to you?" murmured Sparky.

"'Nuther ship's been wrecked, hasn't it!" said Lurret. Sparky sat bolt upright. "I'd a-thought they'd ha' hunted you and founded you by now."

"Where did it happen?" asked Sparky.

"Right here in Mounts Bay. Big 'un too!"

But he found he was talking to himself. Sparky had already slipped his pistol into his belt and was hauling himself away down the path.

* * *

The ship was in a bad way. Great parts of it were missing – lost to the endless ocean. The keel was smashed onto the rocks, where the waves shattered the timber to shingle. The air at Mounts Bay was heavy with the supposition of death.

"What dog of the devil can be doing it?" gaped Father Malone, who had silently appeared at Sparky's side.

Sparky turned to Mops, a wicked grin stretched across his face.

"He has got the wrong sow by the ear this time!" he announced, looking close to laughter.

Mops regarded him with bewilderment and disgust.

"Have a little more respect for the dead," he said.

But Sparky shook his head.

"Few would've died from this wreck."

"It's a mighty wreck, my man."

"Aye, but she had a mighty captain," grinned Sparky. "It's *The Aida Alada*, the ship of Craven LaFayette, and woe betide any man who sows the wind of that little bluster, for they shall reap the whirlwind. There'll be no coaxing her."

"How can you be sure she is alive?"

"She won't die wanting revenge," replied Sparky, simply, as though this provided adequate explanation.

"Well, it was certainly no accident," said Mops after a moment's pause. "The wind got up last night, and t'was rough, but not bad enough for this. And the villagers saw the lights – and false signals from the lighthouse. The ship's already been looted."

"Of course it has," said Sparky, turning back to the wreck. "But this time, there'll be hell to pay."

He caught sight of a ship on the horizon. Taking his spyglass from his belt he held it up to his eye and at once recognised the Christian galley that MacBride had let go.

"Ha! That's my girl!" he said.

Then he turned the spyglass onto the coastguard's house on the hill. Two figures were in the garden.

"Well, breakfast calls!" said Mops. "Coming?"

"Thank you, but no," replied Sparky. "I have some business to attend to."

* * *

As soon as the coastguard caught sight of Sparky coming over the cliff towards his cottage, he hailed him anxiously.

"Hie there! You don't perchance have any notion of how this 'ere wretched ship came to be wrecked?"

"Don't bother," said Cardinham, stepping up beside him. "There's little need."

"I should think," said Sparky, considering the question, "that it was purposely wrecked to enable a certain fine and upstanding gentleman to settle his debts." He regarded first Cardinham, and then the man he'd taken to be the coastguard. "With the help of this little mayfly, who, it is my guess, fluttered down to Mounts Bay especially to assist in the task." He grinned his wicked grin at Abner, one of Cardinham's men. "No doubt a professional in such areas. One can only hope for you that you have only splinters from the wreck on your hand, and not the blood from the dispatching of the usual coastguard."

Abner looked uncomfortably at Cardinham, who simply huffed impatiently.

"This is Vaquero," he said, irritably.

Abner held his hand out cautiously, and Sparky gripped it in a firm but short handshake, before pulling him close.

"And what, may I ask, is your share from the wreck?" he whispered. "Enough to warrant my dispatching of *you*?"

He was still grinning, displaying his array of black and gold teeth.

"That's no business of yours," said Cardinham, curtly. "I shall have your money before the week is out, Captain Vaquero. That is all that need worry you."

"Well, let's hope you live to see the week out," winked Sparky enigmatically, and he turned and sauntered away.

* * *

Lundy was named after the Norse word for "puffin", but Lundy Island was home to beasts as well as birds. For years it had been used as a hideout for pirates, outlaws, adventurers and other seafaring marauders, and was *l'entrepot* for contraband. Flanked on all sides by great granite cliffs, it offered only one sheltered landing spot, which was monitored meticulously at all times from the watch towers.

It was here that MacBride landed.

Before he and his scant crew had reached the top of the cliff, he was faced with a barrage of pistols and blades. A dark-skinned man pushed his way to the front and approached MacBride fiercely.

"What business have you on Lundy?" he demanded.

But before MacBride could open his mouth to reply, another man stepped forward.

"Why, 'tis Martin MacBride!" he said in surprise.

At once the weapons were lowered, and the familiar man, who went by the name of William, came and stood before him.

"What business *have* you here, MacBride?" he asked. "You bring us liquor?"

"Only a little," replied MacBride, regretfully. "My business here is that of prolonging my existence. The revenue are on my tail."

"And you have led them *here*?" cried the dark-skinned man, angrily.

"Even had I not been followed, they are well aware of the goings-on here."

"If what you say is true, then why have they not attacked?"

William, curious, paced around the group of men who had just landed.

"These are not your men," William interrupted. "These men are foreigners. Where are your crew?"

"We split. These men are on loan to me from a privateer."

"It gets better!" exclaimed the dark-skinned man, sardonically. "Now there is a privateer as well! What is a privateer doing loaning *you* men?"

"Perhaps he likes me?" suggested MacBride.

The man scowled in reply and continued to survey the smuggler with deep suspicion.

"What name does this privateer go by?" enquired William.

Cyprian Bezique stepped forward at once.

"He is the great Captain Vaquero," he announced.

"*Vaquero!*" cried the dark-skinned pirate, furiously. "Vaquero, the Moroccan? You are trusting him? You are foolish! He will come here and claim the bounty on the lot of us!"

"He does not know this is an outlaw's hideout. And you obviously hold little confidence in your own abilities."

"Vaquero – he knows *everything*! He is a demon of the underworld. His powers are not of this earth."

"You clearly have not met him," muttered MacBride. "Do not take heed of all that legend tells."

"Your coming here brings danger to us all."

"Let him be, Hakan," said William. "He is one of us."

"And will he still be one of us when we are all lying in our graves?" snapped Hakan.

There was a murmuring amongst the men. MacBride raised his hand and silence fell.

"I trust Vaquero," he said. "Not in his valour, but in his quenchless needs and weaknesses. Devon and Cornwall would be all but free lands if it were not for one black worm, whose heart has been devoured by canker and evil. If we work as one, with the help of Vaquero, we can overcome this man and continue our trades in relative peace."

"Hark! The preacher who has landed on our shores to the good of us all," cried Hakan.

"Who is this man you speak of?" asked William.

"He goes by the name of Cardinham," replied MacBride, and William nodded.

"Aye. He is known to me. Cardinham of Cloven Foot. He drove me here on his way to Cornwall, and since my coming I have heard many tales of his growing villainy from my brothers. His tide is high, it is time this *black worm* learns the price of his incessant meddling with the free-traders."

"Why bait the man here when we have been left in peace?" demanded Hakan.

"We are only at peace while we allow ourselves to be imprisoned here. My family wait for me along with my demise on the mainland."

"But we cannot trust this Vaquero," insisted Hakan.

"There is honour amongst thieves," said William. "But there is no honour with Cardinham." He patted MacBride heavily, and said again, "This man is one of us."

* * *

Jo opened the door a crack and peered out.

Sparky removed his hat and flourished it with a rather extravagant bow.

"May I come in, my lady?"

"You most certainly may not. John is not here, and I wish to have nothing to do with you."

Jo pushed the door, but Sparky inserted his foot in the door jam.

"I assure you my intentions are only good," he said, pushing his way in.

"The road to Hell is paved with good intentions," sighed Jo.

Sparky grinned, and looked her up and down.

"Is the road to Heaven paved with bad ones?"

Jo leaned into him, and for a moment it looked as though she were about to kiss him, but she lowered her nose to his mouth.

"What are you doing?" grinned Sparky.

"Gauging the extent of your intoxication," she replied.

"I assure you, it is no liquor that speaks from my lips."

"Hmmm." Jo began arranging the bar in preparation for opening. "There is no road from you to me, so put the idea out of your mind now."

Sparky settled himself on a stool.

"Your graceful lack of interest only heightens my desire for you."

"What a pity."

"Can we not come to some arrangement, my dear?"

"Yes, we can," she said, turning to him. "What can I give you in order for you to spare Martin's life? My body is *not* on offer," she added sharply.

Sparky looked disappointed and shrugged his disinterest.

"But this tavern is," she said.

Sparky stared at her.

"Where are your principles?" he mocked. "Was this tavern not passed down through generations of your family? Did it not belong to your grandfather?"

"It did," Jo acquiesced. "But my heart belongs to Martin. My grandfather is dead. Martin is not."

"That's all very quaint," muttered Sparky, reaching for the blackjack that Jo had placed on the bar for him.

Jo caught his wrist before his hand reached the tankard and gripped it hard to show she was serious.

"My inn for his life," she urged.

Sparky looked thoughtful.

"Let me drink on it," he said, reaching for his ale. "*Think* on it," he corrected.

But before the tankard reached his mouth, the door flung open and Cardinham strode in, closely followed by Abner.

"I'm not open yet," said Jo, sourly.

"I care not," replied Cardinham. He caught sight of Sparky and snarled. "What are you doing here?"

Sparky was just about to open his mouth to say he was

considering an accord when Jo replied with an air of irony that he was having a drink.

"So you're open for him but not for me?" Cardinham growled, and began prowling around the tavern as if she might have other men hidden behind the curtains or in the alcoves.

"Looking for something?" she asked, innocently.

"Gah!" spat Cardinham. "I know you know where he is and I'll do whatever I have to in order for you to tell me."

Jo looked at Sparky in the hope he might offer some chivalrous form of defence, but she was wasting her time. He appeared not to have heard the words Cardinham had spoken.

"Well," she said coolly, when she realised that Sparky was not about to ride to her rescue, "If you're talking of MacBride, I can assure you I haven't the faintest idea where he's got to."

She fixed her stare on Sparky and glared at him pointedly. The pirate raised an eyebrow in reply.

Cardinham looked set to march over to where Jo was standing and grab her by the neck when the door burst open again, a woman entered and the cracking of gunshots rang out. Cardinham and Jo immediately dived down onto the flagstone floor behind the bar as it was peppered with lead shot and tankards leaped from the shelves over their heads. A decanter burst, showering them with splinters of glass. Then the musketoons were turned in Abner's direction and he leaped between the tables as wooden legs were blasted and tables toppled behind him.

The woman would surely have shot him had she not run out of pellets. She screamed an ear-piercing scream, and lobbed her pistol through the air in the direction of the coastguard. It struck him soundly on the forehead and he crumpled to the ground. But the witch-creature was over him at once and, with astounding strength, for she was slightly built, she caught hold of his shirt and hoisted the whole upper part of his body from the floor.

"*You!*" she shrieked, and Abner flinched at the sound. "Where were *you w*hen my ship was wrecked?"

Sparky looked amused as he quietly raised his ale back to his lips. He had not moved from his stool. Abner slumped weakly, a stream of blood running down his face.

"My ship was wrecked by purpose!" she thundered, swiftly drawing a long and rather deadly knife from her belt. *"By purpose!"* She pressed the blade to Abner's throat. "Who is for blame?"

"H-him," stuttered Abner, feebly raising his arm to point at Cardinham.

Sparky could not stop a large grin spreading across his face as the banshee set her wild and raging eyes on Cardinham, burning into him as though she kept the fires of Hell itself in her eyes.

"To pay him," slurred Abner, swinging his finger in the direction of Sparky.

Then he lost consciousness and slid to the ground.

Sparky's grin disappeared in a flash as Craven's savage eyes flashed to him, noticing him properly for the first time.

"*YOU!*" she cried. He leapt from his stool and danced his way behind the bar as she flew after him. *"You* had my ship *wrecked?"* Sparky darted behind Jo, using her as a shield as Craven drew back her fists. "*You miserable, carking, deplorable, adulterous, bestial, rank-infested man!* You dare wreck my ship? *My* ship?"

"That's an awful lot of words for you, my beloved," said Sparky, poking his head out from behind Jo. "You learned them especially for this moment, didn't you?"

He hastily popped his head back as he narrowly avoided a kick.

"And this?" shrieked Craven LaFayette, fixing her stare squarely on Jo. "This lowlife, blackguarding harlot, this filthy, whoring, wanton mopsy is who you trade your wife for? ME!"

"Not for want of trying," muttered Sparky, as Craven raised her fist.

But Jo was not somebody to be taken down easily, and she caught Craven's fist before it landed.

"I object to 'mopsy'," she said, swinging the fist aside.

Craven launched herself madly into Jo, but Jo held her ground, leaving Sparky to dive between them and wrench them apart.

"Your *wife*?" mouthed Cardinham in amazement, as he got to his feet and dusted himself down.

"Lucky for you she has no skill with a pistol," Sparky said, jovially, and received a crippling blow to the cheek for his trouble. "It's her fists you need to watch out for," he floundered.

"*That's* for wrecking my ship!" she cried, and delivered a further crashing blow to the other side. "And *that's* for marrying another woman, you bigamist filth!"

"That is not true!" smarted Sparky, rolling on the floor and clutching his face. "I am not getting married!"

"You're damn well not," cried Craven.

"I never was! It was a bare-faced lie!"

"I hear it from lips of Zedekiah – your own man!"

"Zedekiah is a bare-faced liar. Always has been."

Unfortunately, Sparky – on his back behind the bar – could not see Zedekiah standing in the doorway of the tavern, having accompanied Craven to Newlyn. Roaring with rage, Craven grabbed the pistol from Cardinham's belt and fired it at him. Then she pulled another pistol from somewhere under her skirt and fired that one too. The wall and door smoked with gunshot as Zedekiah dived out of harm's way.

Sparky popped his head up.

"Told you she was no good with a gun," he couldn't resist saying. He just managed to duck in time as Craven whipped around and fired at him, a cask of brandy exploding above him. At that very moment, another pirate appeared in the doorway with the cry of "*Soldado Soldado!*" and the faint sound of galloping hooves could be heard.

Jo plucked the pistol from Craven's fingers.

"If you don't mind," she said, irritably, "I would be grateful if you would stop blasting my inn."

Craven dropped her hand, looking as though she was going to yield. Then, like lightening, she flicked it up again pulled yet another pistol from her belt and fired it in the direction of John Cardinham. It hit him in the top of the shoulder, sending him wheeling and howling with pain.

"That's for wrecking my ship!" she cried. She handed the pistol back to Jo and, stepping over Sparky, she stood over Cardinham. "Take it as taste of what is to come. You have made bitter enemy of me."

And with that she shook her hair back and strutted out of the tavern and in amongst the galloping dragoons.

Sparky struggled to his feet and glanced after his wife. Zedekiah, who had stepped aside to let her past, reappeared in the doorway and glared at Sparky, his nostrils flaring.

Sparky turned uncomfortably to Jo, who looked furious. Then he slowly looked around the inn, surveying the damage. When his eyes had gone full circle and came back to rest on Jo again he said,

"I don't want your tavern *now*."

She floored him.

CHAPTER FOURTEEN

IT was hot, and the sun was strong. The sea was sparkling a deep shade of azure. In Polperro, under the expert eye of Cattermole, ship builders worked hard on a new vessel to replace *The Mevagissey*.

MacBride sat at the window of Marisco Castle, staring out over Lametry Bay when William entered the room with a tray of fruits.

"Any sign?"

MacBride shook his head.

"But they will come," he said.

"Word has it that you are a mighty captain. Speak of your mind," pressed William, sitting down.

"I have allies in Cherbourg who will offer us protection at a fair price until it is safe to return home."

"But to sail to Cherbourg is to pass through the hornet's nest itself!" exclaimed William. "Unless you mean to journey cross country and take another boat from the south coast?"

"*The Barentszee* can outrun any revenue cutter. And there is something I need to pick up at Newlyn."

"The Bryant girl? You would sail right back into Mounts Bay itself – for her? That is a mighty risk. They will be waiting for you. They will take your life!"

"Would you be happy leaving your loved ones behind then?"

William stared at him for a moment.

"You would take me to collect them?" he asked.

"Where are they?"

"Little place called Crackington Haven. Pencannow."

"We take all we can. We stop for your family, and we stop for Jo. Are you with me?"

William hesitated, but as he heard MacBride's words, the longing to see his family again took over and before he had time to think, he felt himself nodding.

"I've hidden too long," he acknowledged.

"Cardinham won't command me," MacBride said. "He has taken my life from me once already. I haven't found freedom again only to pander to his vindictiveness. Summon all the willing men."

William was on his feet and at the door in an instant.

"There is one thing, Bill," warned MacBride. "I don't leave until Cardinham is dead."

"But Bridie! I'm only wanted for smuggling! They'll send me to the gallows!"

"You will be no accomplice. Only I will be wanted for murder."

"But you will never be able to return home."

"So be it. I can live easier in France than I can with the thought of him still drawing breath. Besides, I am already due the death penalty. It will make no difference." He looked back over the sea. "Do you know of any fishermen at Pencannow?"

"I know all the fishermen at Pencannow."

"Have one of the men take a message. Whoever is aland the day after next is to be ready with four carts of fish. We'll pay them well. The contraband must be hidden; there will be interceptions before Newlyn. To all the revenue who do not know us, we will be but honest fishermen."

* * *

"What in God's name are you doing!" yelled Josephine, as Cardinham slammed the cellar door shut. "You can't keep her in the cell. At least let her go back into her room!"

"I warned you, Jo, I warned you to keep her downstairs."

"You evil *bastard*," she screamed, lunging at him,

He sent her flying back into the door. Then he caught her by the wrists, suddenly losing his temper.

"*You're lucky she's alive!*" he shouted at her. "She stays here 'til we get back."

"What do you mean, 'get back'?" she cried, as he dragged her forcefully along the passage. "I'm not leaving her!"

"Oh yes you are!" said Cardinham. "Or she dies." He pulled out a knife. "Choice is yours."

Jo wrenched herself free and glared bitterly at him, her eyes full of hate.

"*She stays there 'til we get back,*" Cardinham repeated, forming his words carefully.

"Get back from where? Where are we going?"

Out of the corner of her eye she glimpsed the silhouette of another man in the doorway and she flicked her head around to see who it was.

"To Lundy," replied Cardinham, grinning slowly at Sparky. "To claim MacBride."

* * *

The carthorses sauntered lazily along the hot, dusty track to the crossroad. They were nearly home.

Cattermole had taken refuge up in Polperro, while Doug, Martha and Isaac had holidayed in Sennen, and Eli Abe had been based in Camborne. Jack North had lodged in Canonstown.

Now they were united again, desperate to know the fate of their captain. They met in the middle of the crossroad, as arranged, and proceeded along the track to Newlyn, keeping a wary look-out for suspicious sounds or movement. It had been a long journey, and little was said as the men were tired.

They were just passing through the little town of Mousehole, when Abe leaned across and pulled up the reins. The horses halted.

"What is it?" asked Cattermole.

Abe pointed down to Mousehole harbour.

"That ship …"

Cattermole and the others squinted down in the direction that Abe was pointing. A large revenue cutter was anchored in the harbour and there was a great flurry of activity around it.

"It's making to leave port," said Cattermole.

"It's Cardinham," said Doug. "A ship that big, with that many people. Mark me words, it's that filthy rogue Cardinham, I can smell him a mile away! What's he up to now?"

"Let's take a closer look," said Cattermole, flicking the reins.

They turned right and the horses trotted gingerly down the steep hill towards the sea.

"I don't know if I like this," muttered Martha, putting a protective arm around Isaac. "I thought the idea of taking the back roads was to avoid these people, not to get as near to them as possible."

"We will be well hidden by trees at the bottom," Doug reassured her. "We won't draw any attention to ourselves."

It wasn't long before the road levelled out and they reached the cliff. They were surrounded by a cool copse of trees and tall foliage which, in the sunlight, sent dancing dapples over the dry dirt.

Cattermole leaped from his seat and walked to the edge of the copse, shading his eyes as he looked over to the harbour. They were close to it now, and the shouts from the men on the gangplank could be easily heard. Abe, North and Doug joined him.

"It's Cardinham," confirmed Cattermole, taking a spyglass from his pocket.

"I knew it!" cried Doug. "Didn't I tell ye? What's the villain up to?"

"They're loading the guns," replied Cattermole grimly.

"Then Marty's still out there!" cried Doug, snatching the spyglass. "They can't have caught him! Cardinham wouldn't be loading the guns for any other."

"He obviously thinks he knows where Marty is," agreed Cattermole.

He stiffened abruptly, as if he'd seen something, and quickly took the spyglass back from Doug.

"And that's why!" he said, emphatically. "Vaquero!"

"Vaquero?" raged Doug. "*He's* there?"

"You seen him?" said North.

Cattermole grunted.

"Aye, I see him."

"What!" exclaimed Doug.

Cattermole nodded.

"Damned whoreson was on his side all along."

Martha's voice came calling from the cart.

"What's all the fuss?"

Doug hurried back to her. One by one the others followed, looking despondent.

"Whatever's the matter?" she said.

"They're loading the guns," said Doug. "The pirate's with them."

"Judas!" gasped Martha. "What are we to do? Quick! Let's stop them from sailing."

"We could never do that," replied Cattermole at once. "There's an army of revenue soldiers with them."

"How many?"

"Two hundred?"

"No!"

"He does not mean to let MacBride slip through his fingers this time and no mistake."

"Two hundred men just to catch one sorry sailor," wailed Martha. "There must be something we can do?"

Cattermole hesitated.

"We cannot stop them from sailing, but maybe we *can* stop them on their return."

"But we don't know where they'll be landing," put in North.

"Back here, at Mousehole," said Cattermole. "I'm sure of it. They left from here to avoid trouble with the locals at Newlyn. They'll be landing here for the same reason."

"You cannae be sure of that," said Doug. "He may sail up east, land near London and take him straight to trial."

"Not allowed," replied Cattermole. "He has to go through the authorities down here first. Nevertheless, I will make enquiries with the harbour master."

"As if he'll tell you anything," scoffed Doug.

Cattermole smiled and winked.

* * *

"Ah, shut up yer whinging," moaned Doug, as the customs officer rolled to and fro on the ground.

He was trussed up like a kipper, his hands tightly bound behind his back, his feet fastened together at the ankles. He was gagged, and wearing only his underclothes.

Doug's eyes flicked over to Cattermole, who was walking back towards the others, looking unrecognisable in the revenue man's regimentals. But it was certainly Cattermole's wide grin that beamed at them, and without a word they joined him and walked quickly away, leaving their prisoner rolling and cursing beneath his gag.

"I was right," said Cattermole thankfully, pulling off his hot coat. "They're due back in a day's time. We've got to get over to Newlyn as quickly as we can to organise a waiting committee."

"Surely we'll never have enough people to fight the revenue?" cried Isaac.

But Cattermole's faith was undaunted.

"Bridie's well-known and well-liked. I think you'll be surprised."

It was all the hope they had. They stared out at the revenue cutter, now speeding out into the blue, unaware that they, too, were being watched.

From a tiny, round window in a little Mousehole cottage, somebody was watching them and wondering what they were up to.

Craven chewed the leather end of her spyglass thoughtfully.

* * *

Sparky sauntered up to Cardinham, who was bursting with importance as he ordered about the crew of *The Spider*.

"I don't believe it myself," said the privateer, watching Jo pace the starboard deck. "But they say it's bad luck to have a woman on board."

"I think I take far greater chances having *you* on board," quipped Cardinham, ungraciously.

"I'll get out of your way then, *Capitán*," replied Sparky, bowing low before making his way, over to the cabin, staggering slightly.

Jo watched him go. She stalked the cutter for a moment or two so as not to arouse suspicion, and then followed him in.

Sparky was already snoozing, reclining lazily on a sumptuously upholstered chair, his feet resting, as usual, on the footstool.

Jo slammed the door with such ferocity that Sparky almost fell from his chair in surprise.

"You've yet to give me a precise answer regarding my offer," she hissed, furiously.

"Offer?" echoed Sparky hopefully.

"The tavern."

"Lady, the sum of money I am to receive for bringing in MacBride is of far greater value than your inn, rambling as it is," replied Sparky.

"But Martin is to leave you all he has as well."

"He already has. The necessary documentation has been completed."

Jo was so angry that she threw herself at the chair and hurled Sparky to the floor. Running her hands through her hair, she cried out in despair. She thought to beg the pirate for the mercy of her lover one last time, to offer her body if that was what it would take, but she was taken aback to see that Sparky was still on the floor, curled in a ball and clutching at his belly in agony.

"What's wrong?" she demanded, falling to her knees beside him.

"Nothing's wrong, Flossie," he croaked with difficulty, his face twisted with pain. "Just go over to the cabinet there and pour me a drink."

"I'll do no such thing!" she replied with dignity, drawing her kerchief from her blouse and mopping his dark brow. Then suddenly the penny dropped. "You're dying?" she murmured, her eyes wide.

"One bout of stomach ache does not equate to one dying," said Sparky at once. "I'll be fine in just a few minutes."

Jo lowered her eyes to where his ring-decked hand was grasping at his side. She noticed, for the first time, the yellowing of his skin, disguised under the depth of his tan. His eyes, too, bore a pale yellow hue. She turned his hand over and took in the reddened palm.

"It's your liver …" she murmured.

"What, you a nurse now?"

She ignored him, her eyes flicking about his body without focussing as her mind worked hard to figure out what to do. She was hardly able to believe that Sparky, the great unbeaten Captain Vaquero, one of the most feared pirates in the world, had such a mortal weakness. And anybody, even she, could draw a knife and kill him at this very moment, and there would be nothing he could do. He was defenceless.

Almost as if he could read her thoughts, Sparky reached up and grabbed the collar of her blouse, drawing her towards him.

"Nobody must know," he hissed.

But his black frown and piercing stare that terrorised so many of his enemies did not this time shake Jo from her thoughts.

"I can buy you time," she said, a cautious smile suddenly playing about her lips. "I have much experience. There are herbs that can help you, I know of them. *I* can help you."

"So now you're a witch." He looked resigned. "Can you cure me?"

"Nobody could cure you."

"Then what's the use?" said Sparky, sulkily.

"I can ease the pain," said Jo, eagerly. "There is a plant. I can give you that, and my inn. For Martin's life."

"MacBride wants to die."

"No he doesn't."

With some difficulty, Sparky moved his neck allowing him to look into Jo's eyes. Somehow, he managed to grin his wicked grin.

"He will do," he said, weakly. "When he sees you aboard Cardinham's ship."

Jo sat back on her heels, momentarily mortified. Pulling herself together, she helped Sparky to sit up and lean against the seat of the chair. Again, he growled with pain, and she took his chin in her fingers and forced him to look at her.

"Without my help, you will suffer greatly during your passing," she said. *"Do we have an accord?"*

Sparky flagged and closed his eyes.

"Aye, lady," he muttered. "We have an accord. Now leave me."

* * *

MacBride and William were leaving Pencannow Point. *The Barentszee* was laden with both men and riches, the latter hidden under a thick blanket of pilchards and crayfish. The schooner also carried dinghies for the men who wished to return to Cornwall, and was heavily armed with cannons and guns.

William had been elated to see his family again. His wife, son and two daughters, all of whom had received an hour's warning of their arrival, had packed all that they needed and were now aboard with the crew. The journey round to the south coast took longer than originally anticipated, as the wind had turned and was now against them. They reached Cape Cornwall, with Land's End in sight, when William approached MacBride at the helm.

"I have a bad feeling," he confided in the captain. He looked warily up at the sails. "There is a malevolent frown on the wind. It's turned. I fear we sail for ruin."

But MacBride was utterly focussed, and did not even glance in his direction.

"We could sail south, straight for France," suggested William. "You could come back for Miss Bryant later when the rest of us are safe."

"I'm not leaving without her," insisted MacBride. "There is something amiss with her and it troubles me. Time could be in essence, and I won't leave without her to return and find I am too late."

But William was right, for as they rounded the peninsula there was a shout from the crow's nest, and moments later Cyprian sprinted up to MacBride with a spyglass.

"Ship on the horizon, Captain! West-south-west!"

MacBride grabbed the spyglass and pointed it in the direction of the ship. He swore under his breath.

"Captain?" said William, urgently.

"It's *The Spider*. The revenue. That's Cardinham."

"Turn her around, Captain!" begged William. "My children are on board!"

"No."

"We are heavy," Cyprian added. "We may not outrun her."

"She is coming straight for us!" cried William, stricken. "And the wind blows against us. Turn, Marty, turn us now!"

"No," bit MacBride, rigidly, "I want him. We fight."

"Do not hazard us for this forlorn hope!"

"This was always the deal," insisted MacBride. "It is no less than I spoke of. You may have all you need now, but my destiny is still out there." He paused, lowering his voice. "I swear I will let no harm come to your family." Then he raised his voice again and bellowed an order down the deck. "MAKE READY THE ARMS BROADSIDE! RELEASE THE TOPSAIL! WE ATTACK!"

And from that moment every sound seemed distorted and swallowed. Time moved in slow motion as the revenue cutter slowly came into view of the naked eye. When William's back was turned, shouting orders to the crew while his family cowered below deck, MacBride, once he was satisfied that all aboard were too busy to catch sight of him, fell to his knees and clasped his hands together in prayer.

* * *

Meanwhile, aboard *The Spider*, Sparky had fallen asleep slumped against the chair in the cabin, with Duncan cuddled in against his belly.

The little dog opened one eye, then the other, his ears pricked at the top of his head. The smallest of whines escaped his throat, but it was enough to bring Sparky to his senses. He made to jump up, but a sudden pain reminded him to move more slowly.

At that moment, Jo Bryant came rushing in.

"He's here!" she cried. "The ship's sailing straight for us!"

"Ship?" spluttered Sparky, struggling to his feet. "*My* ship?"

He let out a groan.

"Are you all right?" Jo asked, mistaking his groan for one of pain and hurrying to steady him.

He pushed her away, irritably.

"My ship!" he said. "He's going to make a bloody mess of my ship!"

"Sod your bloody ship," cried Jo, and she shook him hard. "We've got to *do* something!"

There was a pause. Then a voice came from behind them.

"Do what, exactly? What are you two plotting?"

They turned to see Morgan, one of Cardinham's allies, stood in the cabin doorway. Sparky drew his gun, and, rather leisurely given the situation, shot the man dead.

"He'll do," said the pirate, impassively.

He advanced towards the corpse and then, clutching at his belly again, he ordered Jo to undress the man. While she was doing this, Sparky staggered over to the cabinet and poured himself a draught, which revived him, and together he and Jo dragged the body to a cupboard and dumped it inside.

* * *

"What was that gunshot?" cried Cardinham, spinning around at once, his hand instinctively gripping the bandage that covered his own gunshot wound on his shoulder. The man beside him started too.

Cardinham toyed with the idea of going to explore himself, but his main concern was the ship speeding towards them, so he ushered his accomplice away to investigate.

The man never returned.

Cardinham, so utterly consumed with MacBride's imminent

capture, did not realise that a small mutiny was brewing aboard his own ship. Despite his own pain, the pirate proved fatal to all that stood in his way, and Jo, hardy as she was, could not help but be shocked as she witnessed his brutality and irrefutable mastery in the deft slaughter of his victims.

"Stop them loading the cannons!" he called to her, as he broke a man's neck with a quick flick of his hands.

By this time the ships were in firing distance, the very ocean pulsed under the explosions of cannon fire and Jo struggled to keep her balance. Both ships took a severe battering. *The Barentszee* suffered a shattering in the hull as it rose on the crest of a wave.

At once, there was a sense of alarm amongst MacBride's crew, with William howling,

"We sail right into Hell!"

But even as he spoke, there came a lull in the firing from *The Spider*.

"Make ready! They're reloading!" cried MacBride, but Cyprian caught his arm and shook his head, squinting in the distance.

"There be disarray on deck," he muttered.

MacBride held the spyglass to his eye. He scoured the deck of the revenue cutter, searching for some clue as to why they had stopped firing. Almost at once his eye fell upon Josephine, standing on the deck.

"Have you been below?" demanded Cardinham, approaching her. "Why have we stopped firing?"

"How should I know?" replied Jo, "I assumed you had given the order."

"I gave no order!"

"Oh, don't get cross, darling," said Jo, stroking his face.

"Where is the pirate?" he demanded, pushing her away.

"How should I know? What do you need him for?" She raised herself to her toes to whisper in his ear. "You're quite masterful enough all on your own."

MacBride lowered the spyglass slowly.

"What is it, Captain?" said William, with dread.

MacBride closed his eyes in pain and handed the spyglass back to Cyprian.

"We won't make it to Cherbourg," he murmured. "Make for the harbour instead." And he left the helm calling, "Captain her, Cyprian," over his shoulder.

Chapter Fifteen

MacBRIDE lowered himself into the great chair at the captain's table. Rocking it back on two feet, he raised his foot against the leather desktop, his fingers to his lips, and there he stayed for a brooding minute or two before suddenly launching his foot back to kick the desk angrily. Letting the chair fall back down, he jerked open the desk drawer which was rammed full of spirits and tobacco. Had he not been quite so impassioned about seeing Jo playing him for a fool with Cardinham, he would doubtlessly have been well inebriated by the time Gibbon burst in.

"Captain! Come and look at this!" he cried.

MacBride reluctantly made his way out onto the deck, where William handed him the spyglass and pointed towards the shore. The smuggler took it warily. He saw it at once, and it almost made his heart leap through his mouth as, for a mad but magic moment, it seemed as if Lamorran might still be on land, alive and waiting for him. For there it was: the red blouse hanging on the line outside a cottage. As he moved the spyglass, he spotted a red blanket … and another. The town of Mousehole was decked with them, billowing in the wind like scarlet flags. And then his eye was drawn to the chimneys; tall, short, straight, crooked – all spewing out a thick grey smoke.

MacBride was astounded.

"What does it mean, Captain?" demanded Cyprian, who was not aware of English customs.

"It's a sign. A warning, as I said," cried William. "The revenue are waiting for us on land!"

But MacBride frowned and peered through the spyglass again. He scoured the deserted harbour, and at last found what he was looking for. A figure strode along the waterfront, a figure carrying what looked to be a stick with a red rag billowing from it. The man approached another figure, who took the flag and proceeded with it, before long reaching another and passing the flag on again. And this figure MacBride recognised; a great hulk of a man, who ambled with a certain gait along the harbour, the silhouette of a pipe in his mouth. It was Sam Johnston.

"It *is* a sign," replied MacBride. "There is support ashore. We have a landing committee."

* * *

"Stick together, lads!" cried Cole Shanley, but this time the men before him were smugglers and townsfolk. "The dragoons are on their way! Hold fast!"

"Come on, Bridie," shouted Sam, pumping the air with his fist. "Get that there ship anchored before the bastards ride in!"

Meanwhile, one of the town's ladies, Mary Rathmore, was tugging at Sylvia Melthropp, who was busy dabbing her red lips in her little hand-held mirror.

"Come on," she cried in exasperation. "They're coming!"

She, Sylvia, Lil and the others were all dressed in various hues of red. Lil was brandishing a heavy duty rolling pin and holding up her skirts as she hurried along, crying,

"Let me at them! Let me at the fiends!"

* * *

On board *The Spider*, the captain bawled orders furiously, reeling in desperation and confusion when nobody seemed about to carry them out. The reason came to light when he felt the cold prickle of steel at his throat.

"Guide this ship to port," ordered Sparky in a low voice.

* * *

The Barentszee reached the harbour first, and the moment the anchor was dropped the crowds appeared. They swarmed from the alleys, the houses and the carriages; the brotherhood of smuggling.

For a second or two, MacBride stood, overwhelmed, as they engulfed him, battling off the officers who dared to approach them. Pistols were fired and clouds of smoke filled the air. Everywhere he looked he glimpsed faces of those he knew. He saw John Clements take a swipe at the head of a revenue man with the barrel of his gun. Lurret and Talfryn fought back to back with broken bottles. Tom Crycot, Jack North and James Cattermole came roaring over the brow of the hill like ancient warlords, brandishing swords and firing their flintlocks, closely followed by Abe, Isaac, Bert and the others, and around fifty horses. He could see Mops Malone in their midst, his fingers clutching at the crucifix around his neck and damning the soul of anybody who harmed a member of the cloth, while brandishing a cudgel at a soldier who came too near. Even the law-respecting Henry Bolt and his five sons were with them.

"You're early, sonny!" cried Sam, thumping the smuggler on the back. MacBride found that the crowd had already encompassed him and were hurrying him away from the shore. "Come on, get outta here before they come!"

"There's gold on board!" he protested, but on turning back to the boat he saw that the women had already boarded and were busy unloading the goods onto the jetty, where a chain of people handed it from one to another up the beach until it reached a series of carts on the roadside.

* * *

The Spider was drawing ever closer.

Cardinham stormed to the helm where he launched a violent attack on the hapless captain, venting his anger in a series of kicks and punches. It wasn't until the poor man was lying crippled on the deck with blood spilling from his head that Cardinham noticed the identity of the man who had been standing behind him. At first glance, he thought it had been Morgan, as the man was dressed in his attire, but almost at once, even before Sparky had removed the hat to reveal his black and white headscarf, did he realise it was the pirate.

"*YOU! Scourge!*" roared Cardinham, and his voice reverberated with depth of fury. "You damned hell hound!"

As the words were leaving his lips, he reached inside his coat, drew out his pistol and fired it.

But at the crucial second, Jo came pounding up behind him and, slipping on the greasy deck, she took Cardinham's feet out from under him as Sparky, in a stroke of either brilliance or great luck, dropped the grip slightly on his sword, leaving the bullet to strike the blade instead of embedding itself into the pirate's upper leg. Cardinham's fingers grasped at another of his pistols, but his aim was everywhere. Jo heaved at his arm and punched the wound in his shoulder. He let out a yell of pain, flinching for just a brief second, but on opening his eyes he saw the pirate standing over him, *The Executioner* now drawn from its scabbard, its tip resting against his throat.

"You filthy swine!" spat Cardinham. "They'll have you for this!"

Sparky raised the blade and made ready to swipe and behead the Excise Officer in Chief, but Jo threw up her arm and let out a cry.

"Oh, come on, Floss!" cried Sparky. "Anybody could have killed him! He is no good to us alive – I don't need any more trouble."

* * *

Back at Mousehole harbour, a dragoon leaned down from his horse and clutched at Officer Pentlan as he passed amidst the pandemonium.

"Who's in charge here? For God's sake, man! Where is the harbour master?"

Pentlan waved his hand in the direction of a little hut just off the jetty, leaving the dragoon to gallop off through the crowds. He reached the hut, reared up, and crashed through the door on his horse.

The scene that greeted him filled him with astonishment. The harbour master sat lazily on the chair, his feet crossed on the desktop, and his cap pulled down over his face as if he were dozing.

"What in Hell?!" shouted the dragoon over the noise and chaos emanating from outside.

The harbour master raised his head slightly and inspected the solider from under the rim of his cap.

"Can I help you, sir?"

"Where is the Collector of Customs?" demanded the dragoon, giving the harbour master up for a drunkard.

The harbour master raised a finger and rested it on his chest in reply.

"Me," he said.

"*You're* the Collector of Customs as well?" cried the dragoon, vexed. "Well, where's the Inspector of the Water Guard then?"

Again, the harbour master raised his finger and pointed to himself. The dragoon stared incredulously.

"The Landing Waiter?!"

Once more, the harbour master pointed to himself, and the officer caught the sparkle of white teeth as he grinned under his hat.

"And I suppose you are the Officer of Excise as well!" the dragoon cried, pulling out his pistol. "Who are you, heathen?"

A shot rang out, and he fell from his horse, blood saturating the wool of his coat.

Craven removed her feet leisurely from the table and, standing gracefully, she walked over to him, flicking her cap up in order that he might see her face before drawing his final breath.

"My name is Craven LaFayette," she answered politely in her true voice. "You boys wrecked my ship."

She stepped over him and walked calmly out into the turmoil like a lullaby in a storm, drawing another pistol from her jacket and setting forth to gain her revenge. The first people she saw were the crew of *The Spider*, abandoning the ship that now reached the harbour, and racing over the jetty.

Firing both weapons, she took out as many as she could, narrowly missing the disguised Vaquero himself, and drawing attention from the troop of dragoons that were ever arriving.

The revenue stared at the harbour master who, half an hour ago, seemed firmly in their support. Their attentions were guided away from MacBride and his crew to this new and deadly target, and the wildcat heard gunshot whizzing past her head.

Sparky emerged from the smoke, and the gunfire ceased when the revenue saw that he had Cardinham with him as a hostage, a knife at his neck.

Craven spied him at once, and made to bring the man who had wrecked her precious ship to justice. But the gunpowder in her remaining pistol had run out, and she threw the gun aside with a howl of rage before drawing a gun from a revenue officer who appeared beside her to take her down. He tried to wrestle the gun from her but she butted him savagely. Then somebody grabbed her hands from behind and held her back. She screamed and struggled, but there were too many of them. When at last she stopped kicking, one of the dragoons dismounted and came close to her face.

"Who are you?" he demanded.

He was answered with a spit in the face. He wiped it away with the back of his hand.

"She is from the ship wreck!" cried a voice, and Abner stepped up and knocked off her cap, leaving her dark curls to cascade down her chest.

Craven narrowed her eyes at him in hatred.

"Aha!" said the dragoon. "And where are the rest of your crew, pray?"

"They drowned," spat Craven. "By you bestial devils!"

The dragoon surveyed her viciously.

"Gaol her!"

She was shackled and led away, screaming abuse as they did so. Then she raised her head and let out a great cry:

"VENIR AMIGOS! VENIR!"

And from a great lugger that had bobbed passively in the marina there came the bloodthirsty pirate call, and with it a new demon appeared before the revenue – the crew of *The Aida Alada*.

They made a fearsome sight; gnarly, cruel and merciless, their faces scarred with the marks of fearlessness, each one hungry for the blood of those who had so nearly taken their lives. Looking like beasts from below they hurled themselves into the crowds.

Sparky almost dropped his knife as, to his amazement, he recognised one or two as the Christian slaves that MacBride had set free. He guessed Craven had encountered them on her way to England and taken them for herself. Many had escaped when *The Aida Alada* hit the rocks, but those who had not had now seen MacBride and raced to the defence of the hero who had freed them.

Cardinham felt the privateer's grip slacken, and used it to his advantage. Twisting free amidst the disarray of people racing along the port, he disappeared into the crowds that were the landing committee and the revenue officers. Sparky drew his pistol, but any shot was hopeless; Cardinham had already been swallowed by the mass.

"*Damn it!*" he cried, kicking at a mooring post.

Jo turned and, on seeing what had happened, stared at him in disbelief.

"Don't you give me that look, Flossie," he bellowed at her, unable to hide his embarrassment. "If it hadn't been for you he'd have been dead by now!"

The carts were almost fully loaded. Two were filled only with fish and it was one of these that MacBride was led to. The other carts were to serve as decoys.

Farmer Rogers looked up and winked at him as he tacked up the horses. MacBride climbed aboard and Cole Shanley slapped the rump of the horse nearest to him, crying,

"God speed you, friend!"

And the cart raced away through the town, several others accompanying it.

Nobody saw them go amidst the battle taking place on the shoreline.

Nobody, that is, but Cardinham, whose eyes had been focussed on nothing else.

Overwhelmed by rage at seeing his sworn enemy escaping his clutches, he shot the nearest dragoon from his horse and vaulted himself up. Firing his pistol in the air in order to gain the attention of those around him, he yelled,

"For those of you who do not know my face, I am Cardinham, Officer in Chief, and if the law allowed I would have you all killed for this riot! You forget your target!" He kicked the horse which reared up, before galloping off in pursuit of the wagons. "Follow me!" he cried. "We hunt MacBride!"

* * *

Jo supported Sparky as they made their way to the carriage. The battle had taken its toll, and the pain had returned once more.

Craven watched Jo jealously from the jetty. With Cardinham's orders echoing across the harbour at the soldiers, who were facing the approaching cut-throats of *The Aida Alada,* there was just hesitation enough for Craven to fight her way free. In a similar fashion to Cardinham, she secured herself a horse and followed them.

* * *

It was nearing dusk when the little party arrived at Pensilva Cellars.

Craven dismounted, and a string of smoking Spanish fell from her lips. But then she saw her husband, slumped and sick, and she fell silent.

"He needs help," said Jo. "He's dying."

Craven gasped and her hand flew to her mouth. All at once, she looked vulnerable.

"I am not dying," muttered Sparky, through gritted teeth.

He sounded annoyed by the suggestion.

"He is," Jo reaffirmed. "Help me get him inside."

Together the two women helped the pirate to the great tavern door. Jo unlocked it.

"Settle him down," she said to Craven. "I won't be a minute."

"Where you go?" cried Craven, who appeared at a loss what to do with her husband.

But Jo hurried through the swing door without reply.

A few minutes later she reappeared.

"Where you been?" demanded Craven.

"I had some things to see to," Jo replied, shortly, striding up to the two pirates. She was carrying a pestle and mortar, which she showed to Craven.

"What is that?" asked Craven, eyeing the contents suspiciously.

"A painkiller. It will help him."

"How I know it not some witch brew you concoct to finish him off?"

"You *should* know about witches' brews," muttered Sparky, under his breath.

"If I had wanted him dead he would be," said Jo. "Anyway, not

209

so long ago you were ready to kill him yourself."

"He mine for kill," shot back Craven. "Adulterous scally betray me and marry some harlot!"

"*I told you* – I was never marrying anyone else," cried Sparky, sitting up straight before wincing in pain and keeling over again.

"But he still husband for me, and it is my duty to protect him," she continued, unheeded.

"Dammit, Craven! Just let her give it to me," groaned Sparky. "It can't make me any worse."

"It's Gotu Kola," added Jo. "Cleanses the liver."

"Let me try first," said Craven, decidedly.

But Sparky made a grab for the mortar.

"No, you don't," he cried, scooping the mixture onto his fingers. "I need every bit of it."

And he put his fingers in his mouth, before lying peacefully back and closing his eyes.

He opened them again almost at once, and shuddered.

"It's foul!" he cried. "Get me a drink!"

"I can get you some water?" offered Jo.

"That's not a drink!" snorted Sparky. "I need a rum!"

"No."

"Get me a rum, wench!"

Jo crouched down to him.

"Firstly, I don't take kindly to being ordered about …"

"Please, kind wench?"

"Secondly, I am not a wench."

"P-lease?"

"Thirdly, it would render the herb useless."

"Ohh!" lamented Sparky in distress. "What a cruel, cruel world I have tumbled in on!"

And he let out a loud groan, looking as though he was at death's door.

"I think we get rum," said Craven, uncharacteristically anxious.

"No," said Jo. "We should get him upstairs to bed. You give me a hand."

"Yes," said Sparky, brightening suddenly. "Yes, that would help considerably! Am I to take it you two ladies will be joining me?"

This was answered with a sharp slap from Craven as they struggled to haul him to his feet.

* * *

Cardinham pulled his horse to a halt at the bottom of the narrow cobbled street. The carts had split up. Tracks before the cobbles had led east; another set led west. Cardinham's eyes narrowed in thought, and he looked back up the cobbled alley. There was a trail of wet stones, stopping here and there, but nevertheless leading up the street. He dismounted and bent down to study them. He rubbed his finger lightly across a stone before raising it to his nose.

There was a thunder of hooves as Officer Pentlan cantered up.

"We've lost him, sir!" he panted, pulling the horse to a standstill.

"He went up the street," replied Cardinham.

"How can you be sure?"

Cardinham took his eyes from the ground to regard his accomplice with a withering look.

"It's brine," he said. "From the fish. The treasure belongs to that mutinous dog of a pirate. MacBride would not have risked taking it with him – that would make it all far too easy for us."

"So which do we follow? MacBride? Or the treasure?"

Cardinham mounted his horse.

"MacBride of course!"

And he kicked the horse and galloped contemptuously up the street.

* * *

It was dark by the time the revenue men caught up with the smugglers, whose horses had tired with their heavy loads.

MacBride was the first to hear them, his sharp ears picking up the distant galloping of hooves. He turned, and in the moonlight he could see their silhouettes now and again as they rode out from under the shadows of the trees.

The others stopped and turned.

"It's Cardinham," said MacBride. "I can smell him a mile away."

"Split up!" cried Cattermole, but MacBride shook his head.

"No," he said. "I am sick of running. Pretend we have not seen them. Keep going. Slowly."

So they continued on in silence, the tension rising as the sound of chasing hooves grew louder.

At last, when MacBride felt they were close enough for him to get a decent shot, he turned his horse around, reaching for his pistol as he did so. But it was not there. MacBride patted his coat feverishly, then turned to his friends.

"My flintlock!"

Mops Malone looked apologetic as he slowly drew it from the folds of his gown.

"Father?" murmured MacBride in bewilderment. "Father, throw me the gun!"

But Malone shook his head sadly.

"I am sorry, my son," he said. "I cannot let you kill a fellow man and face the devil."

MacBride stared back at him in disbelief, the revenue fast approaching. He jumped from his horse shouting, "*Traitor!*" as he made for the priest. But Cattermole and North leapt down and held him back.

"*Traitor!*" roared MacBride again.

"I am no traitor," Mops said, regretfully. "I am a man of God."

By this time the revenue were upon them, and as MacBride turned to face them, Cardinham drew back his foot and kicked out at his nemesis, propelling MacBride over into the dust. He recoiled, staggering to his feet at once.

"MacBride!" called Cardinham. "Where are you going?"

"Polkerris. To the Seine House," he answered, pausing to wipe the blood from his lip. "You cannot arrest me for that."

"I do not need to," came the reply. "You're already wanted on a charge of death." He leaned down from his horse. "This land is mine, MacBride. But I'll allow you to proceed to Polkerris. I'll accompany you there, in fact. And from there we will pay a visit to Pendennis Castle. You are no longer king of your domain. Your rule is over." He straightened up. "This land is mine."

To the intense surprise of those around him, Cardinham included, MacBride nodded in defeat, holding his wrists together to allow them to be fettered.

"No!" cried Cattermole, drawing his own gun. "Captain, no!"

But MacBride raised his hand to stay him.

"Captain? Let me shoot him, Captain!"

"No," said MacBride. "They're not having you as well."

Cardinham leaned over and clicked the iron handcuffs into place, leaving the crew of *The Mevagissey* staring in horror. As the Excise Officer in Chief drew himself up, he once more aimed a vicious kick, catching MacBride under the chin and sending him flying to the ground again.

It was North who drew his gun this time.

"*No!*" ordered MacBride. "Don't give him any reason!"

"Get him up!" Cardinham ordered the revenue, and several officers dismounted and hauled the smuggler roughly to his feet. MacBride regarded Cardinham with dignity, before turning to Cattermole.

"Tell Josephine that one night with her was worth being hanged for."

Cardinham let out a roar of rage and kicked the horse.

"Bring the Barabbas!" he thundered.

* * *

Another night had passed. Dawn had only just broken behind the heavy clouds laden with the first summer rain, when Sparky, lying in Jo's bed, heard a hammering on the tavern door. It was followed immediately by the creak of floorboards on the landing outside the bedroom as Jo hurried down the staircase.

The moment she glimpsed Cattermole on the doorstep, her heart sank. The look on his face said it all.

"I'm sorry, Josephine," he said. "They have him. He is in the dungeon at Pendennis Castle, and is to be escorted to London and hanged next week."

A loud sob escaped Jo's lips, and she put her hand to her mouth, shaking her head in disbelief.

"No!" cried a voice.

It was Sparky. He appeared in the doorway behind her, tightening his belt and drawing his coat around him. "Oh no," he said, shaking his head. "I haven't come this far to fail now! That money's mine! If MacBride is to go to London then I shall be the one taking him."

Jo looked from Cattermole to Sparky in mortification.

"We – his crew – have discussed it," continued Cattermole. "We have decided to follow him to the end."

He drew a deep breath. He looked questioningly at the innkeeper, but she shook her head in distress.

"He thinks I betrayed him," she whispered. "I cannot watch him die."

"Then I am to give you a message," said Cattermole. "He said, he told me, that one night with you was worth being hanged for."

She closed her eyes, unable to stop the tears from spilling down her cheeks. When she opened them again she regarded Cattermole with renewed honour.

"We go down with the ship," she said, bravely. "To the end."

CHAPTER SIXTEEN

MOPS Malone sat on the steep bank, looking out over the great estuary of Carrick Roads towards Pendennis Castle. The sun beat down upon him, the air was filled with the sounds of birds and summer insects in the pretty shrubbery around him, but his heart was heavy. He stared at a ship sailing in Falmouth Bay, but his eyes were so glazed with grief that he hardly saw it.

"What ails ye, Father?" asked a voice, and to Mop's surprise, Sparky settled himself down beside him.

"You're a long way from home," observed Mops, bitterly.

"Home?" said a puzzled Sparky, as though the word was not known to him. He shook his head. "Now tell me what ails ye?"

"I am inflicted with such burden," cried Mops in anguish. "Oh, wretched, wretched man!" He lifted his arms to the heavens. "I have done God's work and yet I feel it an errand of the devil!"

"Ah, you did what you thought was right," shrugged Sparky, cheerfully, not even caring to know what the wicked deed was.

"He trusted me, and I led him to his doom."

"Well," muttered Sparky, "one of us had to ..."

"You have seen him?" enquired Malone, miserably.

"Not yet. I have only just found my way here."

"Well, you overshot the mark, my friend. The castle is across the estuary, over there."

"And you? What good have you here, o desolate one?"

"I am doing all I can to ensure the good man reaches the Eden. With his – and my – darkest hour approaching, I drain the cup of misery to the dregs."

He pulled a flagon of dark wine from his cloak.

"Aha!" cried Sparky. "Good thinking, brother!"

"*Father,*" corrected Mops severely, holding the bottle out of range of Sparky's flailing grasps. "This is the Blood of Christ. Martin must confess his sins."

"Oh, whatever!" grumbled Sparky, crisply. "He's hardly able to drink it from here though, is he?" He pulled himself to his feet. "Come! My boat is moored below. We sail across!"

* * *

They landed at Falmouth as near to the castle as they could. Sparky followed Father Malone as he wobbled in a rather ungainly fashion onto land.

"How about a quick cup of courage before the cup of misery?" asked Sparky, at once sighting an inn on the waterfront.

"I don't drink," was the curt reply.

"Oh, you are indeed a wretched man!" cried Sparky in a mixture of disbelief and pity. "Well, a wretched liar, at any rate."

"Besides, they'll hardly let *you* in the dungeon," added Mops, gruffly.

"Of course they will. I am employed by your King."

"Ha! That won't get you very far down here now that you've played turncoat to Cardinham. I'll be lucky if *I* get in. I hear the guards are under strict orders not to allow their prisoner any visitors. I can only hope they will not turn away a man of the cloth."

"Hmmm. Then allow me to take your robe so that I, too, may pass as a priest."

Father Malone stared at the pirate, looking him up and down.

"It has a hood," said Sparky. "I'll place it over my head and no one will be any the wiser!"

* * *

The priest's fears were confirmed when the guard at the dungeon was dubious about letting the religious men through.

"Sorry, Father," said the guard. "We're under strict instructions. He's not allowed any visitors lest it aid an escape."

"You surely do not believe that I, a man of God, would aid the escape of an outlaw? A fallen angel?"

"I am told this knave is a notorious escapist."

"My son, have a little greater faith in your abilities as guard."

The guard eyed Sparky suspiciously. The pirate was hovering behind Malone, his head down and the hood pulled low.

"I am also told of shocking acts by the priesthood in the county."

Mops allowed his jaw to drop open.

"No!"

"It is true. I hear they have been helping the outlaws, even secreting contraband under the pews and pulpit in the church."

The reverend shook his head in disbelief.

"That, indeed, is a sin worthy of Hell," he tutted, sadly. Then he brightened. "Surely you can see that I am not such a man? I have been asked to come and eradicate this villain of his sins, in order he may follow a peaceful path to Heaven."

"Nevertheless, Father, I have my orders."

Malone nodded, sadly.

"I understand," he said. "Remember though, we are all sinners. May God have mercy on us all."

And the pair made to leave. As Sparky passed the guard he leaned in and whispered,

"Watch yourself. It's said certain prisoner be adept with witchcraft."

"What's that?" demanded the guard.

"Oh yes, I forgot to mention that," said Mops, turning back. "I am sure it will be quite all right. Just take care not to offend him lest he place a curse on you."

"A curse! What sort of a curse?"

"Oh, I don't know," shrugged Mops. "Hair loss. Plague. It's all hearsay really."

"But, but Father! Can you not shield me from such sorcery? Pray for me, perhaps?"

Mops shook his head apologetically.

"Sadly it does not work that way," he said. "We have to withdraw the demon from within. But as we are not permitted to enter, I see little I can do."

The guard acquiesced.

"All right. You may go in, for a few minutes only."

Father Malone bowed, his palms pressed together.

"God bless you, my son," he said.

"But not him!" said the guard, throwing an arm out to halt Sparky as he made to follow.

"Without Brother Byron?" cried Mops. "But, good gaoler, you surely do not expect me to draw out this demon alone? Goodness knows what might happen! It might escape, or even go into me! Or you!"

The guard looked momentarily horrified. He looked at Sparky, warily.

"All right," he said. "But just a moment, mind."

* * *

Cardinham had indeed made sure that any escape for MacBride would be impossible. He was chained to the walls by both his wrists and ankles, fastened with great padlocks.

He looked up as the bolts were drawn back, and stared at Mops and the monk as they were briskly ushered through. The door slammed shut rapidly behind them.

Sparky drew back his hood.

"Come to take me to my doom, *brother*?" said the smuggler.

"Not yet," replied Sparky, brusquely, as Mops hurried forward and reached up to the fetters around MacBride's wrists.

They rattled as he shook them, studying the locks.

"It's no good, Father," said MacBride. "I am meant to stay here."

"Is there nothing we can do?" cried the priest, desperately.

"Do not trouble yourself so," said MacBride, resignedly. "It is my time."

Mops pulled the flagon from the folds of his cloak.

"Oh please!" grinned MacBride.

But Malone would not be budged.

"If you have done wrong, you *must* confess your sins and drink The Blood of Christ before you are hanged. You will not find your family in Purgatory!"

MacBride's eyes flashed to him, and he looked momentarily angry.

"I like this religion," said Sparky.

"It's not really our religion," pointed out MacBride.

"I'm covering all bases," answered Mops, impatiently.

"Peace, Father," said MacBride, nodding. "I shall do whatever you ask."

Sparky wandered around the dungeon, kicking a stone and looking bored as MacBride prayed and Mops crossed and blessed him, handing him the flagon.

"Is that all he's having?" Sparky cried, watching as MacBride took a sip and handed the flagon back.

He made a grab for it.

"It's not for recreational consumption!" shouted Malone, grabbing it back.

"Then I shall confess *my* sins!" cried the pirate, snatching the bottle and adding with a twinkle, "And I have a *lot!*"

"You are not a Christian," yelled the priest, plucking it back.

"I am." Sparky grabbed it back. "At least, I thought I was. Now I'm not so sure. Maybe I'd like to deviate."

"As entertaining as this all is …" began MacBride.

Mops gathered himself, and the flagon, at once.

"Yes, yes!" he said. "And our time is almost up!"

"You go out and stall the guard," ordered Sparky. "I would like a word with MacBride alone."

Mops opened his mouth to argue, but on catching MacBride's eye, he nodded soberly and turned to go, Sparky hooking the flagon from him as he went past.

"Pray for me, Father," smiled MacBride.

"Oh my boy!" Mops smiled sadly back. "Do not trouble yourself with that!"

* * *

"Father," cried the guard, when Mops knocked to be let out. He opened the door for him, took a furtive glance around the cell, and then shut it again abruptly. "How goes it? I heard such shouting." He looked terrified.

"Aye, he's a stubborn one," replied Malone, seriously.

"Where is Brother Byron?"

"Brother …? Oh! He is still in there, finishing the job. I will await him here, in order that I may hear if he calls for aid."

And he and the guard stood and waited, the minutes permeated by an awkward silence.

* * *

"So, brother," said Sparky, pulling the cork from the flagon. "They are to take you to London in three days' time, I am informed?"

"I know not," replied MacBride. "You wish to take me yourself, no doubt?"

There was a long pause as Sparky drank.

"You would find my company more pleasurable than Cardinham's, would you not?"

"I would. But how do you suppose to go about it?"

"In the usual way," replied Sparky, airily. "So it is settled then. I shall prepare and come for you in three days. Be ready."

"I'll gather my things," came the sardonic reply.

"Sparky?" called MacBride, as the pirate turned to go. "Do something for me?"

"I am at your command," replied Sparky, drily.

"Take a message to the blacksmith back at Newlyn. Tell him it is time."

Sparky arched one brow, and banged on the dungeon door. He handed Mops the flagon as he passed him.

"Dragon's fly," he slurred.

"Wh-what was that about dragons?" asked the guard.

"He means the flagon's dry," mumbled Mops, absent-mindedly. "Poor chap must have been cursed with a speech impediment. Still, we agreed it was a small price to pay."

And with that he thrust the flagon into the hands of the gaoler and followed in the pirate's wake before the terrified guard could ask whether the prisoner had been cured of his ills. They left him shuffling nervously away from the dungeon door.

"I hope whatever you said to him back there was of some use," puffed Mops, as he caught up with Brother Byron.

"Yes, thank you."

"To *him,* not *you!*"

"Oh. Well. He seemed agreeable. That reminds me. Where will I find his friend the blacksmith?"

* * *

The 'usual' way Sparky referred to consisted of pirates, scimitars, muskets, renegades and deys, and a night-time ambush. There was plenty of whooping and shooting as the revenue carriages were overwhelmed by Sparky's and Craven's faithful crews.

MacBride's mind was set on just one thing; ensuring Cardinham did not live to see him suffer. In desperation, Sparky dragged him to a waiting carriage. MacBride grabbed the pirate's musket, and Sparky grappled with him, resulting in MacBride sending a crashing right hook into his face. Sparky grimaced in fury, but still managed to haul MacBride into the seat as the raging revenue closed in on them.

"What is it with everyone?" shouted the smuggler, as the horses sped them away leaving the rest of the pirates behind to keep Cardinham's men busy. "I could have had the bastard!"

"I have a better idea," muttered Sparky, who was at the helm.

"And that would be?"

"Kill him after they've hanged you."

MacBride threw another punch, sending the surprised coachman flying from his seat. A cloud of dust flew up as he hit the ground.

"Ahoy!" yelled Sparky, chasing the continuing carriage. "Come back, you thankless hobbledehoy! I may have just saved your life back there!"

"Hobbledehoy?" remarked MacBride, grudgingly halting the carriage. "Where did you pick that one up?"

He watched as Sparky staggered along the road and hauled himself onto the seat. He looked cross, but in such a way – like a petulant child – that made MacBride want to laugh. He turned away before a smile could break through.

"I don't believe in ghosts," the smuggler said.

"No luck with your wife then? I'm sure I've seen her."

Sparky was still prickling. He deflected the smuggler's fist this time.

"Only after your fill of rum," grunted MacBride. "Why couldn't you find some drop of honour within your blood and respect our deal?"

"Deal?"

"That you would allow me to avenge my family's death before taking me to be hanged?"

"Was that our deal? I've made so many deals I've forgotten what I said to who."

"Oh, your words hold such comfort! *We* agreed you would spare me the time to kill Cardinham before you took me to London."

"Well, I have. I've spared you plenty of time. It's not my fault you didn't get on with it."

"Because somebody is always stopping me," protested MacBride. "I could have had him then – *I had the shot and you stopped me!*"

"Yes, well, like I said, I have a better idea."

"What, that I am to crawl back from the grave and hound him until he repents?"

"Nice. But risky."

"You could let me go now. If you were a nice man."

"I am not a nice man. And it would ruin my reputation. And my idea is still better."

MacBride sighed.

"Your idea?"

"Is a stroke of mastery; I take you to London, receive my payment, they hang you ..."

"I'm not liking the sound of it," MacBride grunted.

"Are you afraid?" probed the pirate. "After all this time, has the fear of death caught up with you?"

"There are worse things than dying," came the dry reply.

"Ha! Indeed. I went two days without a drink once," said Sparky, shuddering. "*De todas maneras,* what one must remember with hanging, brother, is this; they can only hang you once."

At once MacBride saw the light.

"You saw the blacksmith? The collar – he gave it to you? He made it?"

MacBride took the reins and watched as Sparky tore open his shirt before removing his neckerchief to reveal what looked to be an iron collar underneath. He grinned his wide, manic grin.

"So you believe by wearing this you will survive the hanging?"

"They say a deacon survived his hanging by wearing one of these back near where I came from in Scotland. The blacksmith took my measurements some time ago after Mops told me my name had been gazetted. But he was wary. He wasn't sure it would work."

"So, here is my theory: you wear the collar under my neckerchief, I bribe the hangman, he leaves it on, you're hanged …"

"The doctor signs the death certificate, they load me onto a cart and then you switch me for a cadaver you found … on the streets?"

'We need one that looks like you in case anyone checks under the shroud.'

'They are two a penny if you know where to look. It's a gamble, and you'll need to bring me round fast and then …'

"And then you will be free to kill your foeman, thus fulfilling our accord!" finished Sparky, emphatically.

"And they would not be able to touch me for it," MacBride continued, thoughtfully. "Because, in the eyes of the law, I am dead."

"A stroke of mastery, like I said. *Your* mastery, *hermano.* Of course, it works the other way as well. If you are already dead then

Cardinham could kill you himself – they could hardly punish him for murdering a dead man. You would have to keep your existence a secret from him for as long as you could manage."

"And if it all fails?"

"Then we revert to Plan B."

"Which is what, exactly?"

"Your plan. With the ghost."

"That was my plan?"

"Was it not?"

MacBride shook his head, confused.

"If it fails then you will have not honoured our accord, therefore we must make a new one."

"And what is that to be?"

"You kill him yourself."

"I do find he can sometimes be a contrary little anarchist."

"Good. Then that's settled."

All the same, MacBride did not look content. Sparky nudged him and flashed him a cheery grin.

"Fear not, brother!" he said, as they rode into the night. "For if it looks as though you are dying I shall pull on your legs and make fast your passing!"

* * *

Jo had wrestled with the decision of whether to stay in Newlyn or go with the others to London. At last, content that Cardinham was out of the way in London in order to see that MacBride's demise was conducted smoothly and therefore could do no harm at Pensilva, she left her inn in the dubiously capable hands of Hetty.

"If you see him, use it," instructed Jo, handing Hetty the rifle. "Don't even think on it. Don't let him near her now."

Jo stepped out of the tavern door to see many carriages and

horses gathered outside Pensilva Cellars. Outwardly, she looked immaculate, all dressed in black with a black lace veil, her long hair swept up and pinned at the back of her head. But inwardly she was falling to pieces.

They were all there. Doug and Martha Coby with Isaac, James Cattermole, Jack North, Eli Abe, Lurret, Bert Crocker, Tom Crycot, Sam Johnston, Cole Shanley, and Lil Ferry and her cronies, not to mention many other locals from Newlyn, Penzance and Marazion – all loyal and grateful customers of the smuggler.

Jo was helped into the lead carriage, driven by Doug, with Martha, Isaac and Sam for company.

"We wondered if you'd be coming," said Martha, gently. "Are you sure you want to, darling? No one would blame you for walking back into your tavern."

"I would blame me."

"That's it, girl!" cried Sam, slapping her leg.

But Martha placed her hand on Jo's knee.

"It's a long, long road," she said. "To a hard and bitter end."

"I know," said Jo, softly. "But if I don't go, I shall always regret it."

"Yes," Martha said, with understanding. She bit back the tears. "I feel the same. He's always been a son to me. I can't bear the thought of him dying amongst strangers."

They set off, a long procession, their great iron wheels rumbling below them. Sam Johnston banged his fist on the wall of the carriage behind where Doug was sitting; Doug almost fell off in fright.

"DON'T FORGET WE'RE PICKING UP TALFRYN AND JOHN!" he bellowed. Then he muttered to the others in the carriage, "Is it safe to be letting this old coffin-dodger drive?"

Chapter Seventeen

THE morning had arrived.

Sparky had received his payment; the executioner had been bribed. Great crowds had gathered to see the infamous smuggler hang.

The pirate was permitted into the cell where MacBride was waiting to be taken out to the gallows.

"Cheer up!" he said, gaily.

Before MacBride could shoot back with a witty reply, Craven appeared and spoke shortly to Sparky, curtsied to MacBride and fluttered her lashes at him, then left. MacBride stared after her.

"Don't you go looking at her!" waved Sparky, impatiently.

"Why? You got your eye on her?"

"That's my wife."

"*She's* your wife?!"

"Why does everyone say it like that?" muttered Sparky.

"Because she's young and beautiful and you're old and ugly?"

"It's not too late to take that bribe back from your hangman."

"But then you wouldn't know whether the iron collar works."

"Nevertheless," grunted Sparky, "she is not for the likes of you."

"So I am told," grinned MacBride, his eyes sparkling.

Sparky looked intensely annoyed at being mimicked. But then his smile broke through.

"Aye, brother. You be knowin' yer pirates now!" he said, and gripped MacBrides hand. "Brethren of the Coast!" He paused. "Hark! I hear the cries growing! They are coming for you."

MacBride nodded. Sparky took a little bottle from inside his coat and offered it to the smuggler.

"Good luck, MacBride."

"You're allowing me first drink?" said the smuggler. "Wonders will never cease!"

"Actually," admitted Sparky, "I have another one for me."

And he drew out a large bottle. MacBride nodded.

"That would be about right," he said, then raised his bottle to the sky with the shout of, "To the free trade!"

"*To the free trade!*" echoed Sparky, following suit, and they crashed the bottles together in toast.

* * *

Jo could not stop herself from letting out a gasp as she watched the guards lead MacBride out from the Tower of London to the gallows. It was as if she had hoped, by some miracle, that it might not really be him. Martha tremored and crossed herself before raising her palm to cover her mouth. Out of the corner of his eye, Sparky saw Cardinham approach. He stood beside him.

"Did you get your money from His Majesty?" Cardinham asked out of the corner of his mouth.

"I did."

"I care not, you understand. This is all I have been waiting for – this and this alone. Watching MacBride dance the hempen jig!"

Jo caught sight of him standing beside the gibbet. Her tear-filled eyes gave him a stare of bitter hatred, pleading and despair. He returned it with a self-satisfied smile. Her look turned to pity, and the side of his lip curled up in a snarl. He turned away, only to see that Craven was also staring at him tempestuously from the other direction. Her lips were pursed, her eyes black as stone, a look intent on reminding him that he had his own dues to pay.

"Very nice corset your 'wife' is wearing there," remarked Cardinham.

"It's to keep my 'wife's' spirits up," replied Sparky. "Hell hath no fury …"

The crowd were jeering and booing now as the hangman stood MacBride on the block and positioned the noose around his neck.

No, no, thought Jo, desperately willing MacBride to do something. Fight for his life. Beg for mercy. Anything, *anything* but accept his fate so readily. Wracked with guilt, she, like Martha beside her, cupped her mouth in silent panic. *Come on, Martin,* she pleaded. *Come on! You're not beaten yet.*

She was not close enough, however, to see MacBride turn his face towards Cardinham beside him and wink.

"*Delanda est carthago,*" Cardinham muttered, staring back. "What are you waiting for! Destroy him!"

As if he had heard, the Mayor of London raised his arm.

"Behold!" roared the Mayor. "The fate of a smuggler!"

And as the crowds cheered, Cardinham could not help shouting,

"Hark! The gates to Hell!"

MacBride closed his eyes as his soul prepared to kick off into eternity. Jo screamed out in distress as the block was booted from under his feet and he was left hanging. In that moment, her heart felt as if it had burst, and was now lying limp and bleeding inside of her, and she heard herself cry out again in terror. Her eyes were fixed on her lover's last moments, despite her efforts to tear them away.

Martha put a hand to the back of Jo's head and forced her face down onto her shoulder, holding her tight as they wept together in anguish.

Sparky, on the other hand, watched intently, looking for any sign that MacBride might not be dying. He caught the eye of Craven, who glanced back anxiously.

"What are you flinching at?" mocked Cardinham, glancing back at the dangling body with a scathing laugh. "Surely you feel no affection for the ruffian? Or perhaps you see your own fate before you?"

"Huh?" Sparky was jerked from his troubled thoughts. "Oh no. Not I. I merely cannot envisage being able to stand as tall and face my penance with such honour and dignity." He smiled genially at Cardinham, whose face grew black. "I believe you have your martyr, sir."

* * *

When they cut MacBride down, he appeared to be dead. As his cadaver was carried away through the jeering throng, Sparky and Craven once again exchanged doubtful glances. The body passed close to Craven, and she leaned curiously over the smuggler's face, oblivious to the surprised looks she was inciting.

Cardinham strode forward and vaulted onto the platform, holding his hands up to quieten the heckling crowd.

"People of London!" he cried. "This man was not just a smuggler and a murderer, but a pirate! I therefore propose he is made to suffer the full punishment of a pirate and be hanged out until three tides have washed over him!"

The crowd roared. But as the Excise Officer in Chief stepped down, Sparky placed a hand on his shoulder in a friendly way and said,

"They would not dare. He has too many alliances. T'would invite much revolt."

* * *

Sparky found it extremely hard to get near the body of MacBride for, despite his enigmatic charm, he was refused entry into the tower. The suspense of finding out whether the iron collar had proved a successful invention was almost unbearable. Not only that, but there was another sensation; something that the pirate had rarely felt before. It was developing not in his head, but in his heart – a desperate need to know whether the smuggler was alive or had departed this world forever. Time was running out. If he was to be revived, it would have to be done soon. You weren't dead until you were warm and dead, as the saying went, but every moment of unconsciousness brought MacBride one step closer to the afterlife.

At last he caught the doctor as he was leaving one of the dungeons.

"Is he dead?" he demanded in agitation, gripping the doctor roughly by the arm.

"Of course he is!" replied the doctor, alarmed.

He stared at the rather striking foreigner before him with a mixture of fear and surprise.

"You've signed the death certificate?"

The doctor nodded, and hurried away, glancing back over his shoulder in bewilderment. What else would a hanged man be, but dead?

The pirate sat impatiently upon the seat of his cart amongst the departing crowds, watching as MacBride's body was loaded onto the prison cart some distance away. Then he gave the signal. At once, Craven appeared, wailing and weeping, demanding to see MacBride's body one last time. Upon beholding him, she feigned a faint, falling into the prison warden's arms and, while everyone's attention was diverted, Sparky's crew moved in and, surrounding the cart, they swiftly made a switch.

Once Sparky was sure that MacBride was safely loaded onto Craven's cart, he followed the prison cart to the cemetery, where the open mouth of a grave waited hungrily for its intended victim. The substitute cadaver was now safely out of sight, sealed into the coffin intended for MacBride. Sparky knew he was being watched; he had to keep up the pretence of seeing his part of the deal through to the end. He observed, from some distance away, as the body of the man found by the docks early that morning was lowered into the ground.

Then Sparky turned and drove his cart away to find out if MacBride had been saved.

Chapter Eighteen

WHEN Sparky caught up with the cart that carried MacBride and saw the smuggler's grey and pallid countenance, his spirits sank. His voice, however, bore no sign of his uncertainty.

"Is he still alive?" Dr Cottle was in the back of the cart with MacBride. The pirate doctor had been kept sober especially for the occasion, and was not in the brightest of moods. "Answer me, devil, or I'll cut your throat!"

'He's still warm,' Dr Cottle said as he tried to resuscitate MacBride.

No one dared speak. They waited, knowing time was running out. There was the sound of a bucket being emptied and water sloshing over the boards, then coughing and spluttering as MacBride came round.

"He's alive," came the doctor's stunned voice.

Sparky could not help but release a sigh of relief.

"Get that collar off his neck!" he cried, and then, as silence was once again the answer, he bellowed, "Did you hear me! Get that damned collar off his neck!"

* * *

By the time they reached Somerset, MacBride was sitting up beside Sparky on the cart, his neck bearing a thick red band of bruising where the noose had cut into his skin. Dr. Cottle, who had immediately taken medicinal alcohol, was lying in a drunken somnolence in the back, every now and again coming round to slur a few lines of a pirate ditty before falling back into his coma again.

"I feel twice the man!" croaked MacBride.

His voice was ailing, although his spirits seemed intact.

"You don't look it," remarked Sparky sourly, ashamed at himself for being concerned.

MacBride saw right through the façade at once.

"You were worried about me, weren't you?"

Sparky avoided the reply.

'Get some rest,' he said.

MacBride allowed himself a smile.

* * *

The cart rolled on. Sparky took over the reins. MacBride slept sound in the knowledge that he was now officially a dead man. When he woke, he was possessed of a terrible thirst. A flagon of ale eased his throat.

"Would you have missed me?" he asked his pirate friend.

Sparky scowled.

"Come on," persisted MacBride, grinning. "Tell me. Don't be ashamed."

Sparky pulled out his pistol in fury.

"What, you're going to *shoot* me now?" he laughed.

"I'm going to shoot you," confirmed Sparky.

"You'll miss me."

"I've never missed."

MacBride laughed.

"That's not what I meant. Now come. We are brothers, are we not?"

"I killed my brother."

"You don't want to kill me."

"I'm going to do it."

"You'll pine for me."

"I'm going to do it anyway."

MacBride was ducking in and out of aim as Sparky fought to hold the horses and keep the pistol straight.

"You'll regret it for the rest of your life."

"I'll die soon. That won't be long."

"All those years at sea have warmed your affection for your fellow man!"

The pistol went off. MacBride ducked in surprise, but was still laughing.

"Hey give me that, you're getting dangerous."

He tried to wrestle the gun from the pirate's grip.

"I preferred you when you were dead," said Sparky, trying to knock him out with the opposite end of the gun. But MacBride was too quick for him. At last the pirate grinned. "Ah! How I hate you, Lochiel!" he remarked, reluctantly.

MacBride leaned over, his lips pursed.

"Give me a kiss," he said.

Sparky punched him. MacBride retaliated by poking him in both eyes. Sparky hit him again, and MacBride hit back sending Sparky toppling from the cart. Grabbing the smuggler's jerkin he pulled him down with him.

After they had stopped rolling, they staggered to their feet, bruised and battered, but still grinning. They clapped each other on the back and ambled back to the horses, who had halted the wagon some hundred yards down the track.

"So what was it like?" asked Sparky, when they had settled themselves back on the cart and set off again.

"What, being hanged? Not very pleasant. I feel like a dozen carts of whisky have driven over my neck." He rubbed it tenderly. "Think I need Martha's cool compress."

"Oh spare me!"

"You asked. I would try to avoid it if I were you. I thought I was a dead man."

"Oh aye?"

"I could feel all my spirits pressing upwards, and when they reached my head there was a blaze of light that seemed to go out through my eyes, and all the pain with it. It certainly didn't feel as if the collar was working."

Sparky pinched him hard.

"Ow! What was that for?"

"Just making certain it had."

"Could you not establish that from thumping me?"

"I'd forgotten I'd done that."

"I wish Martha was bringing me home. If I'd have known you were going to turn all soft on me, I might have opted to stay dead."

"That's it!" cried Sparky, drawing his pistol. "I'm putting you in the ground where you should be!"

But his eyes were on the road and he didn't see MacBride's fist coming straight for him. MacBride caught the gun as Sparky hit the road once more. He got up and brushed himself down. Then he hoisted himself back onto the cart again.

"I thought," continued MacBride, when Sparky had settled himself back at the helm, "That I was off to join the souls from the lost land of Lyonesse, where many a mariner has met his doom."

"Where's that?"

"Some sunken land off the coast of Cornwall where us sea-goers are supposed to go when we die." He paused. "In some ways I feel I am already somewhere between this world and the next."

"There are many different worlds," said Sparky. "Many different suns."

"Aye? And what world will you be off to next, now that your work here is done?"

"I go back to Algiers," replied Sparky, without hesitation. "Some quiet corner to see out the last of my days."

"You speak as though you were a dying man?"

"You concerned for *my* welfare?" grinned Sparky. "Why don't you join me?"

"And go back to Algiers?"

"It's paradise."

"That's not how I remember it. Cornwall is my home."

"Ha! So now Cornwall is your home? Before it did not serve the purpose. Tell me, what is this 'home' you Englanders speak of that shackles you so?"

"My people are there."

"People? Huh! There's just *you*. You have learned, brother, you can only trust *you*. There is no 'people.'"

"You have a black aspect. Your home is Morocco? Would you not return there?"

"Morocco was where I was imprisoned as a child. I do not think it would fulfil your criteria of *home*."

"So where did you go when you escaped?"

"Spain. Extremadura. A vast, sun-blasted province, poor and unyielding. I sought my brothers after my escape in 1756, but the place held no candle to my heart. When I was fourteen and begging, I was told there was once a man named Francisco Pizarro, who had been born two hundred years before me, out of wedlock in a back street not far from me in Trujillo. He had been discontent with his lot in life, and set sail in search of better things. The man became one of the greatest conquistadors. He crumbled the Incas."

"And it is from this man that you learned your brutality?"

"He didn't get anywhere being nice. Neither would you if you hadn't have had me."

"I don't follow you."

"My point is, savvy, that our paths are marked by the gods. God. Whatever. I see it in you; you are a man of destiny. Why settle for a constant battle to win a living from your unforgiving seas when the world can offer such gentler times? Extremadura was the poorest province in Spain. Had I accepted my life there, I would have slaved each and every day of my existence against starvation and disease, and died many years ago. Instead …"

"Life has been easy?"

"It has. Think of it, we could make our living by simply plundering every ship that crosses our path back to England with tobacco and silks and spices – and *gold.*"

"Attack my own people, you mean?"

"Cardinham is your 'own people,'" Sparky reminded him. "This island of the north is all you know. But out there, to wake at the break of day and see the rising sun spill over the ocean horizon like wet gold … What life does your Cornubian shore offer you in comparison?"

MacBride did not answer.

"Ha! The woman! Even now!"

"Algiers was Hell on earth for me," said MacBride. "I'd rather die than return. And I am not the trailblazer you are, Jose."

"On the contrary," replied the pirate. "I bear witness to the fact that you are just that. You have all the necessary credentials."

"Aye? And what are they?"

"You are clever and you are mad."

"I am mad?"

"Quite mad. Just covertly. But even you are not mad enough

to stay here for the unrequited love of a woman." Sparky grinned, flashing his gold teeth. "Come, my brother! Come, be free!"

* * *

Cardinham stood in silence over the hump of earth in the cemetery. He was studying it carefully. Something wasn't right.

"Dig it up!" he ordered at last.

Thinking him slightly mad, the gravediggers dug up the coffin, which to their horror he then demanded they open. Inside, a body was wrapped in a white shroud. Cardinham uncovered the face.

'This isn't the prisoner,' he said.

"Who is it then?" asked one of the gravediggers.

'I've no idea.'

'So where did the hanged man go?'

"I expect he got up and walked," replied Cardinham. Glimpsing their alarmed faces he added, "They have taken him to be buried in Cornwall! Fear not, gentlemen. I shall see that it does not go ahead."

"But what are we supposed to do with this body?"

'That is your problem. MacBride has to be buried here. In Cornwall he would have mourners. Kneeling and praying and putting flowers at a tombstone. That I cannot allow."

* * *

It was some days before Sparky and MacBride crossed the border into Cornwall. They stopped off briefly at Beer in Devon where the smuggler had some associates who kindly provided them with a decoy coffin. When the pair at last reached Newlyn, MacBride leaned back, content to return to the town he never thought he'd see again.

They passed the church, and Mops spotted them from the lych-gate and stared, blinking in astonishment.

"Good morning to you, Father!" called MacBride, and gave a wave.

Mops did not answer, but his jaw dropped open.

Soon the shout went up that, by some act of God, Martin MacBride was still alive, and the townsfolk came running from their houses to see the miracle.

The cart rumbled down the narrow Hemlock Street, where it was surrounded by people. MacBride leaped to the ground.

A shout reached his ears, and he saw Lost Doug Coby racing up the street like a man possessed.

"It's yer mad father," Sparky remarked.

"He's not my father."

"Marty! Marty, my boy!" he cried, trying to say more but not finding the breath. MacBride went to meet him, Duncan yapping and barking at his feet. Doug threw his arms around the smuggler, then stepped back and cupped his face in his hands as if to make sure he was real. He embraced him again. "Oh my boy! My boy! Tis a miracle! However did you do it?"

"I vowed to you, with God as my witness, that I would not leave this world until I had made Cardinham settle his debts. I stand by that vow."

"Marty! Do not be reckless," cried Doug in dismay. "God has given you this second chance at life. You will be straight back to the gibbet!"

"So far as the authorities are concerned, I am already a dead man. I have paid my price, now I get the reward. So long as I am the man that kills him, nothing can be done."

Doug thumped him on the back as the crowds flocked around them. Cattermole pushed through the mob and embraced his captain, followed at length by other members of *The Mevagissey.*

Abe caught his arm and, guessing that he was accompanied by contraband of some form, told him in a low voice that the gaugers were coming. MacBride strained his eyes and looked over the crowd down the street towards the harbour. Sure enough, he could see Officer Roberts, accompanied by three other officers and two dragoons, making their way up to investigate the flurry of activity that had taken place in Hemlock Street.

"It is of no consequence," said MacBride. "Treat this as my funeral, my friends."

He grinned and disappeared into the crowd towards Doug Coby's front door.

Sparky signalled to the people to help him with something in the back of the wagon. They heaved the snoring Dr. Cottle aside and the coffin of contraband that was collected from Beer was held aloft.

"People of Cornwall," announced Sparky. "Look upon the coffin of your hero, MacBride, and remember all that he did for you!"

A cheer rose up from the crowd, and Sparky punched the air.

"For the Free Trade!" he cried, and was answered with an echo from the ever-growing crowd.

"Now come! Let us bury him with the honour he deserves!"

* * *

The revenue men followed the curious procession all the way up the hill to the church. Many of the people joined the crowd after MacBride made his departure, and thus believed it to be a genuine funeral. Others could not help smiling, which puzzled the revenue officers intensely. A muffled drum had been produced from somewhere, and hymns were sung as the procession of mourners followed in the coffin's wake.

Sparky found the reverend exactly where they had left him, standing under the lych-gate and staring into space. He turned when he heard the approaching lilt of hymns, and regarded Sparky with what could only be described as the acceptance of madness.

"Brandy," hissed Sparky to the vicar as he stood aside to allow the procession through. "They're watching!"

The word 'brandy' seemed to jerk Mops back to earth. He pulled himself together at once and smiled.

"Do not trouble yourself trying to look elegiac. Nothing could appear more suspicious."

And he drew his fingers into a tight fist and let out a cry of joy. But as soon as he slid back into view from under the pirate's shadow, his face was a solemn picture of sadness as he ushered the sorrowful mourners in.

"Father Malone?" came the voice of Officer Roberts when the last lamenter had shuffled past, dabbing her eyes with a handkerchief.

"What is it, my child? I have a funeral to conduct."

"This is the funeral of Martin MacBride?"

"It is."

Officer Roberts turned to the dragoons in surprise.

"If you don't mind me saying, Father," he said, turning back, "many of the mourners do not appear to be dressed in the customary attire."

"From what I gather," replied Mops, quite honestly, "it was rather short notice. Excuse me ..." He stopped. "Unless you wish me to insist they return home to change into the correct apparel?"

He bustled away down the path and into the church, leaving Roberts hastily shaking his head under the lych-gate.

After the service, the coffin was lowered into the grave – fortunately Mops always made sure there was an empty grave for similar circumstances involving contraband – before Doug, James and Jack scattered their handfuls of earth over it and it was filled in.

The "wake" was held at Doug and Martha's tiny cottage back in Hemlock Street. Townsfolk spilled out into the alley to see the guest of honour – MacBride, who had insisted on being present.

"And miss my own wake!" he said when Martha wrapped a cold rag around his neck and ordered him to go for a lie down.

There was a shock in store for all, however, as MacBride raised his hands to signal that he wished to make an announcement, and broke it to his friends that in two days' time he would be leaving for the Mediterranean with Sparky.

"Dying has opened my eyes to a few things," he added, risking a glance in Doug's direction. He had been expecting this information to be met with firm opposition, especially from his "father", but the old man just smiled and nodded.

"So be it," he said. "You are alive, and that is all that matters. Just be happy, boy."

But Martha, despite managing a weak smile, was dabbing her eyes with her handkerchief.

"Who are we going to have to bring us our goods now?" cried Sam, jovially.

"You'll have my boys," said MacBride, patting North on the back. "Sparky's wife has agreed to come with us, so she'll be leaving the lugger behind, and Polperro are making a new cutter for us. *The Wind Waker* will be two hundred tons and larger than any other vessel in the fleet. She will take a crew of a hundred men, and she'll have twenty-two guns on board. I'll leave James in charge."

"Promise me one thing before you go," piped up Doug now he had had a moment for the news to sink in. "That you do not make an attempt on Cardinham's life, nor venture anywhere near him. I can live content knowing you are away but alive, but if he is faster than ye to fire then you will break this old man's heart. Let go of it, boy. It shall bring ye no peace, nor I."

"I promise you this," replied MacBride. "I shall not wait for Cardinham's return to Cornwall, nor shall I seek him out. If I do not see him before we sail, I shall make no such attempts."

CHAPTER NINETEEN

IT was dusk by the time everyone had gone home. All was still. Duncan lay asleep on the rug, the occasional deep sigh emanating from his throat.

MacBride sat on the little bed in the back room, looking out of the tiny window towards the sea. In his fingers was a small, crumpled piece of parchment bearing a picture of his daughter, Lucy. It had been painted for Martha on Lucy's third birthday, and had been her most treasured possession, right up until just now, when she had passed it onto him.

"Take it with you," she had insisted, placing the parchment into his palm before gently closing his fingers over it. "She's your little girl."

Somehow, having the painting close to him brought MacBride comfort, but looking at it made his heart ache.

Lucy. With her rosy cheeks and her tight golden curls. Her innocent blue eyes stared up at him from the canvas.

"Lamorran …" he whispered, almost inaudibly, and he closed his eyes. "Why?"

But his own heart gave him no rest as he cursed himself for ever leaving them, for being unable to protect them, and accused himself of failing as both a husband and a father. He covered his face with his hand.

She was immortalised now. Forever to be a tiny child, never to grow a day older.

For another hour he sat there. He watched the moon rise, at last facing the heartbreak that had dogged him for so long, only breaking through each time he let his guard down. Many a time out at sea he had woken up at night and called their names. Now he spoke to them as if they were with him.

He thought of Josephine, and all that she had meant to him, and although still loathed to leave her and what he believed could have been his last chance of happiness, he made a silent vow that he would never lend his heart again.

But he had loved her. She was the only one of her kind and, even should he search every corner of the world, he knew he would never find another.

But such was life.

He looked again at Lucy, and kissed her face, and the time came to him when she had been picking shells at Barricane Beach, holding the hem of her little smock dress to make a hammock for them. A wave had come and soaked her and she had squealed and run, slipped on the stones and nearly hurt herself. But although she had called for her father, she had not been able to keep up the act, and when he had tickled her, and helped her, wet and dripping, to her feet, she had been laughing.

"Be good, Bubble," he whispered, and wrapped the parchment in her little woollen bonnet. "I'd be with you if I could."

Pensilva Cellars was shut. The great door had not been unbolted since the day Jo left for MacBride's funeral. She had taken refuge in her bedroom, and there, desolate and guilt-ridden, had refused to see anybody.

"I know what you're thinking," she said, hearing Hetty come softly into the room and close the door behind her. She was sitting at her dressing table, her head resting on her arms. "You're thinking that I brought this grief upon myself."

"No," said Hetty, sadly. "No, my darling, my sweet. I do not think that at all."

"It is my fault he died."

"Father Malone believed it was his."

"No," said Jo, lifting her head. Her dark eyes had lost their sparkle, and her nose was red with crying. "I talked. I gave John the excuse he needed. And now I've lost Martin forever."

But Hetty went over to her and shook her.

"Now you listen to me, Josephine Bryant. You did the *right* thing! Get up. Take off those black clothes and open up your inn. Life *must* go on." Jo blinked hard, drew in a deep breath and at last nodded in agreement. "I'll go down to the market and get what we need," continued Hetty in a businesslike manner. "You stay here and start getting the tavern ready."

* * *

The stage pulled up outside the church, and Cardinham stepped down. Marching down the little path through the graveyard, he passed Cole Shanley. No words were spoken between the Customs Officer and the Excise Officer, but they glowered intensely at each other.

Cardinham reached the door and threw it open with a crash. Mops jumped. When he saw it was Cardinham striding towards him, a deep frown furrowed his kindly features.

"How dare you enter the House of God in such a way!" he cried.

"I have no time for this, Malone," barked Cardinham. "I understand that MacBride is to be brought back here for a proper funeral. I will not allow it. And should my orders be disobeyed then I shall ensure the punishment is severe. Do you understand?"

Mops shrugged.

"You're too late," he replied. "The service took place two days ago."

Cardinham was furious. He swiped all the silver candelabras off the altar and they fell, with a great clanging sound, onto the stone floor.

"*WHAT!*" he bellowed. "It cannot be so! There is no way they would have got back here in time." Then he paused. "Unless … Unless they had this planned from the start?"

Mops did not answer, but busied himself collecting up the silver. Irritated by the priest's indifference, Cardinham grabbed him.

"Were you in on this?"

"No," replied Mops, sharply. He shook himself free. "I simply did God's will."

"*You lie!*" Cardinham's voice had become quiet and dangerous. "Dig him up!"

"Never!"

"Then show me his grave."

Mops looked very fierce.

"You have no authority here! You are not a man of God! Leave this place!"

To his surprise, Cardinham obliged, and strode back down the aisle.

"This isn't over," he threatened as he reached the door.

But Mop's best preaching voice rang out over the pews, sharp and clear.

"If the man's death brings you no release, then what can? Indeed, I see for you, it will never be over."

* * *

MacBride sat on the jetty as they prepared the schooner, *The Barentszee*, for sail. He smoked the last of his tobacco, staring around the place that had become his home since he was seventeen. Sparky and Sam were laughing on the shingle as the pirates busied themselves on the ship under the orders of Cyprian Bezique.

MacBride's eyes travelled up to the vast hulk on the cliff that was Pensilva Cellars. Drawing a deep sigh, he ruffled Duncan's shaggy fur, took a swig from the bottle beside him, and lay out on the planks with his hands behind his head, so that all he could see was the clear sky above.

There are many suns.

Unbeknown to MacBride, Officer Roberts has been patrolling the harbour, directing the gaugers to check the ship for illegal export. Annoyed at finding few volunteers willing to board the ship of cutthroats looking for wool, tin, or copper, and not enthused by having to do the job himself, he looked around to see if there were any dragoons present, and was jolted with shock as his eyes fell upon Martin MacBride, lying on the jetty with a bottle and his dog.

"That's – that's – *MacBride* – isn't it?" he stammered to the man beside him.

"Don't know," shrugged the man. "Never met him."

But Roberts had gone, letting out a howl as he ran.

* * *

The market in the square at Newlyn was in full swing, with people and animals wandering this way and that. Hetty ushered a donkey out of her way and, as she began picking out some eggs from one of the stalls, she heard the woman behind the stall say under her breath to her husband,

"Look! That cursed man."

Hetty turned to see Cardinham stalking through the rabble towards her, with Officer Pentlan at his side. She intercepted them as they passed.

"I hope you're happy," she said.

"Yes thank you," snapped Cardinham, looking anything but pleased.

"I sincerely hope you will leave that wretched girl alone now."

"I wouldn't hope too hard."

He tried twice to push past her, but the stout woman held her own and refused to let him through.

"Well let me tell you this, Mr Cardinham, you underestimate Josephine. The outcome will be the same for you as it was for Mr MacBride."

"I'm shaking."

He pushed her out of the way again, but she stepped back and stood strong.

"You don't fool me, Cardinham. This is all borne out of jealousy for a man and the way you thought she felt for him."

"I know what she felt for him. You women – you're all the same. Empty-headed as those chickens over there. Thinking he's some kind of hero!"

"And he is! What woman wouldn't want him? He is the guardian of our lands and all they stand for."

"He is a brigand! A charlatan! And you should be afraid of him."

"Pah! Brigand!"

"There are many around. I would watch your back."

In answer to this threat, Hetty leaned forward.

"I felt safer in Pensilva against the outlaws of our country when he was there than I ever did with you," she said.

"Then you are a beef-headed, blunt-witted old crone. You should fear him!"

"Why? Because you do?"

"Don't talk rubbish. Get out of my way!"

"You feared him from the start," persisted Hetty, "because you stood to lose to him. Well let me tell you this, she spoke of that man with a fondness you'll never know, thanks to your black soul. She told me she would offer up everything she had to be with him – and she *did*."

Cardinham's face twisted in silent rage at these last words.

"Don't think I don't know your plan failed," she continued. "You wanted Josephine to put her love for him first, to leave him with reason to hate her."

"You've no idea what you're talking about. Go preach your dross to someone else! Stop embarrassing yourself!"

And he rammed her out of his path.

"That silk for her wedding dress?" She raised her voice after him. "She told me she had brought it back from the ship herself; she had undressed for him and he had wrapped it around her waist *'with the grace and gentility of a prince'*. Then she had dressed over it, and even secured safe passage for thirty pounds of tea and a packet of lace under her bustle!"

Cardinham hit out. He sent the woman flailing into the market stall which collapsed beneath her. There was a great gasp from the crowd as Cardinham drew up and raised his foot as if he were going to kick her. He thought better of it, and laughed cruelly.

"Go home, hag," he cried, and spat on her.

He turned to bump into a red-faced and panting Officer Roberts.

The lady behind the stall helped Hetty up and brushed her down.

"You shouldn't antagonise him," said her husband, shaking his head. "He is a dangerous man."

"Well *I* thought he deserved everything he got," cried the wife, making sure she was in earshot of the Excise Officer in Chief. "About time someone stood up to him!"

But Cardinham was not listening.

"What are you doing here?" he snapped at Roberts.

"Yes, what are you doing here?" demanded Pentlan. "I left you in charge of the harbour."

"*Ghosts!*" cried Roberts, pointing a very bold finger at Cardinham. "You told me they didn't exist. *Vacuous fool,* you said! Well, I tell you, with God as my witness, I have just seen a ghost right on the harbour, and this time there was no way I was imagining it!"

"Oh really?" mocked Cardinham. "And who, pray, was the lost soul this time?"

"Martin MacBride," answered Roberts at once.

"Mar …" He stopped. Hetty's ears pricked up and she turned in astonishment. Cardinham finished his sentence, but his tone was no longer scornful.

"Martin MacBride?"

"Larger than life!"

There was silence. Nobody moved. The rage in Cardinham was building like a volcano about to erupt. You could see it in the slight movement of his fingers clenching, and the deepening of his frown. But his eyes, his eyes grew black and sparkled with pure fury.

He turned to one of the dragoons.

"Give me your horse," he yelled, and when the dragoon hesitated, Cardinham drew his pistol. *"I said give me the horse!"*

The dragoon leapt from the saddle, allowing Cardinham to climb up and gallop off in the direction of the harbour. But the horse was Morwellham, and in true smuggler style, he was trained to backwards. When Cardinham reached the fork for the harbour, the horse galloped in the opposite direction.

"Whoa!" yelled Cardinham. But he only succeeded in making the horse gallop faster. "*Sodding* smugglers horses!" he roared.

* * *

Hetty ran. It had been many years since she had run, and to be accurate it was more of a giddy stumble, but nonetheless she stumbled as fast as she could.

"Wait!" cried the woman at the stall. "You've left your basket!"

But Hetty either could not hear or did not care. She had information to pass on and she needed to be quick.

* * *

The ship was almost ready. Most of the activity moved from

beach to onboard *The Barentszee*. Cattermole, North, Abe, Isaac, Doug and Martha were making their way down to the shore to say their goodbyes, along with many of the other inhabitants of Newlyn and the surrounding area who had been a friend to the smuggler.

Sparky walked along the jetty and held his hand out to MacBride to help him up.

"Time to go, brother," he said.

"Sand's fallen?" smiled MacBride, getting to his feet.

"Sand's fallen," nodded Sparky. But he caught sight of the smuggler's expression darken as he looked past him along the deck. Sparky turned, and his sharp eyes homed in on what had caught MacBride's attention. John Cardinham was standing on the cliff.

Almost as the pirate had turned, Cardinham disappeared.

"He's not in London …" murmured MacBride.

"No!" cried Doug, hurrying up. He too had seen the figure on the cliff top. "Please, Marty. Count the odds! You get on the ship and you leave! Put all this behind you."

"I can't do it, Doug," said MacBride, quietly. "He's here. I finish this."

Doug clutched him.

"Please, Marty, please my boy," he begged, softly. "They're gone, and nothing will bring them back. After today, we shall probably never meet again. Let this be the last thing ye do for me."

MacBride dragged his eyes away from the cliff to meet Doug's stare, and he forced himself to think of all the times Doug had been there for him over the years. A constant force. He *had* been his father.

"All right," he said, with effort.

And he backed it up with a stiff nod.

"Get him on that ship now, and out of here," demanded Doug to Sparky. "Cardinham wants Marty's blood as much as Marty wants his. Get him away!"

Hetty puffed up the wooden staircase, pausing briefly to look out of the window to persuade herself that MacBride really was standing on the harbour. Jo was still sitting at her dressing table, her hand resting on her belly, trying to stir herself. Trying to face life without him. She had been so lost in her thoughts that when Hetty burst breathlessly in, Jo leapt to her feet.

"Oh!" she said, breathing in relief, her hand on her heart. "I thought you were John, coming in here like that."

"Mr MacBride!" gasped Hetty, trying to find her breath. She was pointing hysterically at the window. *"He's alive!"*

Jo stared, her mouth open.

"He isn't," she said, shaking her head in bewilderment. "I watched him die."

"I don't know what you saw," breathed Hetty, heavily, "But Mr MacBride is down there on that beach as sure as I am standing here before you."

"But … he *can't* be," whispered Jo. "It's simply not possible."

"My girl," said Hetty, drawing herself up, "he is alive and looks just about ready to leave. He may never come back. Now you get down there and you tell him how you feel, or you really will lose him forever!" She drew in a deep breath. "Turn around," she said slowly. "And look out of that window behind you."

And Jo, blinking very hard, slowly turned and looked out of her bedroom window onto the harbour.

He was the first person she saw, and she let out a sob and grasped the window seat to steady herself as her legs gave way beneath her.

Without another word, she flew past Hetty, out of the door and down the stairs, where she ran squarely into Cardinham. He grabbed her tightly by her wrists and dragged her roughly down the passage. At first she had been too taken aback to speak, but she recovered quickly and began struggling and kicking out at him.

"What are you doing?!" she screamed.

Hetty came running to help her. But Cardinham swung his fist out, swiping the old lady with the back of his right hand. It launched Hetty clean off her feet. She flew back and struck her head on the staircase, before sliding to the ground, lifeless.

"*NO!*" screamed Jo, and now she fought with all she had. It became clear that Cardinham had taken complete leave of his senses, and she guessed what he meant to do. But try as she might, she could not free herself from him. In her grief she had refused to eat since she had returned to Cornwall, and her usually tough body was weak with lack of nourishment. She stumbled a little as Cardinham pulled her down the cellar steps, but he would not stop. She struggled to slip her wrist from his tight grasp, but before she knew it he had hauled her into the cell where he thrust her wrists into the shackles on the wall. "*NO!*" she shrieked again.

"This time they fit!" he cried triumphantly, with a twisted grin. "Just the right size – *for a whore!*" And he wrenched up her skirts. But Jo at once drew her knees to her chest and thrust them out into Cardinham's stomach. He fell to the ground.

"Not me, never!" she cried.

He gave her an ugly look, and taking up a ceramic jug of stale water which had been standing on the chair in the corner, he threw it at her, smashing the jug on the wall behind her. She gasped as the cold water drenched her through.

"You can't do this, John!" she screamed as he made for the door.

"Why not? They're both dead!"

And he left her desperately rattling the shackles around her wrists, her screams following him as he left the cellars.

* * *

The harbour was crowded. Everywhere MacBride looked he could see familiar faces. He said his goodbyes as he walked along the jetty. Doug and Martha were waiting for him at the foot of the boarding plank. He shook hands solemnly with Doug, who threw his arms around the boy and tried to hold back the tears. Then MacBride embraced a sobbing Martha.

"I'll never forget all you have done for me," he promised, taking her hands and crouching down in order to see her face under her bowed head. "I love you both."

"Good luck, son," said Doug, as MacBride stepped onto the boarding plank.

But Duncan, who had not left the smuggler's heels all day, perked up his ears, gave a sharp bark and ran off the boarding plank and away over the beach like a shot from a gun.

"What the hell's got into him?" exclaimed Sparky.

"I don't know," frowned MacBride, puzzled. "But we're not going without the dog."

"Damn right we're not going without the dog!" cried Sparky.

They stared out over the shore, searching for his fast-moving form. But he was gone.

"Stubborn little bugger, isn't 'e?" grinned Doug. "Wonder where he gets that from!"

* * *

Jo was doing all she could to free herself from the shackles on the wall. She tried screwing her hands into as thin a shape as she could and squeezing them through the cuffs, and when that failed she just pulled at them in desperation until her wrists were raw and bleeding.

But the cuffs were doing their job well, and she sobbed, hysteria rising in her throat, as with every second that slipped by she fell deeper and deeper into despair.

Not far away, Cardinham stormed into the little room behind the door with the window. A small child sat hugging her knees in the corner of a bed. She was shivering with fear, and her blue eyes were brimming. He snatched her up, and she squealed with fright when he threw her over his shoulder as though she were no more than a sack of turnips.

* * *

After what felt like hours, but in truth was no more than a few minutes, Jo slumped, exhausted. She fell into that dangerous place between wakefulness and sleep where memories were able to torment her.

It had been stormy that night; the rain pouring in torrents and the wind howling. A draught crept through one of the leaded windows and toyed playfully with the flames on the candles.

She had not been aware of them coming in, had simply turned to see them behind her: Lamorran MacBride and little Lucy, her blonde curls tucked under a woollen bonnet.

"Jo, would you look after Lucy for me please?" Morrie had said. "I have to go somewhere and this is no weather for a child."

"Of course," Jo had said, her face lighting up in delight at the thought of a few hours with the little girl. "Hello Lucy! Have you come to do some cooking with me?" She looked up to Lamorran. "Stay for something to eat first, Morrie. You look half starved."

Lamorran had shaken her head. She'd seemed anxious to leave. Carefully, she'd untied Lucy's bonnet and clutched it to her chest. Sensing that something was not right, Jo had hooked back the curtain with a finger and watched Lamorran as she'd paused briefly on the doorstep to weep into the bonnet, before hurrying off into the night.

Jo and Lucy had spent the evening baking and playing, waiting for Lamorran's return until, eventually, Lucy had fallen asleep on Jo's lap in the rocking chair. Before long, Jo's eyes had closed too, unaware of Cardinham standing in the doorway, silently watching them.

Jo's mind relived again the horror of being forced to keep Lucy in the cellars. She had furnished the room as comfortably as she could, and sewn Lucy a ragdoll to keep her company. When Cardinham was not around, she would have the child upstairs in bed with her, but when he was present, she would cuddle up with Lucy in her bed in the cellar. She remembered coming into the room, placing a lantern on the table and crouching beside Lucy in her bed. She would gently sweep the hair from the trembling child's forehead, whispering, "*Don't be scared, my darling. I won't let him in here,*" and kissing her. Lucy would whimper and beg Jo not to leave her.

"She's become like a daughter to you, hasn't she?" Cardinham had sneered. "I see in you the love and need to protect her as if she were your own. If you don't do as I say, Josephine, I *will* kill her. Granted, it will be quick, painless, just a grimy bullet into its pretty head. But remember, Jo, I possess no valour or virtue. Do not make the mistake of thinking me incapable of such a deed. I look at it and I see *him*. I will *relish* it."

Jo, as she came to, still manacled to the wall, remembered it all. And then Martin had returned to Cornwall from Algiers.

"What's the black-hearted beggar doing now?" Hetty had said.

"It's not Cardinham. It's MacBride," Jo remembered answering, holding Lucy's hand and hurrying her out from the cellars before MacBride could see her when he came to check the liquor.

"My daddy?" Lucy's clear, young voice had asked.

But Jo had been fervently looking down the hall to check the coast was clear before hurrying the child to the stairs, Hetty wearily following. She'd encouraged the girl on gently, and when they'd reached Jo's bedroom, Lucy had flown joyfully to the window, where she had curled on the window seat to stare at the dark, sparkling sea below. Jo had blown her a kiss, but had been in too much of a hurry to see Lucy blow one back to her departing shadow.

She had taken her with her wherever she could, but most of the time it had not been safe for her to leave the tavern. Nobody was to know she was alive, John had insisted. He'd demanded she was not to leave her cellar room. But it was cruel, and Jo's heart could not bear it. Sometimes, she would wrap her up and take her outside. The safest place was Wistmans Wood, as few ventured there, and should they happen upon somebody, the trees would provide a safe hiding place.

Once, Jo gave a low whistle, then fired the rifle. Lucy was laying on the ground beside her, her hand over her ears. But a tiny sound had distracted the inn-keeper at the crucial moment, and the lucky rabbit darted into the undergrowth.

"It's Mr Cardinham, Miss," Hetty had panted, coming up behind her. "On the way to the tavern."

And that familiar look of fear had swept across Lucy's face, and she began to run, leaving Jo to pick up her skirts and follow her.

"Where is he?" Jo had shouted to Hetty over her shoulder.

"On the beach. But on his way, so it looks!"

And Jo had taken Lucy's hand and they had run together.

"If I find you have been out in Wistmans Wood with her, or anywhere out of the confines of that cellar, I shall personally remove you from this place, if I have to kill you first," Cardinham had warned her when he had entered the tavern.

Jo had twisted her wrist from his grasp.

"You cannot keep a human being locked in a cellar," she had said, defiantly.

"She is no human being to me," he'd replied. "She is a parasite. A mere pawn. If she is discovered and MacBride finds out, I shall kill all three of you."

Sometimes, he had really frightened the little girl. Once, when Lucy had been sitting on the window seat in Jo's bedroom, she had heard soft footsteps ascend the stairs.

"Josephine?" she had called out. There was no reply. "Josephine?"

And then, just as she had turned her fair head, a great swarthy hand had clapped over her mouth. Cardinham had crouched down so that his eyes were level with hers.

"Shush ... Don't scream." He'd taken his hand away and slowly run it over the soft curls on her head. "You're a pretty little poppy, aren't you? What a pity your father is such a tragic fool."

Cardinham had laughed horribly. His grip had been tight,

bruising her wrist, and she had been unable to squirm from his grasp. Her eyes had filled with frightened tears.

"Don't worry," he had said, "I'll be here. I'll be with you. I'll be listening to your screams."

"Get away from her!" Jo had yelled, and Cardinham had turned to see her standing in the doorway, the rifle poised.

"Josie!" Lucy had cried, and tried to run to her, but Cardinham had gripped her even tighter.

"I said let her go!"

But Cardinham had dragged the child out of the room and down the stairs towards the cellars.

"What in God's name are you doing?" Jo had cried. "You can't keep her down there!"

"I warned you, Jo, I warned you to keep her downstairs."

The shackles on the wall were too high and too big for Lucy, so Cardinham had tied her tightly to the rotting chair in the corner, beating Josephine off as he did so.

"You evil bastard!"

She had lunged at him, but he'd thrown out his fist and sent her flying back against the wall, suddenly losing his temper.

"*You're lucky she's alive!*" he'd roared. "She stays here 'til we get back!"

And so Jo had been forced to sail out with Cardinham on *The Spider* in an attempt to capture the smuggler. The moment she had returned, Lucy heard her clattering down the stone steps and she had burst into the cell.

"Josephine!"

"I'm here, darling," Jo had wept.

Lucy had still been tied to the chair. Her eyes had been red, but dry; her cheeks streaked from the tears. Her nose and chin had still been damp with tears. She had held out her arms to Jo, who had crouched down and embraced her tightly.

"My brave girl. My brave, brave little girl."

She'd taken a knife from her pocket and sliced the ropes that had bound Lucy to the chair. Lucy had fallen into her arms, and Jo had hugged her again. Then the little girl had drawn back and rubbed her hand over her tummy.

"It hurts," she'd whimpered.

Jo had gently lifted her smock top, revealing a series of deep red marks across her midriff where the ropes had cut into her. She'd taken her into her arms once more, stroking her head, blinking back the tears.

"I won't let him hurt you again," she had vowed, then had drawn Lucy back in order that she could look into her eyes and would know she meant it. "I *promise* I won't let him hurt you again."

But circumstances had plotted against her. Lucy had begged Jo not to leave her and travel to London. Torn and in despair, Jo had eventually broken free from the weeping child's clutches and gently closed the door behind her. She had taken her rifle and handed it to Hetty.

"If you see him, use it. Don't even think on it. Don't let him near now." She had leaned close so that Lucy would not hear. "Once Martin is dead, he will have no use for her."

Jo pulled at the chains that fettered her to the wall, her wet clothes clinging to her skin.

"I talked," she remembered saying not more than an hour ago. "I talked. I gave John the excuse he needed. And now I've lost Martin for good."

Hetty had shaken her head.

"Now you listen to me, Josephine Bryant," she had cried. "You did the *right* thing! Look at me. Look at me, Jo. You can't go on like this! Lucy doesn't understand. She's pining for you. She thinks she's done something wrong. Please let me bring her in."

"No," Jo had sobbed. "How can I possibly look her in the eye, knowing that I took her father from her? Her last living relative."

In the quiet of the cellar, Jo caught the sound of a floorboard creaking above her.

"HELLO?" She was briefly aware of the desperate tears still running down her face. *"Help me! I'm down here! Help me please!"* There was silence. Not a sound. She strained against her shackles. *"Hello!"* she yelled, as loud as she could. *"Help! Please!"*

And there he was. He scurried through the doorway, wagging his tail furiously. Jo let out a deep breath and her shoulders sagged. Disappointment crushed her.

"Oh, Duncan," she sighed, and burst into fresh tears.

Duncan sat obediently opposite her, sweeping the floor with his tail, and staring up at her as if awaiting instructions. She stared sorrowfully back at him, biting her lip.

Then suddenly, his sensitive ears pricked and he was gone again.

* * *

Cole Shanley stood in the doorway of the kitchen.

He touched the broken door which hung, suspended on one hinge, in midair. It fell to the floor with a crash.

"Jo?" he cried, drawing his pistol and stepping inside. "Jo? You all right?"

He glanced back at the door again. It had been kicked in. Making his way through the kitchen and the scullery into the passage, his eyes fell on the lifeless form of Hetty, slumped down against the stairs.

"Damn," he murmured. "Jo?"

Out of the corner of his eye, he saw the door to the cellars open a crack, and gripping his pistol tightly, he sidled towards it. He'd only taken two steps when something flew at him from behind the door and landed at his feet, barking.

"Duncan!" Cole let out a breath of relief. The terrier disappeared back into the cellars. He could hear Jo screaming his name, and he rushed after the dog and skidded down the cellar steps.

"WHERE ARE YOU?" he yelled.

"HERE! IN THE CELL! I'M HERE!"

He stumbled through the gloom in the direction of her voice, and at last tumbled in on her.

"My God, Jo!" he cried, seeing the blood running down her arms toward her elbows. He ran to free her at once. "What the hell happened?"

But the moment the second cuff slipped from her wrist, she was running. He ran after her and tried to grab her, but she kicked him off.

"You don't understand!" she screamed, propelling herself up the steps two at a time, "*He's going to kill her!*"

"Kill? Kill who? *Who* is?" He was panting behind her as she raced down the passage, leaping over Hetty who lay in her path, and ran behind the bar where she grabbed the rifle. "Jo! Christ, Jo, what are you doing?" He tried to wrestle the gun from her, but she kicked out at him and ran to the door. Throwing back the great bolts, she swung it open and was gone, leaving him rolling on the flagstones in agony.

Summoning all his strength, he forced himself to his feet and staggered after her.

"Jo! *Christ!*"

CHAPTER TWENTY

JO sprinted towards the cliff as though the very soles of her feet were on fire, leaving even Duncan chasing her heels. Three dragoons tried to intercept her, but she fired the rifle at the ground near the horses' hooves, causing them to panic and rear up. Meanwhile, Cardinham was half carrying, half dragging the sobbing Lucy down the steep cliff path towards the beach, almost slipping himself in his hurry. MacBride did not see him. He had his back to the cliff and was talking to Sam when Cardinham's voice bellowed over the sand.

"MacBride!"

MacBride stopped talking. Everybody fell silent. Nobody had noticed Cardinham come down the cliff path. The smuggler, recognising the voice, did not turn, fearing the second he did so he would be shot. His pistol was in his belt, but he dared not reach for it.

"MacBride!" roared Cardinham again. "Turn and face me, so that I may see your face before I send you to meet your doom! I have been saving something of yours to keep you company on your way to Hell!"

MacBride saw Martha gasp, although he didn't know why. The very next moment, she spoke.

"Daddy?"

Such a small, frightened little voice, yet with it came all the fears, all the terror, that MacBride thought he had left behind. They surged up and hit him like a tidal wave, almost knocking him off his feet, so strong was their force. The fear of his family being hurt, the knowledge of losing them – it all came flooding back, buoyed across the shingle on the back of that small, sweet voice. Everything around him seemed to blur, as if it was spinning too fast, and yet turning around seemed to take forever.

Then he saw her, her golden curls tousled and dirty, frightened tears falling from her eyes. She struggled against the beast that restrained her.

Cole could not catch Jo. She flew over the ground like the wind, her arms pumping up and down, the rifle in her hand. She could hear nothing; not the sea, nor the shouts of the dragoons or the shrieks of the gulls agitated by her gunshots. All she could hear was her heartbeat, a deep pulsing flooding her head, her arms, her legs.

She reached the cliff path and began to skid her way down.

A deathly silence now hung over the beach, broken only by the calm lapping of the ocean on the pebbles.

Everyone heard the click as Cardinham cocked the trigger. It seemed to echo off the cliffs.

"Any last words to your daughter?"

MacBride did not take his eyes from Lucy. He was horror-stricken. She stared back at him in terror, silent now, and still, except for the tears that ran steadily down her pinched face.

Jo wept, too, as the beach came into view. She cocked the rifle, crying for the man she had once loved.

But Cardinham was no longer that man. He had vowed a candle to the devil, and had become a devil himself, so corrupted by his own jealousy that there was nothing left of him but corruption itself. She hated him for what he had made her do; lock a child in a cellar, lie to a man she loved, but above all else, she hated him for what he was making her do now.

Cardinham's fingers tightened on the trigger. Not trusting herself to allow any time to think about it, Jo pursed up her lips and gave a low whistle, just as she did when hunting in the woods.

Again, the sound echoed strangely across the shore.

Lucy and MacBride fell to the ground, and at the same moment, a shot rang out. Then another. Then another.

Blood spattered onto the sand.

Cardinham fell dead.

MacBride gulped and tried to speak through his dry mouth.

"Lucy?"

His voice broke.

But she got to her feet, burst into a flood of tears, and ran to him, her arms wide.

Overwhelmed with relief, MacBride fell to his knees and caught her as she ran into his embrace. And there she stayed, her arms wrapped around his neck as he clasped her tightly to his chest, his hand protectively over the back of her head.

With Lucy at last safe, he looked past her to the cliff, where he saw Josephine a third of the way down, her rifle in her hand. Her exhausted legs buckled beneath her and she slumped to the ground, the blood from her wrists running between her fingers, as Cole Shanley raced to the edge of the cliff above her.

MacBride buried his face into Lucy's hair, and it all began to fall slowly into place.

At last he began to see into Jo's head. Everything she had said, and hadn't said, started to make sense. He tenderly kissed his daughter's forehead, and without releasing her, carried her along the shore towards Jo, the little girl's arms clamped tightly around him as her body shuddered with shock.

Jo struggled to her feet and, dropping her father's gun, stumbled down to meet him. Holding Lucy with one arm, he invited Jo into his other. She fell to her knees at his feet and, as he crouched down. Lucy unwound her arms from around his neck and threw them around Jo's.

"I promised, didn't I?" Jo said, breathlessly. "I promised I wouldn't let him hurt you." She raised her eyes to MacBride. "He gave me no choice."

MacBride nodded, but could not speak.

"Please don't go," she pleaded. "Don't go now. I love you."

He shook his head with a smile, and gently touched the hair on the top of her head.

"I never wanted to leave you," he whispered back.

Then he smiled at Lucy as she turned to look at him. Her tears had at last subsided, and her smile broke through.

"Has this nice lady been looking after you while I've been away?" he asked, softly.

Lucy nodded.

"We had good times," she said through her smile. "She took lots of care of me."

MacBride's smile grew wider, and he nodded. The crowds drew in behind him. Martha broke free from the rest and ran forward to the little girl to envelope her.

Craven stepped up to stand beside Sparky on the jetty.

"What hell was this?"

Sparky shook his head.

"I need a drink," he said.

Chapter Twenty-One

MARTIN MacBride paced the corridor outside the courtroom restlessly.

"She shouldn't be in there," he kept saying. "What the hell are they deliberating about? He was going to kill her!"

Sparky, sat on a bench, shrugged and took another swig of rum.

"They can't do this to her. They can't. I can't lose her now."

"I knew she wasn't on his side," said Sparky.

MacBride stared at him.

"You knew she wasn't on his side? What the hell do you mean, you knew she wasn't on his side?"

"Well, she wasn't. I didn't know what was going on," he shrugged. "I didn't know there was a child. But she tried to bargain for your life, so I knew she couldn't have been with him."

"She barg … What do you mean, she bargained for my life?"

"She offered me the inn if I would spare you."

MacBride was beside himself.

"You knew this? You knew this and you didn't think to tell me? I nearly died believing she was helping him!"

"Well, I didn't want it to fog your senses. Women have had that effect on you before."

"I could have left with you and never seen her again, and you didn't think to tell me?" He stopped as a thought struck him. "I could have killed John Cardinham myself and got away with it, had I known! They could hang her for this!"

"Well … it slipped my mind," Sparky mumbled into the neck of his bottle. Then he looked alarmed and held up his hand. "Now don't hit me!" he said, pre-empting what was coming next. "You don't want to hit me. I'm a dying man."

But it was too late. MacBride struck. This time he was out cold.

* * *

The courtroom was full. Craven came in late, just to hear the verdict, as was her habit. She was wearing her oversized black hat, which she took from her head as she settled herself into one of the chairs next to a rather bruised Hetty, who shuffled anxiously as the judge re-entered the room.

He ascended the platform, looking grave. MacBride slipped in through the door.

"Having heard all the evidence against Officer Cardinham, I conclude that the man abused his position as Excise Officer in Chief, allowing personal matters to take precedence. I am aware that the plundering of ships wrecked by the hand of God is merely regarded as part of the benefits provided for the men of Cornwall by nature, but it would appear that Officer Cardinham was not only responsible for the wrecking of ships by lights, but also for press-ganging local people into forming a band of wreckers under his leadership in order to pay Captain Vaquero to assist with a personal vendetta. It would seem that Mr MacBride was dealt the death penalty under false circumstances as a result of bribery on Officer Cardinham's part. I can also see that Officer Cardinham was guilty of murdering a small number of excise officers that worked under him." He drew breath, his expression grim. "A sorry state, indeed," he said, "that this man should have been allowed to operate for so long."

Then he addressed Jo, who stood in the defendant's stand.

"Miss Bryant, despite understanding your reasons for killing this man who, we can assume, intended to kill Miss MacBride, the fact still remains that you took the life of an officer."

"Oh come on!" MacBride cried.

The judge fixed him with a stern look.

"The fact still remains," he repeated, gravely, "that you took the life from an officer. It therefore stands to reason, Miss Bryant, that you are capable of murder."

"Isn't any mother?" cried Hetty. "When protecting a child?"

MacBride ran his hand through his hair in despair.

"The penalty for this, Miss Bryant, is death by hanging."

"Your Honour!" cried MacBride.

"Before you are sentenced, can you give me any reason why you feel you should not be put to death for this crime?"

The judge fixed her with a look that was almost pleading.

MacBride turned to the door in anguish, unwilling to hear the sentence given.

"I am with child."

Jo's voice was cool and clear.

There was utter silence. Everybody stared at the woman in the dock.

MacBride, halfway through the door, stopped and turned. He stared in disbelief. That night! That sacred, blessed night they had spent together? At last, at long last, had he actually done something right?

Jo smiled broadly at him, and there could be no doubt she was speaking the truth.

"Hmmm …" mused the judge, barely concealing a smile. "Is there a doctor here who can confirm this?"

There was a rustling as Dr Cottle wobbled to his feet, his hand aloft. Sadly, he was holding a half empty bottle in it.

"Yes," he said, looking furtively around for the judge. "I can confirm this."

"Is it too much to hope for," sighed the judge, "that there might be a doctor here who does not belong to a pirate ship – comprising entirely of men – and who is not under the influence of spirits? Let's do this properly."

Dr Cottle fell back into his chair, and another man stood up.

"Ah! Doctor Rowe!" smiled the judge, pleased. "You have examined the defendant?"

"I have, Your Honour. This morning. I have the results here."

"Can I see them please?"

The courtroom filled with excited whispering. MacBride smiled and shook his head with a curious mixture of disbelief and relief.

"Miss Bryant!" announced the judge, looking up from the document and removing his spectacles. "As the law deems killing a pregnant woman is killing the life on an innocent, you are free to return henceforth to Cornwall and reside there for the present time. You are to report to the local authorities there once every quarter."

Vergil Sommerby, who was sitting in court, caught Jo's eye and winked at her.

Sparky stumbled through the door, apparently having just come round from the blow.

"What was the verdict?" he slurred.

"Lucky," replied MacBride, clapping him on the back. "Bloody lucky!"

* * *

Newlyn gathered once more on the beach to say goodbye to Captain Jose Vaquero. Summer had drawn to an end, and autumn was upon them. More often than not now, Sparky needed help to get about. He was no longer the lithe and quick man MacBride first encountered early in the year. But he remained undaunted. His skills of out-daring and out-foxing were still doubtlessly very much alive, and his manic grin as ready as ever.

He stood now with Craven at his side, supporting him. MacBride shook his hand.

"Goodbye, brother," said Sparky.

"Goodbye, old friend," said MacBride. "May Africa provide you with all the riches you desire."

"I don't go to Africa for riches," grinned Sparky. "Or women. Or even rum. I go to die. Which reminds me," he turned to Father Malone, "I'll be having some of that Christ's Blood to take with me if I may."

"Find a priest there," replied Mops, good-humouredly. "On second thoughts, to ensure your pass to Heaven, you'll probably require the Archbishop of Canterbury."

"Does he live in Africa?"

"He lives in Canterbury."

"Ha! Rotten luck!"

With effort, he crouched down and kissed Lucy tenderly on the forehead.

"I'm sorry I didn't get to know you better."

He stood again and faced Josephine, now with a small, rounded bump beneath her woollen dress.

"And you, Witch," he said. "Thank you."

She smiled in reply and handed him a sackcloth bag.

"To keep you going," she said.

He bowed, before turning back to MacBride. He indicated behind him, where his schooner bore a new name plate. It read, *The Cornubian*.

"And you, brother," he said, "I'll meet you on the lost land of Lyonesse."

He clasped MacBride's hand and shook it once more before he turned to go. Craven helped him up the boarding plank and onto the ship.

The flag was raised, and this time – the first time since MacBride met him – it was Vaquero's own; the red skull and cannon. It flew proudly from its mast, flapping in the autumn breeze as *The Cornubian* set out on its journey.

MacBride lifted Lucy onto his shoulder so that she could better see, and slipped his arm around Jo's waist. He saw Sparky salute him from the helm.

"Hail! All hail! *Esto perpetua*, Martin MacBride! And may your shadow never grow less!"

And the mists swallowed them from sight, forever.

THE CORNUBIAN

The Facts and the Inspiration

AUTHOR'S NOTE

This customs featured in this book are based on real occurrences of the age. In no particular order, here is a glossary of some of the interesting information I drudged up while researching this book, just for your interest. A fast-track guide to smugglers and pirates, if you will.

Enjoy!

J

SMUGGLING and CORNWALL

- A house with bottle ends cemented under the eaves, a tiny figure of a man on a horse on the ridge of the house, or, in Scotland, a white rose growing by the door, was a sign that whoever resided there welcomed smugglers.

- Riding a horse along the coast road was a sign to smugglers that all was clear to land.

- The fish leaving a trail of water is a reference to a local wife (present day) who discovered her husband having an affair when she followed the trail of water his fish truck left, and found him in the cab with another woman!

- Dropping a cask into a gatepost socket was just one way of quickly hiding goods when the revenue were on your tail. A farmer carrying a keg of brandy along a winding lane used this method when he realised he had been spotted by an excise man. By the time the excise man had caught up with him, the farmer had had just enough time to pull the gatepost out of its socket, drop the cask in, and replace the post. Naturally, the baffled officer found nothing! The smugglers had many of these set up between harbour and destination.

- In an inn, common seamen drunk below, officers drunk above.

- Huge amounts of people in Cornwall supported the smuggling trade in every way they could.

- Brixham, as with many other ports in the south west of England, did have unique knitting designs for their fishermen's jumpers to make identifying the body easier if there were any accidents!

- Gotu Kola is a plant that detoxifies the liver.

- Polkerris had cellars where pilchards were salted and the seine house here (once the largest in Cornwall) was where they were processed for oil.

- In Edinburgh, 1724, Maggie Dickson was hanged for stealing. The doctor signed her death certificate and her body was put into a cart and taken off to the graveyard. On the way, Maggie sat up and scared the life out of the driver! The town council decided that they couldn't hang her again as she was already officially dead. They let her live and she raised a family before dying naturally 30 years later. (Ref: Horrible Histories: Bloody Scotland by Terry Deary.)

- On the 1 October 1788, Deacon Brodie was said to have escaped hanging by wearing a metal collar under his shirt and being resuscitated after he was cut down. It was unlikely this really happened, but nobody knows for sure!

- Wool was often illegally exported as payment for contraband, as was tin and copper. Smugglers often took things 'on credit', as they were renowned for being honest men.

- Customs and Excise did not amalgamate until 1909.

- A smuggler could win a free pardon if he confessed all and gave the names of his companions.

- If your name was given as an accomplice to smuggling, it would be gazetted, leaving the smuggler 40 days to come forward and surrender. If this was not done, the smuggler was automatically given the death penalty. There were rewards of up to £500 for any person willing to turn in such a man.

- Spout lanterns really existed in Cornwall. They were crafted locally.

- The capture of a smuggler was worth £20, which the free traders referred to as Blood Money.

- Red shirts on washing lines and smoking chimneys were just two of the many warning signs that smugglers could look out for ashore.

- A Devonshire collector wrote to London, 'We think it almost impossible to convict an offender by a Devonshire Jury, who are composed of farmers, and generally the greater part of them either smugglers or always ready to assist them in receiving and secreting their goods.' – taken from the book 'Smuggling in Devon and Cornwall 1700-1850', by Mary Waugh. Indeed, revenue officers were sometimes risking their lives to make an arrest, and most of the time it was pointless, as the smuggler would just be let off again in court. It was as a result of this that many officers would take bribes to turn a blind eye. As with Martin MacBride and Cole Shanley, a bag of money might be dropped in the hollow of a certain rock, and when the revenue officer and the smuggler met, the smuggler would say, 'Sir, your coat is unbuttoned', and the officer would smile and reply, 'Aye, but my money's safe enough', which was a sign the bribe had been accepted and the boats could take roller in peace.

- Black Joan and her brother, Fyn, were very fearsome smugglers. Joan was the worst.

- Falmouth Customs House sold seized contraband to the public.

- A law was passed in the 1750s specifically against the deliberate wrecking of ships using lights. If a wrecker was caught he would be given the death penalty.

- Farmers drove herds of sheep or cows over cart tracks left by smugglers in order to hide them.

- John Clements did exist. He was born in 1768 to John and

Susannah Clements of Talland, and married Jane Quiller, the daughter of a notorious Polperro smuggler and privateer in the August of 1791.

- Highwaymen were popular at this time due to the invention of the flintlock pistol, which was very light to carry. Travellers carried money on them, and road signs and maps were few in number, which made an attack much likelier. Highwaymen wore long capes, stylish tricorn hats and masks, and would sometimes tie their victim to the tree after robbing. They rarely killed their victims, however, and looted only rich people, which earned them heroic reputations.

- Wreckers tricked ships by sending out false signals from lighthouses, causing the vessels to crash onto the rocks. The wreckers would then loot the ships.

- Smugglers were often known as 'owlers', as they carried out their crimes at night and hooted to each other like owls.

- Footpads – the term for a highwayman without a horse.

- Moll Cutpurse was a first highwaywoman of London.

- Caves were favourite stores for smugglers.

- Ponies were often waiting nearby after a landing – many of them 'borrowed' from farms. Often, a stable door was left discreetly unfastened at night, and no-one was surprised to find a weary, dirty animal in the morning. Expected in return would be kegs of brandy and pieces of lace, or parcels of tea for the mistress of the house and cake tobacco for the master.

- Sinking and Creeping was the smuggling term used when two kegs of brandy were lashed securely together and weighed down with a suitable heavy sinker. When near home, the lashed kegs were put overboard on a bearing previously arranged with the shore fraternity.

- The gentlemen who made up the shore fraternity went fishing with stout grapnels and orthodox lines to give the business a decent appearance of innocent industry.

- Tea could be brought in under waistcoats in 'Body Bags', and a short bustle under the coat tails could hold as much as thirty pounds.

- Many smugglers lived bordering the moors.

- Cornwall was rife with legends created by the smugglers to keep people away. Ghostly funeral processions and phantom horsemen on remote moorland roads can be traced to nothing more spiritual than good French brandy on its way by horse or vehicle to its destination. These were days of supernatural beliefs, and although inhabitants of such places believed the ghostly coaches to be simply smugglers subterfuge, no-one dared try and prove it.

- Penalties for smuggling meant anything from confiscation of cargo and boats to execution. Ships discovered to be concealing contraband were sawn into three, ending many a smuggler's business completely.

- Ponies were especially trained for work. They were accustomed at the beginning of their training to respond to orthodox words, but in reverse, so that when a revenue man happened upon a pony train laden with contraband and ordered the fellow to halt, the obedient pony man would shout 'Whoa!' – and the ponies would gallop off into the night.

- A famous method of avoiding the excise men was to put the smuggled goods into a coffin and pretending the smuggler was dead. Another was having lace wrapped around the waist and being dressed as a woman over the top.

- Brandy could be hidden in a furled topsail.

- Boys in the late 18th century began to earn a living at 9 years old. They often had hobbies such as fishing and swimming, so smuggling was often a natural step.

- Morte Bay was a graveyard of sailing ships. It is located at Barricane Beach near Woolacombe in North Devon, and is famous for its seashells. It was also famous as a being a smuggler hang-out!

- Marisco Castle on Lundy has a vast grotto beneath it. Lundy, also known as Golden Bay, was a real battleground, an island with an onslaught of pirates and smugglers, and almost continually infested with privateers and pirates and every other sea-going rogue of all nationalities requiring shelter.

- Many cottages and houses had hidden rooms, passages, cellars and tunnels to beaches.
- Cawsand village was ideal for smugglers, as it was close to the great contraband market of Plymouth and yet small enough to possess rambling alleyways, nooks and crannies, where goods could be hidden if necessary. Small boats used here for fishing were also well suited to smuggling.
- Smugglers would employ 'flashers' who signalled from shore with the spout lantern when the coast was clear. This was especially used if the smugglers had been 'crop sowing' – anchoring tubs and casks ('ankers') at a discussed location beneath the sea, and fishermen picking them up later.
- Polperro and Mevagissey specialised in building fast, well-armed vessels capable of out-running the excise men. The entire population of Polperro took part in smuggling. Their favourite smuggling haunts were the eerie Talland churchyard – conveniently haunted by devils (closely resembling the local villains!) and the Punch Bowl Inn at Lanreath, where the fair traders would gather and distribute their goods.
- Priests and vicars also got involved and assisted the smugglers. Contraband could be stored in the church; under the pews and even under the pulpit. Coffins stuffed full of contraband were buried in the churchyards.
- Inns provided a ready market as well as cellars for storage.
- A good smugglers cove had overhanging cliffs and steep rocky sides, which could only be negotiated by torturous pathways. They might be riddled with caves, some connected by secret passageways to houses on the cliff top – as is the case of Talfryn's Rame House.
- Some excise men wrote of Polperro: "Two Irish wherries full of men and guns came to anchor within the limits of this port and lay there three whole days in open defiance discharging contraband goods. We are totally destitute of any force to attack them by sea, and as the whole coast is principally inhabited by a lot of smugglers under the denomination of fishermen, it is next to an impossibility to intercept any of these goods after they have been landed."

- When smugglers passed through a village, the inhabitants would face the wall so that when the revenue men questioned them they could truthfully say they had seen nothing at all.

- Padstow had a Collector of Customs, an Inspector of the Water Guard, a Landing Waiter and an Officer or Excise – all of whom tried in vain to quash illegal trading.

- A phrase among the smugglers was that of the four ports that assisted, 'Sidbury financed, Branscome landed, Sidmouth found wagons and Salcombe carriers.'

- It could be quite amusing being a smuggler. There are many legends about local gangs and how they avoided the excise men. One humorous poem describes how a notorious Brixham character, Bob Elliot, could not run away because he had gout, and was hidden in a coffin, but later that night the coastguards were frightened by meeting what they thought was his ghost! Another old villain was caught in possession but evaded capture by pretending to be the devil rising out of the morning mists. On another occasion, during a cholera epidemic, some Brixham smugglers drove their cargo up from the beach in a hearse accompanied by a bevy of supposed mourners following the cortege drawn by horses with funeral-muffled hooves.

- The (true) tale of Jack Rattenbury, a Westcountry smuggler, is full of amazing heroic adventures. The man was surely born under a lucky star! In comparison, the legend of Cruel Coppinger is a tale to make the hairs stand up on the back of your neck!

PIRATES and PRIVATEERS

- Pirates gave enemies a black spot or an ace of spades as a sign they were coming for them.

- Pirates believed gold earrings improved eyesight.

- Many had parrots or monkeys as pets, which they had caught from South America.

- Privateers were pirates who had been given the Letter of the Marque. They were sponsored by the government, and had permission to rob ships. The Letter or the Marque often saved them from punishment.

- On a pirate ship, slaves that had collapsed and could not be revived by flogging, were thrown overboard to the sharks.

- In Algiers, the patroon (slave master) would look at a captive's hands to gauge whether he was rich or poor. Smooth hands meant he was rich, and could therefore be held for ransom, but rough hands meant rough treatment. The patroons had a pleasures for pain. Hanging, impaling, and cutting off body parts before smothering the stumps with honey and leaving the slave to be eaten alive by insects – were all practices that actually took place.

- The pirates knew the slave trade as 'black ivory'; black because of the usual skin colour, and ivory because of its value.

- 'Kiss the Gunners Daughter' was the pirate name for the flogging of a member of the crew over the cannons.

- 'Specie' was the pirate name for gold and silver.

- Nassau in the Bahamas was the pirate capital of the world.

- Pirates who were brave and daring made good leaders and were widely honoured and respected.

- An astrolabe was a device with which a pirate could measure the height of the sun and stars, helping to understand the position of ships.

- Pirate rules often included that all lights were to be out by 8 o'clock, and that all weapons were to be kept clean and tidy, ready for use.

- When at sea, pirates ate hardtack soaked with grog. (Rum, warm water and lemon.) Limes were eaten to ward off scurvy. Hens were kept aboard for eggs.

- Pirates held duels to settle important issues.

- Caulking was the name for repairing gaps between the ship's planks to keep the vessel watertight.

- Careening was the term for cleaning the weeds, worms and barnacles from the bottom of the ship.

- Black Jacks were pewter or leather tankards used by pirates. Pirates often got drunk – and pewter or leather tankards could not be smashed or broken!

- Salmangundi was a pirate salad.

- When pirates won a battle and took over an enemy ship, they would perform a ritual known as 'Strike Colours', which was the practice of pulling down the ships flag to signal surrender.

- Long red banners flown from ships masts were a sign to enemies that they were going to attack. This was known as the 'No Quarter'.

- A blunderbuss was a short-range firing gun.

- Hempen jig was the dance of death – a grisly joke about the prisoner's dying movements on the end of the hangman's rope.

- After a pirate had been hanged, their body was not cut down immediately but left swinging from the gallows until three tides had washed over it.

- Slaves were chained in gang chains and ankle fetters.

- The 1600s and 1700s were deemed 'The Golden Age of Piracy'.

- Pirates in the Caribbean could not resist plundering ships heading back to England carrying goods such as gold, tobacco, silks and spices.

- Pirates in the West Indies were the first to fly red flags to let everyone know who they were. The skull and crossbones was popular with pirates, as it symbolised death. Pirates created their own flags, or 'Jolly Roger', as it was known. Blackbeard added an hourglass to show that time was running out and death was coming.

- Pirates preyed on ships for both cargoes and slaves.

- Many pirates came from the Barbary Coast of North West Africa, especially from Algiers and the Moroccan port of Sallee.

- Spanish, Turkish and Barbary pirates rarely went over to the Caribbean. All they had to do was wait on the Devon/Cornwall coast for the Westcountry fishing fleets to return.

- Barbary pirates, such as Sparky, would hold fishermen to

ransom or sell them as slaves. Ransom was anywhere between 300-1500 ducats (£35-£75). To put this into perspective, an English seaman was lucky to earn £1 a month!

- Barbary pirates owed their success to trickery and deceit. They used craft and cunning rather than valour and bravery. For example. They would raise an English flag instead of their own when approaching an English ship. They did share the spoils evenly, however. Most slaves were taken to the slave market in Algiers, some were made to serve the Barbary pirates there and then. English and Irish pilots were particularly sought after and were sometimes paid for their services; a pound a month compared favourably with that in the royal or merchant navy, and their local knowledge may have accounted for the description of these pirates being particularly nimble around the Westcountry and Ireland.

- Privateers was also licensed to capture smugglers.

- In relation to pirates, Buccaneers came from the Caribbean (so called because of their famous barbecues) and Corsairs came from the Barbary Coast at the top of Africa.

- Pirate captains needed to be good at steering clear of rocks and sandbanks, and avoiding storms and huge waves, by watching for signs of bad weather in the skies.

- "Shiver me timbers' was an old English phase for when the wind blew the masts and sails, shaking everything on board.

- The Spanish Main was the American mainland, which Spanish conquistadors (conquerors) took for themselves. Pizarro, from Extremadura, found the Aztecs of Mexico and the Incas of Peru. They made them their slaves and stole their gold. After they had done this, many other pirates (including the English – such as Sir Francis Drake) raided the Spanish for gold in return.

- Pirates were notorious for spending, and not saving, their stolen silver and gold.

- 17th and 18th century pirates treasure from just one raid could amount to £5000 per pirate! That was more than 40 years in the Navy could have earned them!

- Pirate ships were often schooners or sloops. Big ships with many sails were usually faster than smaller ships with fewer sails.

- The flintlock pistol was a favourite with pirates, but it was unreliable, as it simply fizzled if the damp sea air had moistened the powder inside. They also used daggers (easy to hide in a pocket or coat), cutlasses (a short sword with a wide, slightly curved blade – there wasn't room to swing a longer sword in cabins or decks crowded with rigging), long knives (which also had many peaceful uses on board the ship), boarding axes (used for cutting through the thick ropes that held up the rigging, thus bringing sails and spars crashing down), and of course, the cannon (which could blast a heavy iron ball as far as a mile.) They were much more frightening and dangerous close at hand, though, so pirates waited until their target was directly alongside before firing at it.

- Trials against pirates were hardly fair. Most pirates were uneducated sailors, who could neither afford to employ a lawyer, nor knew how to defend themselves. A few escaped execution by pleading that they had been forced into piracy. Some were ingenious; Anne Bonny and Mary Read, the two famous female pirates, avoided execution by claiming they were pregnant!

- Highwaymen had their corpses displayed in a gibbet (wooden frame) by the side of the road. Pirates' corpses were sometimes used in this way as well – in an iron cage shaped like a suit of clothes – to stop friends from stealing the body, and to serve as a warning to others. As an added preservative, the bodies were sometimes covered in tar.

RESUSCITATION: 'WARM AND DEAD'

- The current guideline issued by the American Heart Association (AHA) is that one should continue reviving the patient until their core body temperature is above 95 degrees Fahrenheit- 95 degrees, because below that they are technically hypothermic. The mantra here is, 'They're not dead until they're warm and dead'. It is likely that this basic idea may have been understood in MacBride's time.

- In Britain, mouth-to-mouth resuscitation for the 'sudden dead' became popular after William Tossach's documentation of his own successful case back in 1744.

WOMEN WHO 'PLED THEIR BELLY'

- As I mentioned, pirates Mary Read and Anne Bonny were granted a separate trial from Jack Rackham and his crew because they were women. At the point of being found guilty, they both declared they were pregnant. This was apparently confirmed, and as a result both women were granted a stay of execution until after their babies had been born. Mary Read unfortunately passed away as a result of fever while in jail, but Anne cheated the gallows and disappeared. There have been several theories presented in explanation to this. Some say her father, who was very well connected, arranged for her to be returned to the Carolinas. Some say she was granted a pardon by the governor on condition that she leave and never return. Others believe she escaped with an unknown lover. Whichever it was, she was not alone in escaping her fate.

- Elizabeth Proctor and her husband were accused of being witches during the Salem Witch Trials. Her husband was executed, but pregnant Elizabeth was granted a stay of execution until she had birthed the baby. It was then believed that many people had been wrongly convicted without enough hard evidence, and Elizabeth was among the 153 people released.

- It is likely that many other women escaped their execution in a similar fashion, especially those with well-connected friends.

Sources of information from:

Smuggling in Devon and Cornwall 1700-1850 – Mary Waugh

Pirates and Smugglers – Moira Butterfield

Pirates and Robbers – Grandreams

Bloody Scotland – Terry Deary

Life Among the Pirates: The Romance and the Reality – David Cordimgly

The Mariners Handbook

War, Ice and Piracy: The Remarkable Career of a Victorian Sailor –
The Journals and Letters of Samuel Gurney Cresswell.

Jamaica-gleaner.com

PubMed NCBI

Other information sourced from Penzance Tourist Information Board, local museums – and local people.

ABOUT THE AUTHOR

Julie lives in Devon with her husband and three children. She has diplomas in Child Psychology and Child and Adolescent Counselling, as well as qualifications in writing stories for children. She has been a foster mother and is now a full-time step-mother. Her life has had it's dramas, but her mantra is to follow her heart.

ENJOYED
THIS BOOK? WE'VE GOT LOTS MORE!

Britain's Next
BESTSELLER

DISCOVER NEW INDEPENDENT BOOKS & HELP AUTHORS GET A PUBLISHING DEAL.

DECIDE WHAT BOOKS WE PUBLISH NEXT & MAKE AN AUTHOR'S DREAM COME TRUE.

Visit **www.britainsnextbestseller.co.uk** to view book trailers, read book extracts, pre-order new titles and get exclusive Britain's Next Bestseller Supporter perks.

FOLLOW US:

 BNBSbooks   @bnbsbooks   bnbsbooks

BRITAINSNEXTBESTSELLER.CO.UK